A GLASS OF BLESSINGS

**Books by Barbara Pym available
in Perennial Library**

EXCELLENT WOMEN
A FEW GREEN LEAVES
A GLASS OF BLESSINGS
QUARTET IN AUTUMN
THE SWEET DOVE DIED

A GLASS OF BLESSINGS

BARBARA PYM

PERENNIAL LIBRARY
Harper & Row, Publishers
New York, Cambridge, Philadelphia, San Francisco
London, Mexico City, São Paulo, Sydney

The author thanks the Literary Trustees of Walter de la Mare and The Society of Authors, London, for permission to quote lines from the poem "Autumn" which appear on page 83.

A hardcover edition of this book is published in the United States by E. P. Dutton, a division of Elsevier-Dutton Publishing Co., Inc., New York. It is here reprinted by arrangement.

First PERENNIAL LIBRARY edition published 1981.

ISBN: 0-06-080550-1

83 84 85 10 9 8 7 6 5 4 3 2

A GLASS OF BLESSINGS

When God at first made man,
Having a glasse of blessings standing by;
Let us (said he) poure on him all we can:
Let the world's riches, which dispersed lie,
Contract into a span.

GEORGE HERBERT: *The Pulley*

CHAPTER ONE

I SUPPOSE it must have been the shock of hearing the telephone ring, apparently in the church, that made me turn my head and see Piers Longridge in one of the side aisles behind me. It sounded shrill and particularly urgent against the music of the organ, and it was probably because I had never before heard a telephone ringing in church that my thoughts were immediately distracted, so that I found myself wondering where it could be and whether anyone would answer it. I imagined the little bent woman in the peacock blue hat who acted as verger going into the vestry and picking up the receiver gingerly, if only to put an end to the loud unsuitable ringing. She might say that Father Thames was engaged at the moment or not available; but surely the caller ought to have known that, for it was St Luke's day, the patronal festival of the church, and this lunchtime Mass was one of the services held for people who worked in the offices near by or perhaps for the idle ones like myself who had been too lazy to get up for an earlier service.

The ringing soon stopped, but I was still wondering who the caller could have been, and finally decided on one of Father Thames's wealthy elderly female friends inviting him to luncheon or dinner. Then a different bell began to ring and I tried to collect my thoughts, ashamed that they should have wandered so far from the service. I closed my eyes and prayed for myself, on this my thirty-third birthday, for my husband Rodney, my mother-in-law Sybil, and a vague collection of friends who always seemed to need praying for. At the last minute I remembered to pray for a new assistant priest to be sent to us, for Father Thames had urged us in the parish magazine to do this. When I opened my eyes again I could not help looking quickly at the side aisle where I had caught a glimpse of the man who

5

looked like Piers Longridge, the brother of my great friend Rowena Talbot.

She usually spoke of him as 'poor Piers', for there was something vaguely unsatisfactory about him. At thirty-five he had had too many jobs and his early brilliance seemed to have come to nothing. It was also held against him that he had not yet married. I wondered what could have brought him to St Luke's at lunchtime. I remembered Rowena telling me that he had recently obtained work as a proof-reader to a firm of printers specializing in the production of learned books, but I had understood that it was somewhere in the city. I did not know him very well and had seen very little of him recently; probably he was one of those people who go into churches to look at the architecture and stay for a service out of curiosity. I stole another quick look at him. In novels, or perhaps more often in parish magazine stories, one sometimes reads descriptions of 'a lonely figure kneeling at the back of the church, his head bowed in prayer', but Piers was gazing about him in an inquisitive interested way. I realized again how good looking he was, with his aquiline features and fair hair, and I wondered if I should have a chance to speak to him after the service was over.

When this moment came, Father Thames, a tall scraggy old man with thick white hair and a beaky nose, was standing by the door, talking in his rather too loud social voice to various individuals — calling out to a young man to keep in touch — while others slipped past him on the way back to their offices, perhaps calculating whether they would have time for a quick lunch or a cup of coffee before returning to work.

Although I had quite often been to his church, which was near where I lived, Father Thames and I had not yet spoken to each other. Today, as I approached him, I had the feeling that he would say something; but rather to my surprise, for I had not prepared any opening sentence, I was the one to speak first. And what I said was really rather unsuitable.

'How strange to hear a telephone ringing in church! I don't

think I ever have before,' I began and then stopped, wondering how he would take it.

He threw back his head, almost as if he were about to laugh. 'Have you not?' he said. 'Oh, it is *always* ringing here, although we have another one at the clergy house, of course. Usually it's business, but just occasionally a kind friend may be inviting me to luncheon or something of the sort. People *are* so kind!'

So it could have been as I had imagined. But there were two priests at the clergy house. Were the invitations always for Father Thames and never for mild dumpy little Father Bode, with his round spectacled face and slightly common voice, who always seemed to be the sub-deacon at High Mass and who had once read the wrong lesson at a carol service? I was sure that Father Bode was equally worthy of eating smoked salmon and grouse or whatever luncheon the hostesses might care to provide. Then it occurred to me that he might well be the kind of person who would prefer tinned salmon, though I was ashamed of the unworthy thought for I knew him to be a good man.

'As a matter of fact that telephone call was about Father Ransome, our new assistant priest,' Father Thames continued. 'That much Mrs Spooner was able to tell me after the service. In fact, from what I understood her to say it may even have been Ransome himself on the telephone, but she was understandably a little flustered.'

I wondered if it was a good omen that the new assistant priest should have telephoned in the middle of a service or if it showed some lack of something.

'I'm so glad to hear that you have found somebody,' I said.

'Yes — prayer has been answered in the way that it so often is. Of course there are still difficulties to be overcome, but if all goes according to plan he should be with us next month. Then we shall be able to get our full winter programme started. You must come and have a glass of sherry one evening — or perhaps you would like to join one of the study groups,' he added, seeming to offer me two strangely contrasting alternatives. 'We are hoping to go *very* thoroughly into the South India business this autumn ...' His voice tailed off and I could see that his glance had left me and fixed itself on a young man who was trying to slip past him. 'Now, Geoffrey,' he called out, 'how would you like to be a server?'

Geoffrey looked sheepish and mumbled something to the effect that he would not like it very much. He managed to make his escape while Father Thames was being buttonholed by an elderly woman of the type that always seems to waylay the clergy in porches and doorways.

'Wilmet,' said a voice at my side, 'don't you remember me?'

It was Piers Longridge. We walked out into the October sunshine together.

'I noticed you in church,' he said. 'I was sure it was you.'

'I noticed you,' I said, 'and then I seemed to get caught up with Father Thames.'

'Father *Thames*?' he laughed. 'Surely there's something rather odd about the name?'

'Yes, I suppose there is, but I'm used to it now. And he does seem to have lived it down — the oddness, I mean. Do you often come here?'

'No, this is the first time. Perhaps Rowena told you — I've got a job in London now as a proof-reader for French and Portuguese books, and I'm also teaching those languages at evening classes to earnest clerks and middle-aged ladies — terribly like an early novel by H. G. Wells, don't you think?'

'It seems respectable work,' I ventured.

'Yes, it keeps me going. Are you a "regular worshipper" at St Luke's, as they say?'

'Yes, I've been coming here for a few months. You see, the church nearest to us is very Low and I couldn't bear that.'

'I should imagine not,' said Piers.

We walked on a little way.

'And what's your news? You're not married yet?' I asked rather brightly.

'Good heavens, no! What should I marry on? And women are so terrifying these days and seem to expect so much, really far more than one could possibly give. Not that I would include *you* in my condemnation,' he added quickly. 'You look particularly charming today, Wilmet.' He smiled down at me in the provocative way I remembered.

I was pleased at his compliment for I always take trouble with my clothes, and being tall and dark I usually manage to achieve some kind of distinction. Today I was in pale coffee brown with touches of black and coral jewellery. Rodney seldom commented on my appearance now and Piers had that engaging air of making me feel that he meant what he said. I was sorry when we came to a crossroads and he said he must leave me.

'Back to work,' he sighed. 'I expect we shall meet again — perhaps for lunch one day,' he added uncertainly, as if feeling that something was expected of him but not liking to commit himself.

'You must come and see us,' I said.

'I'm afraid I'm not a very sociable person in the conventional way,' he said quickly, 'but I'm sure we *shall* meet.'

'Yes,' I said. 'Goodbye!'

I decided to wait for a bus to take me to the shops, and when the right one came I went on the top and sat looking down into the street. We had not gone very far before I saw Piers about to enter what could not by any stretch of the imagination have been his place of work, for it was a pub, or rather a 'wine lodge' — one of those attractively named places of refreshment which seem to have an almost poetic air about them like the Portuguese *quintas* — and indeed the comparison was not inappropriate, for Piers and his sister had been brought up in Portugal where their father had been in the wine trade. I began to look back over what I could remember of Piers's career. He had been at Oxford or Cambridge but had got a disappointingly low class in his final examinations. He had taught in a school, been a courier with a travel agency, worked for a time in the B.B.C., and helped in the compilation of a Portuguese dictionary. It was from the title page of this work that I had gleaned some further information, for he was described as 'Piers Longridge, B.A., late of the British Museum, sometime lecturer in English Literature' at a college in Portugal whose name I could not remember — and now creeping into a wine lodge at two o'clock in the afternoon when he had told me that he was going back to work. How the glory had departed, if glory it had ever been! The words 'late' and 'sometime' seemed all of a sudden rather sad; and Piers himself, glimpsed from the bus, a rather shambling figure, more worn and less glamorous than he had seemed in the kindlier light of the church. I noticed that he did not go in immediately to have his drink but lurked outside on the pavement, gazing into the road and then at a line of parked cars in what seemed a very odd way. Then I remembered Rowena telling me about his obsession with car numbers which he either collected in simple numerical order or used in more complicated games, such as spotting a car with his own initials and adding up the numbers that followed it to see if they were 'propitious'. It seemed a foolish game for a grown man to play, and I felt mean to have caught him at his folly, to be spying on him as it were. I was glad when the bus moved on and I saw him at last enter the wine lodge.

Later, when I had finished my wandering round the shops and was approaching home, it occurred to me how very bleak and respectable the house looked. This appearance was of course very fitting for Rodney, a civil servant; but it hardly seemed to suit Sybil, my mother-in-law — who is what one calls a real character, though not in a tiresome way. As I opened the front door she was standing in the hall, a dumpy square-faced woman of sixty-nine, energetic and brusque in her manner. She had been in youth, and still was, passionately interested in archaeology, and the big table in the basement kitchen was often covered with pie-dishes full of pottery fragments waiting to be labelled and classified. Now she was trying to arrange some flowers, grimly and without enjoyment, tweaking them here and there with impatient gestures.

'Ah, Wilmet — just at the right moment,' she said. 'I don't seem able to get these right at all. I was trying to make a natural arrangement, but there seems to be something evil and malicious about chrysanthemums.'

'Let me try.' I took off my gloves and set to work. I have a talent for arranging flowers and soon had them looking most artistically natural.

'Noddy telephoned to say that he's bringing a friend home for dinner', Sybil went on.

'From the Ministry?'

'Yes, I suppose so. All Noddy's friends seem to be from the Ministry, don't they?' Sybil seemed to take a sardonic pleasure in calling her son by the childish nickname which now seemed so unsuitable for a civil servant approaching middle age. I sometimes wondered if that was why she did it.

'I'd better go and change, then.'

'Don't make yourself too grand, dear. I was just going to say that civil servants don't notice what their wives wear or the wives of their colleagues — one of those foolish generalizations that couldn't possibly be true.'

'I suppose a female colleague would notice more.'

Sybil laughed. 'Those splendid and formidable women! I often think that was one of the reasons why Noddy didn't want you to have a job — for fear you might turn into the kind of woman one sees getting out of the train at St James's Park or Westminster, carrying a briefcase with E.R. stamped on it.'

'I suppose some of them try to combine marriage with a career — I mean the ones who carry baskets as well as briefcases and look both formidable and worried, as if they hoped to slip into the butcher's before going to their desks.'

'Yes, though single women also have to eat or may be entertaining friends to dinner,' said Sybil. 'I read in the paper the other day of a woman civil servant who was discovered preparing Brussels sprouts behind a filing cabinet — poor thing, I suppose she felt it would save a precious ten minutes when she got home.'

11

'Yes,' I laughed, 'and one could top and tail gooseberries or shell peas quite easily in an office, perhaps even without the shelter of a filing cabinet. Good heavens! There's Rodney's key in the lock — I must hurry.'

When I came down again the men were in the drawing-room, drinking sherry. Sybil, who had evidently not considered them worthy of a change of dress, was with them. But then her clothes always looked the same — of no particular style or even colour, though quite neat except when she dropped cigarette ash on them.

A stiff-looking young-middle-aged man was standing by the fire. He had something of Rodney's air about him, except that Rodney was better looking and going bald in a rather distinguished way which seemed suitable to his age and position in the Ministry, whereas this man had a thick crop of wiry greying hair.

'Wilmet, I don't think you've met James Cash, have you?' Rodney said.

We nodded and bowed to each other, and Rodney went over to the table by the window to get me a drink.

'I think I'll have a dry Martini,' I said. 'It doesn't seem quite the weather for sherry — too mild or something. St Luke's little summer.'

A shadow, surely of displeasure, seemed to cross James Cash's face, and I guessed that he was probably one of those men who disapprove of women drinking spirits — or indeed of anyone drinking gin before a meal.

'Gin always gives me a dry mouth,' said Sybil in her detached way. 'Even the smallest amount. I wonder why that is?'

'You're sure you wouldn't prefer gin and lime, dear?' said Rodney, hesitating with his hand on the Noilly Prat bottle.

'No, I'd rather have French, please.'

'Let her have what she likes, Noddy,' said Sybil. 'After all it is her birthday.'

'Of course. And that reminds me, I saw Griffin at lunchtime and arranged about your present.'

'Thank you, darling.' Mr Griffin was Rodney's bank manager.

I imagined the scene, dry and businesslike: the transfer of a substantial sum of money to my account, nothing really spontaneous or romantic about it. Still, perhaps something good and solid like money was better than the extravagant bottle of French scent that some husbands — my friend Rowena's, for example — might have given. And the whole thing was somehow characteristic of Rodney and those peculiarly English qualities which had seemed so lovable when we had first met in Italy during the war and I had been homesick for damp green English churchyards and intellectual walks and talks in the park on a Saturday afternoon.

'Such a pity Hilary can't be with us this evening,' said Rodney rather formally to James Cash.

'Is she ill? I didn't quite gather,' said Sybil bluntly.

'Well, not really. She has just had a child,' said James in a rather surprised tone.

'How nice,' I said, trying to sound warm and feminine. 'Boy or girl?'

'A boy.'

'That is supposed to be the best,' laughed Sybil.

We drained our glasses and went into the dining-room. I was touched to see that Sybil had chosen all my favourite dishes — smoked salmon, roast duckling and gooseberry pie with cream. The men would not of course have realized that they had been chosen specially for me, looking upon the whole meal as no more than was due to them.

'One never *quite* knows what wine to drink with gooseberries,' said Rodney, turning to James Cash rather apologetically. 'I suppose something a little drier than might be considered usual with the sweet — is that about the best one can do?'

I let out a snort of laughter before I realized that Rodney's manner was serious, almost deferential, and that the question was being gravely considered. So James was one of those boring wine men, I thought.

'I think you've hit upon an admirable compromise here,' he

said politely, 'though I believe you could almost get away with one of those outrageously sweet wines — perhaps even a Samos — the kind of thing that seems otherwise to have no possible raison d'être. Perhaps that *is* their raison d'être — to be drunk with gooseberries or rhubarb! If you like I will raise the matter with my own wine merchant — a man of considerable courage, even panache.'

'Thank you,' said Rodney seriously. 'We — my wife and mother, rather — are very fond of gooseberries. We often eat them in one form or another.'

'Perhaps they are more a woman's fruit,' said Sybil, 'like rhubarb. Women are prepared to take trouble with sour and difficult things, whereas men would hardly think it worth while.'

The men were silent for a moment, as if pondering how they might defend themselves or whether that, too, was hardly worth while. Rodney's next remark showed that they had evidently considered it not to be.

'And what have you done today, Wilmet?' he asked. 'I hope you've enjoyed your birthday? We have planned a theatre party for tomorrow evening,' he added, turning to James, as if he felt some explanation was necessary.

'I went to the lunchtime service at St Luke's,' I said, 'and Father Thames actually spoke to me. Then I went shopping.'

'Our parish church isn't really High enough for Wilmet's taste,' Rodney explained.

'I'm afraid it's all the same to me,' said James. 'I don't go to any kind of church.'

'Neither do I,' said Sybil. 'I thought out my position when I was twenty, and have found no reason since to change or modify the conclusions I came to then.'

I could not protest, for there was something about my mother-in-law's bleakly courageous agnosticism that I admired. It seemed to me rather brave for somebody nearing the end of life to hold such views. I wondered if she was ever afraid when she woke up in the small hours of the night and thought of death.

'Today, during the service,' I said, 'the telephone rang in the vestry, and that apparently was the answer to our prayers. We had been praying for a suitable assistant priest,' I explained.

'Yes, I suppose that is quite often done,' said James in a detached tone, 'but I imagine that certain practical measures must be taken as well — a word to the bishop or the patron of the living, perhaps even an advertisement in a suitable paper.'

'Ah yes, the *Church Times*,' said Sybil, 'with a few tempting titbits to encourage suitable applicants. Vestments — Western Use — large robed choir — opportunities for youth work. Though perhaps *not* the last — we know the kind of thing that sometimes happens: the lurid headlines in the gutter press or the small sad paragraph in the better papers.'

Rodney threw her a warning glance.

'How very distressing it all is,' Sybil went on, ignoring her son. 'One wonders how these poor creatures fare afterwards. I suppose they would be unfrocked — is that the procedure? One hopes there is some place where they can be received afterwards. It would be a noble work that, the rehabilitation of some of those fallen ones. Even a house of this moderate size could accommodate four or five. . . .'

Rodney and I looked at her apprehensively, for Sybil was a keen social worker.

'Surely, Mother, you aren't thinking of starting such a place *here*?' asked Rodney impatiently. 'And we do seem to have got rather off the point, don't we?'

'Perhaps we have strayed into a byway,' said James with a little laugh. 'I suppose the arrival of a new clergyman must be rather exciting for the ladies. Would he be a celibate?'

'I should think so,' I said. 'Neither Father Thames nor Father Bode is married.'

'Do they live together at the vicarage?'

'Well, it is called the clergy house,' I explained. 'It is a rather Gothic looking building in the same style as the church. On the door is a notice telling you not to ring unless on urgent business.'

'I should have thought all clergy business must be urgent,' said Rodney. 'They are concerned with the fundamental things, after all — birth, marriage, death, sin — though I suppose they are also besieged by idle women wanting to know about jumble and things like that.'

'Well, let us hope this new one will be up to standard,' said Sybil vaguely, with a glance at me. 'Shall we leave the gentlemen to their port and manly conversation. Women are supposed not to like port except in a rather vulgar way,' she added as we rose from the table, 'and the male conversation that goes with it is thought to be unsuitable for feminine ears.'

I could not help smiling as I looked at the two men, who seemed so very formal and correct. I supposed they might discuss the port itself, then perhaps something that had happened at the Ministry — trouble with the typing pool or the iniquities of some colleague would be the very worst that might be expected of them.

'I saw Rowena's brother today,' I said to Sybil when we were alone in the drawing-room. 'He was at St Luke's and we had a few words of conversation. Then I got on to a bus and saw him going into a pub.'

'Oh dear!' Sybil paused and then laughed. 'I wonder why I said that? Isn't there supposed to be something unsatisfactory about him? He must be well on into his thirties now. At what age does one start to accept a person as he is? Could a man in his fifties or sixties still go on being labelled as "unsatisfactory"?'

'Perhaps up to thirty, one may still go on expecting great things of people,' I suggested, 'or even thirty-five.'

'Why is Piers unsatisfactory? Because he has had rather a lot of jobs and hasn't yet married? Is that it?'

'Yes, I think so. You see, Rowena is so very much married, with three children, and Harry being in Mincing Lane.' I giggled. 'You know what I mean — so very solid and good, and so very much sticking to the business founded by his great-great-grand-father. I suppose Rowena chose him as a kind of contrast to all the Portuguese men she must have met living out there — some-

16

how one doesn't think of them as being solid and reliable. Piers is now proof-reading learned books, and teaching French and Portuguese in the evenings, he told me.'

'Oh, let's go to some of his classes,' said Sybil enthusiastically. 'I really had thought we might go to Portugal next summer, and it would be a good thing to get some rudiments of the language. Will you ask him about them next time you see him?'

'Yes, but I'm not sure when that will be. I don't suppose he'll be at Rowena's when I go to stay there — Harry doesn't really like him.'

'What a pity. Why don't you ask him here one evening? He might like to come into a good solid English home — I suppose ours is that. Home life is generally supposed to be a good influence, isn't it.'

'Yes, but perhaps only for young men and women coming to London for their first job from the provinces — for the times when they aren't spending an evening at the Y.M.C.A. or some church youth club. I suppose Piers wouldn't really come into that category. Incidentally, Father Thames said something about evening study groups in the winter — perhaps he might be persuaded to go to those.'

'That hardly seems likely,' said Sybil with a laugh, 'but it would be nice for *you* to have some intellectual occupation, if it would be that.'

'You mean that I should have some work to do?' I asked, rather on the defensive, for I sometimes felt guilty about my long idle days. I did not really regret not having any children, but I sometimes envied the comfortable busyness of my friends who had. Nobody expected *them* to have any other kind of occupation.

'Not at all, dear,' said Sybil calmly. 'Everybody should do as they like. You seem to fill your days quite happily.'

It was true that I had tried one or two part time jobs since my marriage, but Rodney had the old-fashioned idea that wives should not work unless it was financially necessary. Moreover, I was not trained for any career and hated to be tied down to a routine. My autumn plans to take more part in the life of St Luke's, to try to befriend Piers Longridge and perhaps even go to his classes, ought to keep me fully occupied, I thought.

'Why don't you come to the Settlement with me one day?' Sybil suggested. 'Mary Beamish was asking me if you'd be interested the last time I was there.'

'Yes, I'll come along with you,' I said. 'It might be rather —' I had been going to say amusing, but obviously the word was unsuitable. My sentence was left unfinished as the men came back into the room.

'Ah — the gentlemen,' said Sybil with a slightly mocking air. 'Now we shall have to stop our conversation and you will have to stop yours.'

'We were exchanging our experiences of the young women who do our typing,' said James. 'Oh, there was nothing shocking about them,' he added, sensing Sybil's ironical glance.

'I was telling James how I had occasion to criticize, quite mildly I may say, a piece of work one of them had done,' said Rodney. 'I had asked for a three-inch margin and she had done only a two-inch. It was really quite important or I shouldn't have asked for it. I said, "I'm afraid this won't do, Miss Pim", whereupon she snatched the report out of my hand and ran from the room in tears, slamming the door after her. It was really quite upsetting.'

'Perhaps she's in love with you,' I heard myself saying with unsuitable detachment.

There was a slight pause, then James burst into laughter and said, 'Oh, I can assure you, nothing like that goes on in *our* department!'

I was glad that he had broken the silence. I glanced at Rodney, but he did not seem to have noticed anything, if indeed there had been anything to notice.

'You like this Tia Maria, don't you, Mother?' he said smoothly, taking up a bottle. 'I know Wilmet finds it too sweet.'

I took a large gulp of brandy and began to cough. Then I turned my thoughts to the visit to the Settlement and Mary Beamish.

CHAPTER TWO

MARY BEAMISH was the kind of person who always made me feel particularly useless — she was so very much immersed in good works, so *splendid*, everyone said. She was about my own age, but small and rather dowdily dressed, presumably because she had neither the wish nor the ability to make the most of herself. She lived with her selfish old mother in a block of flats near our house and was on several committees as well as being a member of St Luke's parochial church council. This particular morning, which seemed to me in my nastiness the last straw, she had just been to a blood donor session and had apparently come away sooner than she ought to have done; for when Sybil and I arrived at the Settlement she was sitting on a chair surrounded by anxious fussing women, one of whom held a cup of tea seeming uncertain what to do with it.

'You should have rested for at least twenty minutes,' said Miss Holmes, the warden of the Settlement, a tall worried looking woman. 'It was most unwise of you to come away so soon.'

'And not to wait for your cup of tea either,' said Lady Nollard in her fruity tones which always made me think of some great actress playing an Oscar Wilde dowager. 'That was *very naughty*, you know.'

'But I've given blood so *many* times,' said Mary in a weak bright voice. 'I really didn't think it would do me any harm to come away a little sooner than I usually do. I didn't want to be late. It was only on the trolley bus that I began to feel a little faint —'

'Ah, the *trolley bus*!' Lady Nollard's tone was full of horror and I realized that she had probably never travelled on one. Not that I had myself very much, for I did not tend to visit the parts of London where they operated. I had noticed them sometimes going to places that seemed impossibly remote and even romantically inviting, but I had never been bold enough to risk the almost certain disillusionment waiting at the other end.

'The motion can sometimes be quite upsetting,' said Miss Holmes, 'like a ship.'

'Personally that's why I like them,' said Sybil in her gruff tones. 'And I'm always fascinated by the blue flashes they give out at night. I suppose we may as well start the meeting now as we are all here? You'll feel better after you've rested awhile, Mary,' she said rather briskly. 'Are there any apologies, Miss Holmes?'

Miss Holmes began to go into unnecessary details about why various members of the committee could not attend, but Sybil firmly put a stop to her meanderings and set the meeting in motion.

I always find committee meetings very difficult to attend to because my thoughts wander so unsuitably. I began by trying to take in what was being said; but after a while I found myself looking round the room, resting my eyes on the pleasant carvings and mouldings on the ceiling and round the fireplace, for the Settlement was situated in a part of London which had been a fashionable residential area in the late eighteenth and early nineteenth centuries and the house had preserved many of the pleasing elegancies of that period. It made me sad to think of the decay and shabbiness all around, and the streamlined blocks of new flats springing up on the bombed sites, although I supposed it was a good thing that children should now be running about and playing in the square gardens, their shouts and laughter drowned by the noise of the machinery that was building hideous new homes for them.

'... the old people don't like fish,' I heard Mary Beamish saying. 'It's funny, really, Mother is just the same. She seems to *need* meat, and yet you'd think that somebody over seventy —' she gave her bright little smile and made a helpless gesture with her hands. I imagined old Mrs Beamish crouching greedily over a great steak or taking up a chop bone in her fingers, all to give her strength to batten on her daughter with her tiresome demands. I was thankful that Sybil was so independent and self-sufficient, and that my own mother, had she been alive still, would never have expected as much of me as Mrs Beamish did of Mary.

'Well, we have to give them a fish dinner one day a week,' said Miss Holmes in a harassed tone. 'We can't *afford* meat every day, and of course Friday does seem to be the obvious day for fish.'

'When I was a girl,' said Lady Nollard, 'there was an excellent cheap and nourishing soup or broth we used to make for the cottagers on the estate. Quite a meal in itself, made of bones of course, and large quantities of *root* vegetables — turnips, swedes, carrots and so on.'

I could see Sybil looking at her rather warily. I knew that she felt the need to be careful with Lady Nollard, for there was always the danger that she might start talking about the 'working classes', the 'lower classes', or even quite simply 'the poor'.

'Yes, of course we do give them good soup,' said Sybil, 'but I'm afraid they'll have to go on having the fish. As Miss Holmes points out, we can't afford to give them a meat dinner every day. And now for the report on the Youth Club. Mr Spong?'

A red-haired young man rose to his feet and began to read in a rather aggressive tone. There was some discussion about what he had called 'undesirable elements' creeping into the club, and then the meeting was at an end. I realized that I hadn't uttered a single word or contributed in any way to the good work that was being done.

'How nice to see you here, Wilmet,' said Mary Beamish. 'I was wondering if Mrs Forsyth might bring you along some time.'

'Yes, Sybil told me you had suggested it,' I said. 'But I'm not sure that it's quite my sort of thing,' I added lamely. 'Perhaps giving blood would be better.'

'Oh, that's great fun!' said Mary enthusiastically. 'If you really would like to be a blood donor I can send your name in.'

'All right, I should like to very much.'

'Good! I must hurry home now. Mother will be waiting for her lunch.'

'Poor Mary,' said Sybil. 'I do feel that she has too much to put up with. Old people shouldn't expect their children to give up their lives to them. It isn't as if Ella Beamish really needed her — she has plenty of money and could get a paid companion who would expect to be bullied.'

'I know,' I said. 'But Mary is somehow the kind of person to be put upon. I suppose there must always be people like that. And after all, what would she have done if she hadn't devoted her life to her mother and good works? Married and had children? That's what people always say, isn't it?'

'Well, she would have been able to lead her own life, though it might not have been so very different from her life now. I thought we might have lunch out today,' Sybil went on. 'It's nearly one o'clock already. Shall we go in here?'

We had been walking as we talked and now stopped outside an extremely unappetizing looking cafeteria, where a small queue had formed near the counter. Sybil marched in and joined the end of it, so I could do nothing else but follow her. Although she knew about good food, she had a rather splendid indifference to it where it concerned herself and I had often been with her to places which my own fastidiousness or squeamishness would have stopped me from entering alone. Now, as we manoeuvred our heavy trays along the counter, I tried to choose the dishes that seemed most harmless — a cheese salad with a roll and butter, some stewed apple, and a cup of black coffee.

We found two vacant places at a table where a young man and woman were already sitting. The floor around us had the appearance of being strewn with chips. I pushed one or two aside with my foot, moved some dirty crockery to a corner of the table, and sat down.

Sybil began to examine the lettuce in her salad with detached efficiency.

'They can't always wash it as well as one would at home,' she

22

explained. 'One could hardly expect them to, having to prepare so many lettuces — just imagine it!' The examination over, she began to eat abstractedly as if she had switched her thoughts away from food entirely.

I could not bear to examine mine with such thoroughness, so my eating was apprehensive. All the time I was worrying, imagining grit and live things, certain that I was going to get food poisoning, waiting almost with resignation for the first symptoms, although I knew that they could not possibly manifest themselves for several hours. The people around me seemed particularly unattractive, the young man smothering his sausages and chips in bright red sauce, talking in such a low voice to his girl friend that all she ever seemed to say was 'Pardon?' in an equally low voice. I was glad when the meal was over and we were outside in the sunshine again.

'Well, that wasn't so bad,' said Sybil calmly. 'Shall we walk a bit as it's such a lovely day?'

We came to a secondhand bookshop with rows of books arranged in the open window. Sybil began to examine some of them, taking them up in her gloved hands and holding them some distance away so that she could read the titles, though without her glasses some of them sounded distinctly odd and intriguing. '*Victory Over Pan*,' she read, and '*My Tears at the Vatican*. I wonder what *that* can be? The autobiography of some poor unfortunate priest of the type we were talking about last night?'

'There's always something sad about publishers' remainders,' I said. 'One hopes that it doesn't mean the book had very poor sales, but rather that the publishers were too rash and greedy and printed more than could possibly be sold.'

Sybil put down the memoirs of an opera singer through which she had been glancing.

'What tremendous loves these women seem to have had in their lives,' she sighed. 'It makes one's own seem so dull.'

'Yes, but I suppose we should all be able to make our lives sound romantic if we took the trouble to write about them,' I

23

said. 'After all, the man one eventually marries is practically never one's first proposal, surely?'

'My husband was,' said Sybil simply. 'I should like to have refused a man but it was an experience I never had. I suppose it might be a painful one.'

'Yes, sometimes — but with a kind of triumph mixed with it. One always hoped he would never marry anyone else, but of course he always did. And so unflatteringly soon, sometimes.'

'Excuse me.' A spectacled youth in a raincoat reached across me for a book with a faintly pornographic title and began to turn the pages expectantly. I turned away with what I suppose was a kind of womanly delicacy.

'I think I shall go home now and do up some clergy parcels,' said Sybil. 'A visit to the Settlement always spurs me on in that way.' She pulled out her wallet which was stuffed with newspaper cuttings. In spite of her agnosticism she was unable to resist the pleas of the clergy from poor parishes who advertised in the papers, and all were sure of receiving parcels of old clothes from her in strictly fair rotation.

'Canon Adrian Reresby-Hamilton,' she read out. 'I think it's his turn next. St Anselm's Vicarage, E.1, "this very poor parish". Such a good name and such a poor address! You see there is still that ideal of service among the nobly born as there was in Victorian days. Hearts just as pure and fair *do* beat in Belgrave Square....' Her voice was rather loud and I noticed one or two people turning their heads to look at us.

'I've put some old things of mine in the morning-room,' I said. 'I'll be back later.'

'Don't forget that we are asked to tea with Miss Prideaux at half past four,' Sybil called out as we parted.

I had forgotten, but there was plenty of time, perhaps too much time. It was only just after three o'clock. If I were working in an office it would be almost teatime now. Perhaps the sound of spoons clattering in saucers and the rattle of the trolley would already be audible along the corridors of the Ministry where

Rodney and James Cash worked; at this very moment they might be taking their mugs out of drawers or cupboards. I sometimes liked to imagine myself in a small cosy office where a little group of women might gather in a room, drinking tea and eating biscuits, discussing the iniquities of the Boss. I could picture the boss himself coming bursting into the room, perhaps with an ill-typed letter in his hand, and the cool stares of the women as they stood with their teacups in their hands, letting him have his say, putting him out of countenance with their insolent detachment, so that his wrath smouldered out like a damp squib and he was left floundering and stammering.

Eventually I took a bus to St Luke's, feeling rather virtuous at turning away from the shops and the prospect of a new hat.

It was dark and warm inside the church and there was a strong smell of incense. I began to wonder idly whether it was the cheaper brands that smelt stronger, like shag tobacco or inferior tea, but I was sure that Father Thames would have only the very best. I noticed a few professional details, candles burning before the rather brightly coloured statue of our patron saint, a violet stole flung carelessly over one of the confessionals which had curtains of purple brocade. This one had Father Thames's name above it; those of the assistant priests looked somehow inferior, perhaps because the curtains were not of such good quality material — there could surely not be all that much difference in the quality of the spiritual advice. One or two people were kneeling in the church, and I knelt down too and began to say one of those indefinite prayers which come to us if we are at all used to praying, and which can impose themselves above our other thoughts, so often totally unconnected with spiritual matters.

After a few moments I got up and went outside into the little courtyard, and sat down on one of the seats to read the parish magazine which I had just bought. I turned first to Father Thames's letter, which was, as so often, troubled and confused. Spiritual and material matters jostled each other in a most inartistic manner, so that the effect was almost comic. In one sentence we were urged not to forget that All Saints' Day was a day of obligation and that it was therefore our duty to hear Mass, while in the next, without even a new paragraph, we were plunged into a domestic rigmarole about unfurnished rooms or a flat ('not necessarily self-contained') for the new assistant priest. 'He would, of course, want free use of the bathroom', but could have meals at the clergy house except for breakfast which could be 'light' — even 'continental' — he would not require more than that. This seemed to be rather presumptuous, for the new curate might well have a hearty appetite and would surely deserve more than a light breakfast after saying an early Mass. The letter then returned to spiritual matters — the attendances at Solemn Evensong and Devotions were lamentably poor, it was really hardly worth while for Mr Fasnidge the organist to come all the way from Peckham — and ended with hopes for better things in the Church's New Year. But then an agitated postscript had been added. 'Oh dear me, Mrs Greenhill, our housekeeper, has just come into my study and told me that she will have to leave — she has been finding the work too much, and then there is her fibrositis. Well, perhaps we are all finding the work too much for us. Now we are *really* in the soup! Prayers, please, and *practical* help. Isn't there some good woman (or man) who would feel drawn to do *really Christian work* and look after Father Bode and myself? We can just about boil an egg between us!'

I saw them at the stove, anxiously watching the bubbling water; then, watches in hand, lowering the eggs into the saucepan. I wondered if they would know what to do if they cracked. I never did myself.

Then I went on to read about the most enjoyable outing the servers had had, 'greatly assisted by the presence of Mr Coleman and his Husky'. I was just puzzling over these last words, wondering if the Husky was indeed a large polar dog or perhaps a kind of motor car, when I was conscious of somebody standing over me.

'Good afternoon, Miss — er — Mrs ...' Father Thames, in a splendid cloak clasped at the neck with gilt lions' heads, hovered over me like a great bird. 'Do you know,' he went on, 'I thought for one moment when I saw you sitting there reading the parish paper that you might be the answer to prayer.'

I flushed for a moment and preened myself, almost as if I had been paid some frivolous compliment at a party.

'I've just been reading about Mrs Greenhill leaving,' I said. 'I do hope you've got somebody else to keep house for you?'

'No, alas, not yet. That's why I was thinking how wonderful it would be if *you*, reading my cri de cœur — ' he paused and gave me a most appealing look. I wondered whether many men, perhaps the clergy especially, went about cajoling or bullying women into being the answer to prayer. I supposed that the technique must often be successful. For a moment I even toyed with the idea that I might go and live in the clergy house and look after the priests. Then, of course, I remembered that I was married and could hardly leave Rodney even if I did nothing very much in the way of housekeeping for him. And then again I was obviously much too young to be able to live in the clergy house with two priests without fear of scandal. Why, then, had Father Thames seemed to think that I might be suitable? Perhaps I didn't look so young after all. The thought was disturbing and I put it from me quickly. It must be that the morning at the Settlement had temporarily aged me.

'You see, I have my husband to look after,' I began.

'Ah yes, women do have husbands,' he said a little peevishly. 'It was too much to hope that you would be free. Still, we know that God *does* move in a mysterious way, as Cowper tells us. Perhaps one day a stranger might sit here, as you are sitting, reading our parish paper — '

'I shall certainly let you know if I hear of anybody likely to be suitable,' I said, seizing the easy way out. 'After all, one does sometimes come across people who want such work.' For one wild moment I thought of Piers Longridge — if, as was highly possible, he should lose his job as proof-reader. 'Would you really consider a male housekeeper?' I asked.

'Oh, any sex, any sex,' said Father Thames, wringing his hands.

As I walked home I found myself wondering why Father Ransome couldn't live at the clergy house with Father Thames and Father Bode. I was sure there must be plenty of room.

I found Sybil in the morning-room struggling to fold up one of Rodney's old suits into a manageable parcel.

'He was rather doubtful when I asked him if it could go,' I remarked. 'He does rather like to hang on to these old things, though I'm sure he hasn't worn that suit for about two years.'

'We will say nothing,' said Sybil, folding the brown paper round it. 'It is such a good clerical grey. Perhaps it will go no farther than the vicarage. And now I suppose I must tidy myself up for Miss Prideaux.'

I did not very much look forward to the tea party, though Miss Prideaux had a curious kind of fascination for me. The words 'distressed gentlewoman' always came into my mind when I thought of her, though the expression was not really accurate. She was undoubtedly a gentlewoman, but perhaps reduced circumstances described her position better than any phrase suggesting distress or decay. Indeed, I felt that the word 're-duced', with its culinary associations hinting at something that has been concentrated and enriched by the boiling away of un-necessary elements, gave a much truer picture. The rich residue here was the distillation of her vivid memories of life as a governess in Europe in the grand old days. Miss Prideaux ap-peared to remember only the best parts of her life, so that she was sometimes accused of exaggeration or even of downright lying. 'Two litres of Chianti *from our own vineyards* was sent up to the schoolroom *every day*,' I once heard her say; at other times she would hint at remarkable and esoteric knowledge of some historical event, such as what *really* happened at the hunting lodge at Mayerling that winter night in 1883.

In appearance she was small and dry and bent, and this after-noon I noticed that, like the clergyman who might be going to receive Rodney's old suit, she was wearing a lavender-coloured cardigan which I had sent to St Luke's last jumble sale. I remembered that it had been nearly new — really too good for a jumble sale — but that I had taken a dislike to the colour. *Vogue* or *Harper's* had urged us to 'make it a lavender spring this year' and I had responded with too much haste and enthusiasm. I could only suppose that one of the organizers of the sale had allowed Miss Prideaux a kind of preview of some of the best things, for I hated to think of her fragile old body being buffeted by the rough jumble sale crowd. Besides, she would have found the whole thing so distasteful — I could not imagine her even entertaining the idea of going there herself.

Miss Prideaux was of the generation which wears a hat in the house for luncheon and tea, and she now came forward to greet us wearing a little black toque to which a bunch of artificial Parma violets had been pinned at a rather rakish angle. Her cheeks were, as usual, very heavily rouged.

Her little drawing-room, as she called it, which was really a bed-sitting-room in the flat of some other people, was cluttered with souvenirs and photographs in silver frames. Some of the photographs were undoubtedly of minor European royalties, but I never quite knew which were royalties and which Miss Prideaux's own relations; they did not look so very different, except that the royalties were usually adorned with large sprawling signatures.

'Now we need not wait for Sir Denbigh,' she said. 'I will make the tea. I expect it is one of his busy days and he has been delayed.'

'I suppose we all have our busy days,' said Sybil, 'even retired diplomats. What does Sir Denbigh do with his days?'

'He is writing his memoirs, of course,' said Miss Prideaux, without irony, 'and that keeps him rather fully occupied. Then he is vicar's warden at St Luke's, you know.'

'Father Thames seems worried about getting a new housekeeper,' I said.

'Yes, poor Oswald,' said Miss Prideaux. 'If it isn't one thing it's another.'

It always surprised me to hear Father Thames called by his christian name. I wondered if he called Miss Prideaux Augusta.

At that moment I heard the bell ring and shortly afterwards Sir Denbigh Grote came into the room, rubbing his hands together as if it were a cold afternoon. He looked so much like a retired diplomat is generally supposed to look, even to his monocle, that I never thought of him as being the sort of person one needed to describe in any detail. What did seem unusual was his friendship with Miss Prideaux, who in spite of being a gentlewoman had only been a governess in some of the countries where he had served in a much higher capacity. It could only be supposed that retirement, like death, is a kind of leveller; and that social differences had been forgotten in the common pleasure of recalling garden parties at the embassies to celebrate the sovereign's birthday, and other similar functions which few people would have been capable of discussing at all knowledgeably.

I personally found Sir Denbigh rather dull, and the tea party with its almost ritual sipping of weak China tea and crumbling of shortbread biscuits was something of an ordeal. Fortunately Sybil made a move to go shortly after half past five.

'Let me see now, Sir Denbigh, were you ever in Lisbon?' she asked, putting on her gloves. 'Wilmet and I are thinking of taking Portuguese lessons this winter.'

'Was I ever in Lisbon?' Sir Denbigh repeated. 'Lisboa — ah, yes, but many years ago. The climate is delightful, but the language is very difficult — perhaps too difficult for ladies.'

Miss Prideaux looked a little bored, though in the most gentlewomanly way, so I concluded that she did not know Lisbon.

'Did you know a family called Longridge?' I asked Sir Denbigh.

'I do not recall anyone of that name,' he began, then added thoughtfully, 'Longbottom — an unusual name.'

It hardly seemed worth while to correct him, especially as Sybil and I were now in the doorway about to leave.

'What was that little parcel you dropped on the table as we were going?' I asked her when we were outside.

'Just half a pound of coffee and some of those Egyptian cigarettes she likes.'

'You are full of good works today. First the Settlement, then the poor clergy, and now Miss Prideaux. I wish I could do things like that.'

'You will one day,' said Sybil confidently. 'It is something for one's old or middle age, not really for youth.'

I reflected that perhaps that very evening an opportunity might occur for me to do something that would give me a glow of virtue, and as it turned out I was not far wrong.

When Rodney came home he seemed to have some worry on his mind. Sybil and I did not generally ask him about his day's work at the Ministry — I think we had the impression, probably erroneous, that it was too secret to be discussed, or if not too secret too dull, but this time I felt that he wanted to unburden himself, so I said lightly, 'What's the matter, darling? Has Miss Pim been temperamental again?'

'No, not that,' he said. 'It's a man in my department. Really it's nothing to do with me, but one feels vaguely responsible somehow. He isn't at all suited to the work — in fact he has been dismissed, and I feel I ought to help him to do something about getting another job, though heaven knows what.'

'What can he do?' asked Sybil, practical as always.

'Well,' Rodney began doubtfully, 'I hardly know. Certainly not what he was engaged to do in the Ministry. He is an Anglo-Catholic and fond of cooking.' He laughed. 'There you are — I'm afraid that's about all I can tell you.'

'But that sounds rather promising,' I said, and told him about Father Thames's appeal for a housekeeper ('Oh, any sex, any sex!') and my promise to let him know if I heard of anybody suitable.

'That *might* be a possibility,' said Rodney, 'though it sounds almost too good to be true. Shall I ask him to get in touch with Father Thames — would that be the best thing?'

'Yes, do. After all, you never know. It might be just the thing.'

'Somehow I can't imagine poor Bason being just the thing at any job,' said Rodney, 'but, as you say, one never knows.'

'Bason or Basin — is that his name?' chuckled Sybil. 'That might be a good omen. At least it has a domestic sound about it.'

'How wonderful if it were the answer to all our prayers,' I said. 'Father Thames might announce it from the pulpit one Sunday morning. How proud I should feel — as if there were some justification for my life after all!'

CHAPTER THREE

I LOOKED forward to my weekend with Rowena and Harry as I sat in the Green Line bus on Friday afternoon. I had taken care to avoid the rush hour and should be there in time for tea. We travelled through some of the pleasanter suburbs and were soon in the country — tame country, really, though once I caught a glimpse of a mysterious Excalibur-like lake through a gap in some trees, beyond which stood a great house now turned into a country club, with swimming pool and American bar, as the noticeboard proclaimed.

When I got to the right bus stop I saw Rowena waiting with her little pale blue car; presumably Harry had taken the Jaguar to the station or even up to Mincing Lane with him. The three children, Sara, Bertram and Patience, were crowded into the back, their solemn eyes gazing at me in the rather unnerving way of young children.

'Wilmet, how *lovely*!'

I thought we must have made quite a pleasing picture — two tall tweedy young Englishwomen embracing on a Surrey road-side. Rowena was as tall as I, but fair, with blue eyes and a typically English complexion. We had met during the war in Italy where we had both been in the Wrens. We had also met our husbands there, two rather dashing army majors they had been then — and now they were Harry going up to Mincing Lane every day and Rodney working from nine-thirty to six at the Ministry. Both were slightly balder and fatter than they had been in Italy. I liked to think that Rowena and I had changed rather less.

We drove up to the large comfortable house, which was built in Elizabethan style and had the date — 1933 — carved into a stone over the front door. The gardens were extensive and well laid out. Harry had always wanted a cedar tree on the lawn, as

33

there had been in his old home, but had done the best he could by planting a monkey-puzzle, which was said to be quicker growing. He employed a fulltime gardener and the house was always full of beautiful pot plants. As we came into the hall I admired the early chrysanthemums, primulas and cyclamen.

'Your usual room, darling,' Rowena said. 'Let Sara take your case up for you. She's been so looking forward to your coming.'

Sara, a plump fair child of nine, seized my case and staggered up the stairs with it. I tried to think of something to say to her, but although she was my godchild there did not seem to be any particular mystical rapport between us. I thought that talking to children was one of those things one shouldn't have to make any effort about, and my few platitudes seemed to satisfy her and set her off chattering about her own doings which were no more remarkable than those of other children of her age.

I was glad to be alone in my room, with the view over the garden, well polished mahogany furniture, pink sheets and towels, and a tablet of rose-geranium soap in the washbasin. Rowena always remembered that it was my favourite. The room seemed so very comfortable, somehow even more than my room at home — perhaps because I could be alone in it. I saw that Rowena had put reading matter on the bedside table, glossy magazines, and two new novels in bright jackets.

Tea was ready in the drawing-room. The children had been taken away by the Italian girl who looked after them, and Rowena and I were able to enjoy an uninhibited talk. The room was almost Edwardian in its charming clutter of furniture and objects, for Rowena had inherited her mother's things and had been unable to bring herself to get rid of any of them, just as her mother before her had kept all her own mother's things. There was a great deal of china, some of it rather ugly Portuguese ware which she kept for sentimental reasons, mixed up with good Chelsea, Dresden and Meissen pieces. There were many photographs in silver frames on the grand piano, but they were somehow not like Miss Prideaux's photographs. There were Rowena's

34

parents, Piers and Rowena as children, Rowena as a young girl of nineteen — this last taken by a fashionable Mayfair photographer and showing her, for all her tweeds and pearls, in a kind of misty aura — Harry in uniform, and the children in all stages of growth; there was even one of myself in Wren officer's uniform.

'Now,' said Rowena comfortably, 'what have you been doing? Tell me *all*.'

'Well, not much really,' I admitted. The days when we had confided our emotional secrets to each other were gone now, or perhaps it was the secrets themselves rather than the days which were gone, I thought rather sadly. 'I saw Piers at St Luke's, as I told you when I wrote. *That* was rather surprising.'

'Yes, poor Piers. I suppose nothing is really surprising about him now. Let's hope that *this* time ...' Rowena raised her hand and let it fall in a helpless gesture.

'He seems to have two quite steady jobs,' I said, 'proof-reading for a very good press and then the evening classes in French and Portuguese.'

'Well yes, the proof-reading may be all right if he doesn't get bored with it; but he's really not much good as a teacher, though he speaks the languages very well. He's the kind of person who ought to have a steady unearned income.'

'He might marry money,' I suggested.

'Oh, *marriage*! We've given up hope long ago. The numbers of eligible girls I've tried to put into his path,' Rowena sighed, 'awfully dull most of them were, I must admit, but all with money of their own.'

'Sybil and I are thinking of going to his Portuguese classes — she thought it might be nice to have a holiday in Portugal.'

'Then perhaps Piers will make an effort with his teaching if people he knows are going to be in the class. Though why you should want to learn the language I can't imagine.'

'You know what Sybil is.'

'Yes, so unlike Harry's mother who only thinks about household linen and knitting for the children. By the way, I did ask

Piers to come this weekend, but he hasn't even answered my letter.'

'Perhaps he will turn up unexpectedly.'

'Yes, that would be just like him. My *dear*,' Rowena leaned forward, her blue eyes sparkling, 'talking of the unexpected, *who* do you think I met in Piccadilly when I was in town last week? Rocky!'

'Not Rocky *Napier*?'

'Yes, our darling Rocky.'

We paused in a kind of rapturously reminiscent silence, for Rocky Napier had been flag lieutenant to one of the admirals when we were in Italy and each of us had been in love with him for a short time.

'How extraordinary! What happened?'

'He asked me to go and have a drink with him, so of course I did, though I was supposed to be meeting Harry's mother for lunch at Fortnum's. We went into a bar and had two dry Martinis, and do you know I didn't feel a *thing*!'

'What, from Rocky or the drink?'

'From Rocky — wasn't it sad? And to think of all the agony of that six weeks when I was in love with him!'

'Was it only six weeks?'

'Yes, because then I met Harry. That letter I wrote to Rocky — oh dear, I feel quite ashamed now, quoting Donne and all that — "but after one such love can love no more ..." Aren't women *foolish*!' Rowena's eyes sparkled even more brightly. 'I couldn't help thinking about that letter all the time I was sipping my Martini. Why does one say *sipping* a cocktail? I was positively *gulping* it down!'

'I don't suppose Rocky remembered the letter,' I said, meaning to be consoling rather than catty, but perhaps a little of both.

'No, that's a comfort. He must have had so many. Now he lives in the country with that rather formidable wife, and they have a child — just think of it!'

'Well, you have three.'

'Yes, I'm very lucky. It's a pity you haven't any, Wilmet,' she added tentatively. 'Do you mind?'

'A little, I suppose. It makes one feel rather useless. Still, there's plenty to occupy my time.'

'Oh, surely. You would never be idle, you're so much more intelligent than I am, anyway. Listen, there's Harry! I heard the car. He's been longing to see you, but first he'll go into the dining-room to get his large pink gin, then he'll come into the room carrying it very carefully.'

Harry did precisely as Rowena had prophesied. He was a tall dark man of thirty-nine, his hair now streaked with grey and his manner more pompous than in the days when I had stood on his shoulders to write my name on the ceiling of an officers' mess somewhere near Naples.

'Wilmet, how *very* nice to see you, and looking as beautiful and elegant as ever. You really must bring old Rodney with you next time.'

'Yes, he'd love to come, but work wouldn't allow it this week-end.'

'A shocking life—I don't know how these civil servants stand it!'

'How are things in Mincing Lane?' I asked, unable to keep a hint of mockery out of my tone.

'Not too bad, thanks. In fact, business is pretty good. But I won't bore you with details.'

Harry was one of those non-intellectual men who are often more comforting to women than the exciting but tortured intellectuals. He might not have any very interesting conversation for his wife at the end of the day, might indeed quite easily drop off to sleep after dinner, but he was strong and reliable, assuming that he would be the breadwinner and that his wife would of course vote the same way as he did.

Dinner was a very pleasant meal. Rowena was a good cook and would have liked to make exotic dishes, but the tyranny of Harry and the children made it necessary for her to keep to plain wholesome English food.

'Well, this looks all right,' said Harry, as a joint of veal was brought to the table. 'I hope you like veal, Wilmet?'

'Oh dear, I'd forgotten it was Friday,' Rowena lamented. 'Does your high vicar command you to eat fish?'

'Not really,' I said, 'though I daresay he and Father Bode will be abstaining from meat this evening.' A sudden anxious picture came into my mind – the two priests in the clergy house kitchen, trying to cook fillets of plaice or cod steaks. Perhaps in the end they would have to open a tin of sardines or spaghetti, unless they had decided to dine out. They might even have got a housekeeper by now. How wonderful it would be if Father Thames had interviewed and engaged Mr Bason, and he was even now preparing them a delicious sole véronique! I saw him at the kitchen table, peeling grapes. Of course I had no idea what he looked like – I just saw his fingers, long and sensitive as befitted an Anglo-Catholic fond of cooking, removing the pips. I was smiling to myself at the thought of it so I had to tell Rowena and Harry.

'It would be much better if all clergymen were married,' said Harry dogmatically. 'This new man we've got here is proving very troublesome.'

'Is he married?'

'Actually he is, but he's got High Church leanings, though he hasn't had much opportunity to put them into practice yet.'

'But High Church services are much the most interesting kind,' I said rather feebly.

'That's what Piers always says,' said Rowena.

At the mention of her brother, Harry gave an angry snort, so we thought it more prudent to change the subject.

After dinner we had coffee in the drawing-room and watched a television programme. There was a film about the habits of badgers, which showed the creatures rootling about in a kind of twilight in what seemed to be rhododendron bushes. But in reality, as we were told by the commentator, there were lights suspended from the trees because badgers only come out at night and so couldn't be filmed naturally. There was something melancholy about the creatures in the half darkness, with their long sad faces.

It was not until half way through the entertainment, if such it could be called, that I realized that Harry had edged nearer to me on the sofa and was holding my hand. My main feeling on discovering this was one of irritation. The silly old thing — not unlike a badger himself, I thought; but then I felt flattered and a little guilty. Rowena, who was sitting in a little pool of lamplight by her sewing table, was absorbed in smocking a dress for Patience. She never once glanced at the television screen.

I withdrew my hand gently. Perhaps Harry was not so solid and reliable after all. Had he always rather liked me in Italy? I wondered, smiling to myself in the badgery dusk.

'Funny thing happened today,' he said in a rather booming voice. 'I was having lunch with Smollett and he suggested a dozen oysters. Well, you know what the oyster and I think of each other!'

'Indeed yes,' I said, for Harry and I had both been poisoned by oysters, and had many times exchanged cosy reminiscences about our dreadful experiences.

'Darling, *not* another oyster story,' said Rowena despairingly. 'Anyway, I hope you didn't eat them.'

'No, of course I remembered in time; but the funny part of it was — the whole point of the story, in fact, as you may remember — that Smollett was with me that *other* time....' Harry yawned and stretched his arms. 'What's this we're looking at?' he asked rather irritably. 'Seems to be all in the dark.' He leaned forward and moved a knob on the set. The picture now became brighter and full of curious dancing lines. 'Does anybody want it, anyway?' he asked.

'You know I never look at it,' said Rowena placidly.

'I think I've had enough now,' I said.

'Early bed tonight, I think,' said Rowena. 'We've got quite a full programme tomorrow. Shopping in the morning, and we shall have to spend the afternoon getting ready for the party, I suppose.'

'The party?'

'Yes, surely I told you? We're having a cocktail party.'

'How exciting!'

'It won't be that, I'm afraid,' said Rowena. 'Just the same old people we owe drinks to, though I suppose they'll be different to you. Your breakfast will be brought to you in bed, Wilmet. Ours is a terrible meal on Saturdays because we have the children with us. I shan't inflict that on you.'

I was glad to lie in bed next morning, listening to the sound of the children getting up and Harry shouting to them to be quiet, until a tray of orange juice, coffee and toast was brought to me. I got up at ten o'clock and we all went shopping in the near-by market town. There was an air of leisure about the restaurant of the large shop where we had our morning coffee. The children gambolled and capered with other children on the thick moss green carpet, and the chirping of their high-pitched well bred young voices mingled with the yapping of dogs, mostly poodles, whose tweed-suited owners made feeble efforts to control them.

'I always do this on Saturdays,' said Rowena. 'It's so nice to be able to relax for a minute.'

'What do the husbands do?' I asked, for very few of them seemed to be drinking coffee.

'Oh, they potter about doing the more manly shopping — going to the ironmonger, ordering things for the garden and that kind of thing, then they assemble in one of the pubs.'

'Men seem to do that in London, too,' I said. 'Winter Saturday mornings one sees the duffle coat and the paraffin can — carrying paraffin does seem to be quite a manly job, doesn't it.'

'We'd better not stay here too long,' said Rowena, and began looking anxiously round for the children. 'There's lunch to eat and then the party to get ready for. Would you like to go in and have a gin with Harry, while I wait in the car with the children?'

I found Harry at the bar with some rather unattractive-looking men and one or two women, all of whom were laughing at some joke. It occurred to me that these were probably the people I should be meeting at the party, and I began to look forward to it with rather modified feelings. It was some time before Harry seemed disposed to leave, and by the time we were outside in the fresh air I found that the two drinks I had so quickly tossed off had made me a little hazy and unsteady.

Harry took my arm. 'Pity we have to hurry back,' he said. 'I wanted to show you the church.'

'The church?' I asked in surprise.

'Yes, you always liked things like that,' he mumbled.

'Some other time, perhaps,' I said in a rather stupid party voice. I tried to remember if I had ever known what the church was like — Victorian gothic with much brass, or cool austere eighteenth century with fine wall tablets? It seemed so unlike Harry to suggest going into a church.

He began to hum 'We plough the fields and scatter', and got into the driving seat. The children began to scuffle and fight among themselves, fractious at being kept waiting for their lunch.

'I'm longing to see what you've brought to wear,' said Rowena later, when we were cutting up things to go on bits of toast and little biscuits. 'Your clothes are always so elegant.'

'It's a sort of mole-coloured velvet dress,' I said, 'and I shall wear my Victorian garnet necklace and earrings with it.'

'How lovely it will be to see somebody not in black! We all wear it here for parties — like a kind of uniform, just with different jewellery and little touches, you know. I suppose it's because we get so few opportunities to wear it, and women always think black suits them, don't they? Or they heard some man once say that it did.'

'Yes — an old love, or one of those rather mythical men who pronounce on such matters, a Frenchman or a Viennese.'

Rowena laughed. 'I wonder if I have time to put on some nail varnish? It might do something for my hands.' She held them out and glanced down at them a little sadly.

41

I hate coloured nail varnish myself, though I could not but agree that Rowena's hands did need something. Even though she had a reasonable amount of domestic help they looked stained and rough, the nails uncared for, hardly even clean. But suddenly, from studying them with critical detachment, I found myself remembering her hands as they had been when we were young and gay Wren officers in Italy. The hand that Rocky Napier had once held on the balcony of the admiral's villa had been soft and smooth, delicately pink-tipped, like those in Laurence Hope's *Indian Love Lyrics* which my mother used to sing in Amy Woodforde Finden's settings. My eyes filled with tears, both at the memory of the song and of Rowena's hands as they used to be. Perhaps it was the contrast of the rough little hands with the elegant black dress that so moved me, and the feeling that they had done so many more worth while things than my own which were still as soft and smooth as they had ever been.

'Leave them as they are,' I said rather brusquely. 'They look perfectly all right. Besides, the nail varnish wouldn't really have time to dry now and might get smudged.'

'Yes, you're right. Doing one's nails can be such an anxiety, can't it?'

Later, when the guests had begun to arrive, nearly all the women in black as Rowena had prophesied, I found myself looking at their hands and liking better those that seemed a little careworn, however cunningly they might have been camouflaged with bright nail varnish and jewelled eternity rings. The only ring I wore myself was my engagement ring, an eighteenth-century setting of rose diamonds, so much prettier than a modern one.

The conversation was inclined to be heavy going, even though the drink was strong and Harry was good about replenishing glasses. The guests were nearly all married couples; and although husbands seemed to enjoy a conversation away from wives, one was often interrupted in such a conversation by the appearance of

42

the wife, usually with some bright domestic remark that made one feel unwanted and shut out of the dreary cosiness of their lives.

'Darling, the coke *did* come after all, just as you were getting the car out.' Or, 'I do hope Ingrid has managed to cope with putting the children to bed. Do you think we should just ring up to make sure, darling?'

The husbands usually murmured rather sheepish replies, but really they were more like bears than sheep, I thought — performing bears, who might rove round the room but only within the limits of their chains. A sharp tweak would soon bring them to heel again. In another way they reminded me of the dark blundering badgers which we had seen on the television the night before.

At one point Rowena led me over to a corner to meet the new vicar and his wife. He was a tall worried looking man, quite young but prematurely bald. His wife was about my own age, neatly dressed in green, with a pleasant ready smile and anxious grey eyes. I noticed that she was nervously twisting an empty glass in her hands.

'Do let me get you another drink,' I offered. 'I'm staying in the house so can count myself as a kind of hostess.'

'No, thank you very much,' she said. 'I don't drink really, but it seems so unfriendly to come to a party and not have anything, so I did have *one*.'

'I think Harry was going to put out some soft drinks. I'm sure I could find you something.'

'Well, that would be nice. I *am* rather thirsty,' she said simply.

I went over to the table where the drinks were and came back with a glass of orange squash.

There was a rather awkward silence, the vicar just standing, his wife sipping her drink.

'I hope to be coming to your church tomorrow,' I said brightly. 'How do you like being in the country?'

'Well, it's very different,' said the vicar. 'We were in London before.'

'Yes, near Shepherd's Bush,' added his wife eagerly.

'What a contrast!' I exclaimed. 'Though of course there is the green there — I mean Shepherd's Bush Green itself.'

They both laughed rather nervously.

'We are just about to have a new assistant priest at the church I go to,' I said, babbling on rather since they did not venture any further remarks, 'with a rather promising name — Marius Love-joy Ransome. I looked him up in Crockford.'

'Oh yes? I think I have met him — third in theology at Oxford; Ely Theological College; Curate at St Mark's, Wapping; then St Gabriel's, North Kensington,' recited the vicar in rather Crockfordian style.

I wondered if he himself had got a better class in theology. 'What is he like?' I asked.

'An excellent fellow,' said the vicar dutifully, and looking at his gentle face I realized that he would probably have said the same about anybody. 'Which church do you go to?' he asked.

I had almost expected him to say worship at, and was relieved that he did not. I told him where I went.

'Ah, St Luke's. You would get full Catholic privileges *there*,' he said rather wistfully.

We talked for a little, though in a guarded manner, about Father Thames, and had just reached another conversational pause when I heard the front doorbell ring.

Seeing that Rowena and Harry were both busy I went out into the hall intending to answer it, but found that Giuseppina, the Italian maid, was already there. She opened the door, then looked back at me appealingly.

'That's all right, Giuseppina,' I said quickly, 'I will take this gentleman in,' for I could see that Piers was standing on the door-step holding a branch of laurel leaves in his hand. I had the impression that he was rather drunk.

'Wilmet, what a lovely surprise!' He held the branch of laurel towards me and bowed.

'Piers,' I said feebly.

He continued to stand on the doorstep without moving. His eyes were glittering strangely like glass or water with the light on it, and his fair hair was dishevelled. I was somehow reminded of the Ancient Mariner. I took his hand and led him into the hall.

'Rowena said you might be coming.'

'Yes, I'm afraid I didn't let her know. And now after spending an hour at the local to make me strong enough to face Harry, I find the drive full of Jaguars.'

'Jaguars?'

'Yes — cars, you know. Very unnerving to find oneself hemmed in by all those Jaguars and not a 279 among them.'

'Is that the number you're looking for at present?' I asked.

'Yes, have been for a week now. But *why* all the Jags?'

'We're having a cocktail party.'

'So that's it. Lead me to it then.' Piers started to walk rather slowly and carefully in the direction of the voices and clinking glasses.

Was this it? I wondered — Piers's trouble? *Drink?* I said the word ponderously to myself, giving it a rather dreadful emphasis. The words on the title page of the dictionary rose up before me — sometime, this, formerly the other. I imagined him drunk at a Portuguese university, sprawling in the sun, drunk in the British Museum, perhaps addressing the Elgin marbles.

'*Darling!*' Rowena ran forward, beautiful in her gaiety and the slight air of abandon the party had given her. 'You've *come!*'

The brother and sister embraced, then Rowena took him off to meet people.

'Wilmet, not drinking?' I found Harry by my side with a full glass. 'I wish we had a conservatory we could go into.'

'How Edwardian,' I said lightly. 'But you haven't.'

'What about having lunch in town with me one day to talk over old times?' said Harry in a rather muffled voice.

I felt slightly hysterical. Had there been 'old times' as far as he and I were concerned, or was Harry just behaving in a conventional caddish way, in keeping with the idea of conservatories and

Edwardian goings on? 'Why, I'd love to,' I said, recovering my social poise. 'Hadn't you better be going round with the drink? I can see some empty glasses.'

'How sharp those beautiful eyes are,' he said and moved off bear- or badger-like with the jug of cocktail.

'*What* was that Harry said?' asked Piers who had come over to me.

'Oh nothing — just silly party conversation.'

'It's terribly hot in here, isn't it?'

'Do you feel all right? Your eyes are glittering feverishly like the Ancient Mariner's,' I said.

'Shall I engage you in conversation then?'

'If you like.'

'Then let's sit down somewhere — what about Harry's den or whatever he calls it?'

We walked, almost tiptoed, across the hall and into the little room which Harry used for the transaction of such business as overflowed from Mincing Lane into his home. Piers pushed some overcoats off the sofa and we sat down among other coats, hats and gloves. The room was dimly lit and a small gas fire popped and hissed with blue and coral flames. I felt the presence of stuffed animals around us. The atmosphere was almost romantic— indeed, a conoisseur of unusual atmospheres would have said that it was. The muffled noise of the party came to us across the hall.

'How pleasant to find you here, Wilmet. You do stand out among all these rather dreadful people,' said Piers.

'Do you find them dreadful? I expect they're very nice, really.'

'Of course they're not, and you know it,' he said truculently, staring at me so intently that I felt bound to say something.

'Sybil — that's my mother-in-law — and I are thinking of coming to your Portuguese classes,' I began. 'We want to go to Portugal next summer.'

'Really? And you think you will try to learn a few useful phrases?' He laughed sardonically.

'But you wouldn't *mind* if we came?'

'How could I? If you pay the fee you are entitled to come, of course.' He seemed uninterested in the subject, so rather in desperation I began telling him about Father Thames and his domestic troubles. We talked for quite a long time about these, until I began to feel it was time we went back to the main party, and Piers to be conscious of his empty glass.

'We must meet more often,' he said. 'And I don't mean at the Portuguese classes.'

'Of course! You must come to dinner one evening,' I said rather formally.

'I didn't quite mean that,' he said. 'I thought we might go for a walk in the park and have tea at a teashop like clandestine lovers.'

I smiled. The evening had been almost too successful, and I had the pleased and comfortable feeling I used to have after parties in Italy when I had been admired and cherished. But now, of course, it was rather different. Still, there could be no harm in having lunch with Harry or walking with Piers in the park. I could show Harry what a good wife Rowena was; and as for Piers, drifting and rootless, perhaps often drunk, it might be that my friendship could be beneficial to him. It seemed an excellent winter programme. Then, for no apparent reason, I remembered my promise to Mary Beamish to join the panel of blood donors. I saw myself lying on a table, blood pouring from a vein in my arm into a bottle which, as soon as it was full, would be snatched away and rushed to hospital to save somebody's life. There seemed at that moment no limit to what I could do.

The next morning naturally brought with it a feeling of anti-climax. We all got up late, and my announcement that I should like to go to church was received with a marked lack of enthusiasm.

'But it's the first Sunday in the month,' Harry pointed out. 'We never go in the mornings then. The vicar will be having sung Eucharist, there'll be hardly anyone there and the service will be much longer.'

'All the same I should like to go,' I persisted. 'It will be the kind of service I prefer, anyway.'

'All right then. I'll take you in the car and call for you when it's over,' said Harry rather grudgingly.

But at that moment Piers came into the room; and in the end it was he who took me in the little car, Harry not trusting him with the Jaguar.

'I may as well come to the service with you,' he said, 'though country churches always depress me.'

'Yes, I know what you mean. There is something sad about them, as if their life were all in the past — all those tablets and monuments of the eighteenth and nineteenth centuries, leaving no room for modern ones.'

'And the hidebound villagers with their gnarled hands grasping *Hymns Ancient and Modern* and rigidly opposing any change, and the gentry putting in an appearance at Matins occasionally or reading the lessons.'

'But we mustn't generalize,' I said. 'After all, there *is* young life in the country too.'

'And a new vicar trying to spike things up a bit.'

'Perhaps it's because country churches are always surrounded by graves and yew trees and they do have a kind of damp smell.'

'And almost never a smell of incense.'

We were a little too early for the service, so we walked round the churchyard together, reading the inscriptions on the grave-stones. Some graves were very old, their headstones broken and overgrown with ivy, reminding me of tumbled unmade beds. Others, because of their new raw look and the flowers arranged in jam jars or ugly vases, had a different kind of sadness.

At last we heard a distant droning of music and decided that it was time to go in. A few people, mostly women and young children, were scattered about in the pews, and I saw that the music came from the vicar's wife, pedalling away at a harmonium. The choir of girls with two men did not make much of Merbecke — as Piers said afterwards, 'One would hardly go there for the music, as people are said to in London churches.' Nevertheless, I felt that we had both been in some way moved by

48

the service, although we neither of us remarked on it. When it was over we had a word with the vicar who seemed very glad that we had come.

'Do you suppose those people who received Communion had been fasting for four hours or whatever it is?' Piers asked as we drove back. 'I feel they hardly could have been.'

'Perhaps they wouldn't know about it and so could be excused. It must be difficult for Father Lester — I suppose we should call him that — to know where to start in his instruction.'

'Yes, in the spiking up, poor man. How much better for him to have been given a cosy London church with hideous brass and stained glass and pitchpine, but a good Catholic tradition.'

'Do you go to any special church in London?' I asked.

'I go where it suits me, and when.'

I was a little chilled by the unfriendliness of his answer. 'I don't even know where you live,' I said at last.

'Holland Park, vaguely, though perhaps a little nearer to the Goldhawk Road than the address might suggest.'

'That seems rather vague, but you must be somewhere near where I live.'

'Not really, Wilmet. The dividing line between elegance and squalor may be a narrow one in London, but the distinction is very rigid.'

'I hope you don't live in squalor. Have you a flat or rooms, or what?' I asked, driven on by curiosity and intrigued by the hint of squalor.

'Well, a kind of flat.'

'And you live by yourself?'

He seemed to hesitate, so I said quickly, 'I imagine you sharing with a colleague, perhaps.'

'Yes, that's about it.'

I supposed I could hardly probe further, though I couldn't help wondering if he lived with a woman and what he would have answered if I had asked him outright.

'Are you going back this evening?' I went on.

49

'Yes, I must be at the press at ten o'clock tomorrow morning.'

He seemed tired and dispirited, and we drove the rest of the way in silence. As we got out of the car he said, 'At least there'll be the Sunday morning gins.'

After lunch we dozed over the Sunday papers. When it was teatime Rowena went to the window to pull the long yellow curtains.

'The evenings are drawing in,' she said. 'I hate November, and after tea on Sunday, too. I suppose it's because people begin to feel the oppression of Monday morning and another week upon them, and it's infectious, even if one doesn't work in an office oneself. Piers, what exactly do you *do* at the press?'

'Oh, just correct proofs. Menial work, really.'

'But you have your evening classes.'

'Yes, I have those.'

'Teaching is creative work in a way, I always think. You must feel that you are moulding people.'

'You should see what I have to mould,' said Piers gloomily.

'And teaching takes it out of you, of course,' Rowena laughed. 'You are giving of yourself, or should be.'

'I doubt if people would want *my* kind of self,' said Piers in a dry tone, 'so I'm not all that generous.'

In the morning, when we were waiting for the Green Line bus, Rowena took my hand and said earnestly, 'Wilmet, darling, do try and see something of Piers if you can. I'm sure it would be so good for him to have a nice female friend — if you could bear it, that is.'

'I expect he has lots,' I said. 'After all he's very attractive.'

'I don't know, really. He tends not to speak of his friends here, and I do sometimes wonder if they're the right kind.' Rowena frowned and then burst into laughter. 'Oh dear, that makes you sound dreary, being so very much the right kind yourself, but you know what I mean. Do give my love to Rodney, won't you?'

When Rodney came home in the evening he asked, 'How was

old Harry Grinners?' which had been our joking nickname for Harry before we really knew him. We spent some time reminiscing about our time in Italy — long evening drives in curious army vehicles with now forgotten names, the headlights picking out an urn or a coat of arms on the gateway to some villa, or illuminating a crowd of people in the square of a little town — the rococo dining-room of a particular officers' club where the Asti Spumante was warm and flat, and there were too many drunken majors ... remembered now after ten years this life had a fantastic dreamlike quality about it.

'By the way,' said Rodney suddenly, 'I meant to tell you, Bason has apparently got that job as housekeeper at the clergy house. I gather he's moving in immediately. I hope he'll turn out all right. In a way I feel responsible for his good behaviour.'

At that moment the telephone rang. It was Mary Beamish. I wondered rather apprehensively what she could be wanting me for, but she was only ringing up to tell me that all the congregation of St Luke's were invited to a social evening in the parish hall at eight o'clock next Saturday to meet Father Ransome, the new assistant priest. It had been announced after Mass on Sunday and she thought I would like to know.

'But where is he going to live?' I asked. 'Is that settled?'

'Oh yes — with *us*,' said Mary. 'We have two spare rooms which he is to have temporarily, and he can cook his own breakfast on a gas ring. He will have his other meals at the clergy house.'

I was both annoyed and amused at her news, annoyed because for some reason I did not want him to live at the Beamishes, and amused at the picture of him cooking his own breakfast on a gas ring. The whole thing seemed most unsuitable. But I certainly intended to go to the social evening in the parish hall. I had the feeling that it might be quite an interesting occasion.

CHAPTER FOUR

W HEN Saturday came Sybil began to be worried about how I should manage my evening meal.

'Eight o'clock is such an impractical time,' she said. 'It does seem that the Church is out of touch with life — one sees what people mean when they say that. Though I suppose,' she added, fair as usual, 'that eight o'clock is probably a convenient time for people who have been working till five or six and had a meal immediately afterwards. And of course people who have to go to work wouldn't want to stay up too late.'

'But tomorrow is Sunday,' I pointed out, 'so I suppose it is chosen for all of us, so that we may get up early to go to church.'

'Father Thames, from what you've told me, doesn't seem the kind of man who would naturally enjoy a cup of tea and a bun at eight o'clock in the evening. I wonder how *he* will be managing?'

'I suppose he is conditioned to it after so many years,' I said, 'so there won't be any problem. I daresay Mr Bason will be giving them a high tea, or something like that.' Then I remembered that Father Thames always heard confessions at half past six on Saturday evenings, so that was something else to be fitted in.

'Won't you at least have a drink before you go?' Sybil asked. 'I'm sure you'll need it.'

I refused, thinking that it might not mix very well with the refreshments I should get at the parish hall, and it occurred to me that one could perhaps classify different groups or circles of people according to drink. I myself seemed to belong to two very clearly defined circles — the Martini drinkers and the tea drinkers though I was only just beginning to be initiated into the latter. I imagined that both might offer different kinds of comfort, though there would surely be times when one might prefer the one that wasn't available. Indeed, as I approached the parish hall, which was next door to the clergy house, I began to wish that I had paid more heed to Sybil's suggestion of a drink. I never think of myself as being nervous socially — I am always perfectly confident when entering the room at a party — but this occasion seemed unlike any I had experienced before. I suppose that church gatherings inevitably attract the strangest mixture of people, and I felt a little apprehensive as I pushed open the door, my eyes fixing themselves on the green walls, hung with rather chipped 'Della Robbia' plaques indicating Father Thames's interest in all things Italian. Would there be anyone to whom I could easily talk? I took courage from the assumption that practically everyone in the congregation would have come to meet or have a look at Father Ransome; it wouldn't be like a whist drive which attracted a very limited circle, so there was a chance that I might find somebody congenial.

It seemed that I was right, for the hall was very crowded. I noticed that the lay people had arranged themselves in little groups, each clearly distinguishable from the others. As a kind of centrepiece there was old Mrs Beamish, large and black, at the same time brooding and quietly triumphant, presumably because Father Ransome was to live under her roof. She was surrounded by various elderly ladies in yellowish-brown fur coats, one of whom I recognized as Miss Prideaux. Mary Beamish, wearing a woollen dress of a rather unbecomingly harsh shade of blue, was hovering near her mother. I was glad that I had decided to wear black in which I always feel right. Near this group I saw Mrs Greenhill, the clergy's late housekeeper, in close conversation with her friend and crony Mrs Spooner the little verger in her familiar peacock blue hat which had a large paste replica of the bird pinned to the front of it. It seemed almost as if they might be murmuring together against the clergy, for I saw them glance in Father Thames's direction once or twice. I also noticed two well-dressed middle-aged women with a young girl, whom I remembered having seen in church sometimes. All three were

53

chinless, with large aristocratic noses. Near them stood a thin woman with purple hair and a surprised expression, as if she had not expected that it would turn out to be quite that colour. She wore a good deal of chunky jewellery, and I felt she had gone a little too far in showing that churchgoers need not necessarily be dowdy. She was rather surprisingly in conversation with a group of nuns from the convent in the parish. The nuns were of two kinds, short and motherly looking, or tall and thin with steel-rimmed spectacles, pale waxy complexions and sweet remote smiles that had something a little sinister about them.

It must not be supposed that there were no men present, but my first overwhelming impression was that, as at so many church gatherings, the women outnumbered the men. There seemed to be a kind of segregation of the sexes, though various young girls and boys moved about freely between all the groups. The largest male group was that dominated by Mr Coleman, the good looking fair-haired master of ceremonies, with his cronies, some of whom I recognized as fellow servers, but one of whom — a tall youngish man with a high dome-shaped forehead — I guessed to be Mr Bason, the new housekeeper at the clergy house. The two churchwardens and the secretary and treasurer of the parochial church council were together in a corner, looking rather important. In the middle of the room stood the three clergy. Father Thames and Father Bode were evidently leading Father Ransome round and introducing him to the various groups of people. When I entered the hall Father Ransome had his back to me, and it was not until later that I was able to form any definite impression of him. This first sight told me only that he was tall and dark.

Being alone I felt that I had to attach myself to some group, and as nobody noticed my entry nobody came forward to greet me. The obvious and dreary course would have been to join Mary Beamish and the old ladies, but something in me rebelled against this and I found myself walking over to where Mr Coleman and the presumed Mr Bason were talking together.

As so often happens, I caught the tail end of a rather esoteric conversation.

'...wouldn't *believe* the trouble we had over them,' Mr Bason was saying.

'It's really simpler when you haven't got any,' said Mr Coleman in his low voice with its slightly north country accent. 'There were only four Sundays in Advent last year, I remember, so it can be a bit of a problem to know when to use them.'

'Good evening,' I said, feeling more at ease interrupting a men's conversation than a women's.

But they did not react in quite the way I was accustomed to. Mr Coleman gave me a slightly hostile stare from his intensely blue eyes. Mr Bason looked a little surprised.

'I'm Mrs Forsyth,' I explained, 'and I think you must be Mr Bason. My husband was so glad to hear that you had settled in at the clergy house.'

'Oh, then I really owe the job to you?' said Mr Bason. He had a rather fluty enthusiastic voice, and I felt that had he been older he might have called me 'dear lady'.

'Well it did seem the obvious thing, when my husband told me about you and I knew Father Thames's need.'

'It's just the kind of thing I wanted,' said Mr Bason, 'and such jobs aren't at all easy to get. But those poor things — I really feel like a deus ex machina!'

Mr Coleman looked a little puzzled.

'I don't think we have ever met socially,' I said, not wishing to leave him out of the conversation, 'but of course I have often admired you from afar.'

He smiled and flushed slightly, and I felt that I liked him better. I made some remark about how difficult it must be to carry out the complicated ceremonial as well as he did.

'There's nothing to it once you know how, Mrs Forsyth,' he said. 'It's just a job like any other. Father Thames is a bit exacting at times, but that keeps me on my mettle.'

55

'Of course they do say, don't they, that he's a disappointed man,' said Mr Bason rather eagerly.

'Really?' I tried to keep the note of interest out of my voice, though I did not really wish to discourage Mr Bason from going further.

'Well, it is common knowledge in the diocese, surely?'

Mr Coleman looked away and said something to one of his fellow servers. I had the impression that he disapproved of the turn the conversation had taken.

'He had hoped to be made archdeacon,' declared Mr Bason in a loud clear tone.

'Archdeacon?' I echoed, but did not ask of what, for I was unwilling to reveal my ignorance of what was apparently common knowledge in the diocese.

'Certainly! And of course he is getting on now — must be over seventy.'

'Yes, I suppose he is older than Sir Denbigh Grote,' I said.

'Well, Sir Denbigh is no chicken, and he too has made rather a mess of things judging by all accounts.'

'Really? What did he do?' I tried to remember what I had heard about him. He had been at some Middle European embassy at the beginning of the war but had been obliged to leave hurriedly when the country had been overrun by Hitler's armies. 'Surely he had to leave his post because of the war?' I said. I had often pictured the scene at the embassy on that day — the hasty packing, the burning of secret documents, and even the used blotting paper in foreign-looking tiled stoves....

'Yes, he did, but I gather that he was a little over-enthusiastic in his destruction of secret papers,' said Mr Bason gloatingly. 'He went and destroyed the whole lot when he should have brought some of them away.'

'It must be very difficult to make up one's mind on such an occasion,' I said, wanting to defend Sir Denbigh.

'Yes — fortunately we are not likely to find ourselves in that sort of position,' said Mr Bason with some complacency

'Do you like living in the clergy house?' I asked.

'Yes, it's really quite cosy. I have a bed-sitter — *not* the room Mrs Greenhill had. That was a poky little room on the ground floor — very damp, I should think.'

'No wonder she got fibrositis and found the work too much for her.'

'Was that why she left, then? Well, a change had to be made. The state of that kitchen, you wouldn't believe it! I should think baked beans and chips was about all *she* knew how to cook!'

It occurred to me that Mr Bason was not being very charitable, but I seemed unable to stop his flow of talk.

'She and that verger woman are doing the refreshments to-night. I suppose that will be within her capabilities — she will make a good cup, as they say, and of course Father Bode does enjoy that; but Father Thames likes his Lapsang, which he takes correctly without milk or sugar. I prefer Earl Grey myself — find the Lapsang too smoky.'

'Do you?' I said in a rather cool tone, feeling that Mr Bason needed to be put in his place. 'I suppose Lapsang is really an acquired taste. I am very fond of it myself.'

'That rather surprises me. I feel that women don't really understand the finer points of cooking or appreciate rare things,' he went on, quite unabashed. 'All the greatest chefs have been men.'

'What do you think about this knotty problem?' I asked, turning to Mr Coleman, feeling like the chairman of a discussion. 'Mr Bason maintains that women don't really understand the finer points of cooking.'

'Oh, I don't know,' he said, rather confused. 'I think some ladies cook very well. In some ways it's funny to see a man cooking.'

Mr Bason turned away, perhaps offended, and as my conversation with Mr Coleman seemed to have come to an end I found myself temporarily with nobody to talk to. I glanced round the room to see what was happening, and began to wonder when the refreshments would be served. At this moment I caught Mary Beamish's eye and she came over to me.

'Why, Wilmet, standing there all alone,' she said. 'I didn't see you'd arrived. I'm so sorry.'

'I've been having a most interesting conversation with Mr Coleman and Mr Bason,' I said, irritated at the way she was making it appear that I had been waiting for somebody to notice me. 'It was really through Rodney that Mr Bason came to the clergy house so I felt I ought to have a word with him,' I added.

'Father Thames is delighted with him, I know,' said Mary warmly. 'Now do come over and talk to us. Miss Prideaux has been telling us about her experiences in Vienna when she was a governess to the royal family.'

I allowed myself to be led over to the little group. Miss Prideaux was certainly talking in her dry precise voice, but not now of Vienna.

'And he gets his own breakfast?' I heard her ask.

'Yes, there is a gas ring up there. He could cook sausages or eggs and bacon, or even kippers if he wanted to,' said Mrs Beamish, dwelling on the various dishes appreciatively. She spoke with a kind of pride, and I knew that they must be talking of Father Ransome. 'It will be quite like old times to have a priest in the house again,' she added.

Miss Prideaux took a small handkerchief from her bag and pressed it to her lips. I saw that it had a dove and the word ASSISI embroidered on it in cross stitch.

'So handy for you,' she said.

I wanted to laugh, for it sounded so odd the way Miss Prideaux put it, as if Father Ransome might be useful for chasing burglars, mending fuses or other manly jobs.

'But will he be about the house much?' I asked. 'I mean in the usual sense?'

'Well no, he will be having his main meals at the clergy house,' said Mary. 'But I suppose we may give him a meal occasionally.'

I was about to ask further questions when I saw that the

58

moment had come. The group of priests was approaching us, and Father Thames was soon introducing Father Ransome.

His christian names—Marius Lovejoy—and the first glimpse of him earlier in the evening had led me to expect somebody handsome, but even so the impact of his good looks was quite startling. He was certainly very handsome indeed, with his dark wavy hair and large brown eyes. The bones in his face were well defined and his expression serious. I remembered that he had been in the East End and in the worst part of Kensington, and I wondered whether the suffering and poverty he had seen there had left their mark on him, until I realized that it probably wouldn't be like that in these days of the welfare state. I had been thinking of Father Lowder and a hundred years ago.

'How do you do,' I murmured as he was introduced to me.

Father Thames was holding forth about the accommodation problem at the clergy house. 'I wonder how many people realize that we haven't as many rooms as you might think,' he said. 'On the ground floor is the dining-room, a room we use for meetings, and a small cloakroom with a washbasin — cold water tap *only*; also the kitchen, of course, and the little room Mrs Greenhill had which we are now using as a storeroom.'

I wondered what they would be storing.

'Then upstairs there is my study and bedroom, the oratory, Father Bode's two rooms, a bathroom, Mr Bason's room, and a spare bedroom — very poky — for visiting clergy. We are really very cramped! *And*,' he paused impressively, 'this will surprise you — there is no basement! Now, would you have believed that?'

'All these old houses do have basements,' said Mrs Beamish, as if Father Thames were deliberately concealing that of the clergy house.

'But the house is *not* so old — that is another surprise! It was built in 1911 and was never intended as a clergy house at all. Its first occupant had five children!'

None of us seemed able to comment suitably on this.

'Things are very different today,' said Father Bode at last, his rosy little face beaming. 'No kiddies about the place now! I can see Mrs Greenhill at the urn. Now we can get on to the main object of this gathering, eh, Ransome?' he added jokingly.

Not the most felicitous of remarks, I thought, wondering how Father Ransome would take his badinage.

'I'm sure everyone will be glad of a cup of tea,' he said, in a curious, almost ironical tone. It occurred to me that he must be very tired of being introduced to people; perhaps even his flow of clerical small talk was beginning to dry up.

'Ah, Mrs Greenhill!' Father Bode stood rubbing his hands as she approached, attended by a kind of acolyte bearing cups of tea on a tray. 'The cups that cheer! I hope you've made mine extra strong with plenty of sugar.'

'I think it will be just as you like it, Father,' said Mrs Greenhill comfortably. Her rather pinched-looking features relaxed into a smile. 'I know you like these iced buns.'

I stood back listening to the cosy parish talk, wondering whether Mr Bason with his Earl Grey and sole véronique wouldn't really be wasted on Father Bode. I tasted my own tea and put the cup down again quickly, for it was not at all to *my* liking, nor did I feel I could tackle one of the large brightly iced cakes which were offered. I noticed that Father Thames was not eating or drinking either.

'Do you know,' he said in a low tone, 'I have been a priest for over forty years and I have never been able to take Indian tea. That will surprise you! It just doesn't agree with me. Of course these evening gatherings take place at difficult times, gastronomically speaking, but tea has become the tradition and most people seem to enjoy it. I shall have something later.'

'I hope Mr Bason is settling down well?' I asked.

'My *dear*, Mrs — er — so it was *you* who found him? Yes, of course, I remember that it was. Have I thanked you enough, I wonder? Do you know,' he lowered his tone, 'he has promised us a coq au vin?'

60

'I'm so glad,' I said.

'I'm just going over to have a word with Mother Beatrice and the sisters,' whispered Mary Beamish, coming up to me. 'Do you know Mrs Pollard and Miss Dove and Susan?' She indicated the group of chinless aristocratic looking ladies I had noticed when I came in. I had a quick foretaste of the sort of conversation we should be making and said hastily that I must be going home now. And indeed I felt that I had had enough. I moved as unobtrusively as I could towards the door, glancing back as I did so to see whether anybody else was leaving so early.

As I did so I happened to catch Father Ransome's eye. He gave a quick upward glance of mock suffering and half smiled. I was a little surprised that he should show his feelings in this intimate way, and wondered if anybody else had noticed. Poor young man, how tired he must be of the whole business! I supposed I could ask him in to have a drink one evening or even a meal. It was now even more galling to think of him living at the Beamishes. No doubt Mary would adopt a kind of proprietary attitude towards him.

Outside it was beginning to rain and it did not seem likely that there would be any taxis cruising about near the church. I stood hesitating, looking at the cars parked outside the hall, one of which was Mr Coleman's Husky. As I waited he came out with some of the servers; they piled into the car without so much as glancing in my direction and drove off quickly. I supposed they might be going back to the home or lodgings of one of them, but I found it difficult to imagine their private lives. It was now nearly half past nine — an awkward time, too late for going to a film; and although I had not the least desire to do anything of the sort, I arrived home wet and tired, feeling rather ill-used.

But in the drawing-room everything was warm and comfortable. A friend of Sybil's, Professor Arnold Root, an elderly archaeologist, was sitting by the fire and they were examining some fragments of pottery together. Rodney was reading some official-looking papers.

'Why, darling, you're wet!' he said. 'Why didn't you ring up? I'd have come for you in the car. Take off your coat and shoes and come to the fire.'

He fussed round me devotedly and I was comforted at once. 'It's only just started to rain,' I said, 'and in any case it probably wouldn't have been suitable to be fetched in a car.'

'Do Christians go in for discomfort for its own sake?' asked Sybil in her detached way. 'It seems unnecessary to me and rather stupid.'

'I suppose most of them don't have cars,' said Rodney.

'Deverel Rimbury?' said Professor Root, holding up a fragment of pottery. 'I think *not*. Mortification of the flesh has of course been a feature of many religious systems,' he added.

He was a gaunt, rather handsome old man, who shared Sybil's lack of religious faith as well as her interest in archaeology.

'What is this new curate like?' Rodney asked.

'Tall, dark and handsome,' I said. 'His name is Marius.'

'Just what you wanted then,' said Sybil tolerantly, as if I were a child who had just been given a new toy. 'And he is lodging with the Beamishes? Ella will like that and I daresay Mary will find it agreeable too.'

'I don't imagine they'll see much of him,' I said quickly. 'He is having his main meals at the clergy house and just making his breakfast on a gas ring at the Beamishes.'

Rodney laughed. 'Poor Marius — perhaps not *quite* the epicurean.'

'I'm not so sure,' I said. 'Apparently Mr Bason has promised them a coq au vin at the clergy house.'

'Funny thing that, about Pater,' said Professor Root, continuing in his own line of thought. 'Was it not after the publication of *Marius* that he left Oxford to live in Kensington, to see life as it were? I wonder what life one would have seen in Kensington in those days?'

'Father Ransome was a curate in North Kensington,' I said. 'I suppose he must have seen life of a kind there.'

'Afterwards,' Professor Root continued, 'Pater returned to Oxford, having one presumes seen as much as he wanted.' He chuckled and began filling his pipe. 'We are not all fortunate enough to be able to do that!'

'What did you think of Bason?' Rodney asked.

'Rather an odd young man, but I should think he will be an admirable housekeeper. He talks a great deal, doesn't he?'

'Yes, he was always holding forth about something or other when he was with us, but it does seem as if he has found his niche now.'

CHAPTER FIVE

'ALL these young people pouring forth,' Sybil observed, as some undergraduates wearing duffle coats and striped scarves narrowly avoided knocking us over. 'How splendid it is to be young and to have the wonder of it all before you! To be handed the key to the treasury of all knowledge!' She thumped her umbrella vigorously on the ground. 'Let us hope that Piers Longridge is going to give *us* that key.'

'Yes, I hope so too,' I said rather doubtfully. The sight of so many young people in a mass had dismayed rather than encouraged me. I did not think I should be able to learn anything. Even the pleasure of seeing Piers again seemed a doubtful one, weighed against the unknown difficulties of the Portuguese language.

'I suppose the lessons will be in *this* building,' said Sybil. 'The porter told us to inquire when we got inside, didn't he?'

It seemed a noble building, glimpsed in the November twilight — perhaps too noble for evening classes. We pushed open a swing door and found ourselves in a kind of entrance hall with noticeboards on which challenging posters, summoning the students to religious and political gatherings or to help various kinds of refugees, were pinned. On either side of the central space were two large white marble statues, male and female, perhaps representing knowledge and wisdom, courage and hope, or other suitable concepts. I looked down at the female's great broad white feet and imagined that were she not barefooted she might have trouble with her shoes. I could almost see the incipient bunion and feel the pain of the fallen arch.

'I suppose the ancient Greeks went barefoot,' I remarked, as Sybil inquired the whereabouts of the beginners' class in Portuguese.

'It is in room 18B, which has a sinister sound about it,' said Sybil. 'It is striking six now — we had better hurry.'

'Yes, we don't want to be late,' I agreed.

I was eager to see Piers, how he looked facing the class, but although the room was full of a confused mass of people of apparently all ages, there was as yet no sign of him, and the voices we had heard through the door were those of his prospective pupils. As time went on I was to know them quite well: Miss Wetherby and Miss Cane, two elderly spinsters who planned to hitchhike round Portugal and write a book about it; Miss James and Miss Honey, young and pretty girls, who seemed to be learning the language for personal and romantic reasons, and always giggled a good deal when it came to explaining the different ways of saying 'like' and 'love'; Miss Childe, whose reasons for learning were never clear to me; and Mrs Marble, who seemed to have a passion for evening classes in themselves, and had done Spanish last year and Italian the year before that. The men — Messrs Potts, Bridewell, Stanniforth and Jones — were all engaged in commerce and were struggling to read letters from Pernambuco, São Paulo and Rio de Janeiro, but Dr McEntee wanted to be able to decipher contemporary documents about the Lisbon earthquake. Sybil and I, with our unashamed admission that all we wanted was to learn enough to get about on a holiday, seemed to have a less noble aim than the others, for even the two young girls hoped eventually to acquire husbands.

At about five past six Piers came in carrying an evening paper and a few books. I thought how distinguished he looked standing up before us, even the blackboard making a frame for his fair good looks. Sybil and I had chosen desks in the front row, and I was gratified when he gave us a special smile.

'Now Portuguese is not so much like Spanish as you might suppose,' he began, 'so those of you who know Spanish had better try and forget about it for the time being.'

Mrs Marble looked crestfallen and the commercial gentlemen began to murmur among themselves.

'Nor is this expensive grammar book which you have been advised to buy the one I should recommend myself. Still, it will do to learn verbs and all those tedious things that must be learnt.'

We felt a little discouraged, but soon forgot about it as our interest was aroused, for Piers was a surprisingly good teacher and I wondered whether he was making a special effort to be successful in this field. It was odd to be learning something again, but there was a certain lightheartedness in the process, as if we had shed some of the intervening years since schooldays. We laughed inordinately at the smallest jokes, finding something amusing in the most ridiculous trifles, and when we were actually given homework it seemed the funniest thing of all.

After the lesson was over the pupils began putting on their coats, the young girls hurrying off to evening engagements perhaps, the others going in search of food or to the bus or train which would take them home. I was thinking that it would be nice to have a word with Piers; but a little group had collected round him, presumably having been lying in wait at the door of the classroom. I wondered if I should join the group but decided to remain aloof, for I could hear questions being asked about the use of the subjunctive and I did not feel equal to that kind of conversation. I amused myself by observing these students, who seemed to be of all ages, until I came to the conclusion that people who went to evening classes were all more or less odd. It was unnatural to want to acquire knowledge after working hours. A tall bearded young man, whose string bag revealed a loaf of bread (the wrapped, sliced kind), a tin of Nescafé and two books from a public library, filled me with a kind of sadness, as if his whole life had been revealed to me by these telling details.

'Do your pupils bother you much out of class?' asked Sybil in her clear open tone. 'I suppose they must want to ask you to explain things quite often?'

'Oh yes,' Piers laughed. 'There's always trouble about something, but I usually have to tell them that I can't go into it all now, so they go away discouraged.'

'Teaching must be very tiring,' I said. 'We must try not to be too much of a nuisance with our questions. I'm sure there will be lots of things I don't understand but I shall probably be too proud to admit it.'

It had been arranged that after the lesson Sybil and I should go to dinner at her club, where Rodney and Professor Root were to join us. I thought what a pity it was that Piers could not come too, but I hardly liked to suggest it to Sybil. He, too, seemed to want to hurry away, but before he did so he drew me aside and said in a low voice, 'If you aren't doing anything tomorrow, would you have lunch with me?'

I said that I should like to, and he named a restaurant and time.

'Did you hear that?' I said to Sybil, for I was sure she must have done, 'Piers has asked me to have lunch with him tomorrow.'

'That should be good for your Portuguese conversation,' she said briskly.

'It will be very limited conversation after only one lesson,' I said, my thoughts going back to the somewhat dry and barren sentences which we had been reciting.

'Well, it will keep him out of the wine lodge, having lunch with you,' said Sybil, 'and that should be a satisfaction to you both. Now will Noddy and Arnold be waiting for us in the hall? Do men feel awkward in a women's club, I wonder? I suppose they well might.'

'Here we are,' said Rodney, coming forward. 'We didn't quite know when to expect you, but it's really been quite an experience waiting here.'

'We have been doing our best to get off, as the vulgar saying is, with those two ladies over there,' said Professor Root, 'but evidently they did not recognize the technique or have never had it practised upon them. I suppose our methods were at fault.'

'I can't imagine what you must have been doing,' said Sybil. 'One is the headmistress of a well known girls' school and the other a professor of botany. I should imagine they would have more important things to do than look around for unattached men.'

'Or they might realize that we were waiting for somebody and be afraid of an embarrassing situation,' said Rodney.

'You mean when we were claimed by our rightful ladies?' chortled Professor Root.

'It would be a piquant situation,' said Rodney, 'an archaeologist and a civil servant having women fight over them — rather unusual, perhaps.'

'You flatter yourselves if you think we should have fought over you,' said Sybil. 'Wilmet and I could have had a very enjoyable dinner by ourselves.'

I smiled rather weakly. For some reason or other I found myself out of tune with the artificiality of the conversation, and during dinner I seemed to detach myself from my surroundings, admiring Sybil's competent ordering of the dishes and calmly efficient way with the waitress, but imagining myself lunching with Piers the next day. In my mind I went over all my clothes, allowing for every possible kind of weather — though if it were wet I should of course take a taxi, so that rain did not really matter. In the end I decided on a new dark grey suit with my marten stole and a little turquoise velvet hat.

It was a fine day and I was five minutes late at the restaurant, which was of the kind which has no foyer for waiting. I supposed Piers would be sitting at a table inside with some kind of drink in front of him, glancing up each time somebody came in. But after looking round me vainly and meeting the expectant or hopeful glances of various waiting men, I was forced to the conclusion that Piers was not among them.

'Mr Longridge?' I asked the manager, who was hovering round me. 'Has he reserved a table?'

He consulted a list. 'No, Madame, I have not the name here. Madame will wait?'

He showed me to a table rather too near the door and I sat down. When a waiter came up to me I ordered a glass of Tio Pepe. As I sat drinking it occurred to me that I ought to have realized that Piers would be late. Unpunctuality would not, after

68

all, be unexpected in one who had followed so many different callings; perhaps this, too, was one of the reasons for his failures.

It did not take me long to finish my drink, and although it had done something to dispel my first feeling of disappointment and irritation, I now began to feel irritated in another way. Was I to sit here alone drinking sherry until he chose to show up? He was already twenty minutes late, there seemed no reason now why he should ever come. Obviously he or I had mistaken the day or the restaurant or both. I supposed I should have to order lunch by myself, and I wondered if there was perhaps some special kind of meal provided (at a reduced price) for women whose escorts had failed to turn up. I amused myself by composing the menu, which might start with the very thinnest of soups and go on to plain boiled fish without sauce — unless, of course, it was thought that a rejected woman needed to be cosseted and all the specialities of the house would be produced, everything flambé in liqueurs.... I must have been smiling to myself at the idea, for I looked up and there was Piers smiling down at me. My relief and pleasure on seeing him quite overcame the possible irritation I might have felt when I saw that he was wearing a duffle coat, a garment I do not approve of for grown men's London wear.

'I hardly deserve to be greeted with a smile,' he said as he sat down, 'when I'm so unforgivably late. But you *do* forgive me, Wilmet?' He looked at me in such a way that I did not need to answer. More sherry was ordered, then wine and food, and all was happy between us. He did not excuse or explain his lateness and I did not refer to it myself, supposing that it had been caused by work or a traffic jam, both of which seemed reasonable explanations.

He was in excellent spirits and we talked of many things. I told him about the arrival of Father Ransome and the social evening to welcome him.

'I wish I'd come to that,' he said. 'That sort of occasion always amuses me, and if you had been there I should have felt quite at home.'

'Or you could have joined up with Mr Bason or Mr Coleman and the servers,' I said. 'There were some male groups.'

'Well next time perhaps you'll take me.'

'I suppose you're rather busy in the evenings, with all these French and Portuguese classes. By the way, Sybil thought it would be so good for my Portuguese to have lunch with you,' I laughed.

Piers poured more wine into my glass. 'This is Colares,' he said, 'a cheap Portuguese wine, but not unpalatable. Was this what she meant, I wonder?'

'She may have. Nothing is really beyond her powers of imagination.'

'Would she approve of our lunching together if it weren't for the Portuguese?'

'Oh yes,' I said enthusiastically.

'Can she really approve all that much? I mean, as much as you make it sound?'

'Of course,' I said with modified enthusiasm, for I had just realized that I could hardly tell Piers of our plans for his reform. 'Rowena would be pleased, too,' I added.

'And Harry, no doubt,' he said sarcastically. 'And what about Rodney?'

'He wouldn't mind at all.'

'He wouldn't mind. You notice the way you put it — others would approve or be delighted, Rodney wouldn't mind.'

'Well, he isn't the sort of person to mind things. He's not a jealous type.'

'Isn't he? I should be if you were mine.'

I was touched by his phrase, but thought that the compliment implicit in it was best met with silence. I finished my coffee and looked round the room which was now almost empty. I remembered the good I had been going to do to Piers; keeping him from his work was not a very suitable beginning.

'It's rather late,' I said. 'Oughtn't you to be getting back?'

'Now don't be dreary,' he said. 'I'm taking the afternoon off.

I thought we might go somewhere on a bus, or something simple like that — perhaps walk by the river if your shoes are suitable.'

They were not particularly, and when we got off the bus after a rather long and unfamiliar ride, I found the rough path difficult going. But I was so touched by his thoughtfulness that I soon forgot my discomfort. It seemed such an unusual thing to be doing, walking by the river on a misty autumn afternoon. The sun was out but would soon be setting, and its light made the water look wonderfully mysterious — a great sheet of pink and silver fading away into the distance — so that one felt the open sea must lie beyond it. The warehouses on the opposite bank looked like palaces, and the boats glided like gondolas.

We had not gone very far when a great and splendid looking building loomed up round a bend in the path. It was of rose brown brick, with minarets almost in the Turkish style. The façade was decorated with carved swags of fruit and flowers, and there were many windows, blank and blind looking, some a little open.

'What is it?' I asked in wonder. 'I never expected to see such a building here.'

'It's a furniture depository,' said Piers.

'But those minarets and Grinling Gibbons decorations — it's all too noble to be just *that*!'

'The birds have not respected it,' said Piers, and I saw then that the rosy façade was white with their droppings.

'I wonder what it's like inside,' I said. 'Vast high-ceilinged rooms filled with huge shrouded bulky objects — great trunks of clothes, surely rather musty now, and books too.'

'Or a kind of sprawling decay — the furniture rotting and riddled with woodworm, legs of tables breaking off in your hand, chair backs collapsing at a touch....'

'I'm sure that couldn't be so when it belongs to such a very reputable firm,' I protested. 'And I suppose things couldn't be left there indefinitely.'

'You would have to pay, of course,' said Piers. 'It would be like keeping an aged relative in an institution.'

'Yes, that grand piano for which you've never found room in your new flat. It's rather sad, really, isn't it?'

'But Wilmet, life is like that, you know. Like your name — so sad, and you so gay and poised.'

I liked this description of myself and longed for him to say more.

'Did you know that my name came out of one of Charlotte M. Yonge's novels?' I asked him. 'My mother was very fond of them. But why do you think it sad?'

'Because it seems to be neither one thing nor the other,' he said, rather mysteriously, and then fell silent.

'Why, there's a kind of chapel,' I exclaimed, as we walked on a little. 'At least that's what it looks like, though I suppose it hardly could be, really.'

'Why not?' said Piers. 'It might be fitting to hold a kind of religious service over furniture as it enters the depository. Undenominational, do you think, like the chapel of a crematorium?'

'Oh no,' I protested, 'surely there would be incense. Think how hygienic it would be — the very strongest kind of incense to smoke out the woodworm!'

We enlarged on our fantasies for some time, until the sun began to sink and the air to grow cold. I nestled down into my fur and drew it up round my face.

'Now we will go back and have tea in Kensington,' said Piers, 'if you would like that.'

'Yes, I should,' I said, 'though I suppose I really ought to be getting home.'

'Why, can't you do as you like?' he asked. 'Your husband is at his work and your mother-in-law is no doubt learning the present indicative of *falar*, *aprender* and *partir*, as I told my class to do. Nobody will miss you.'

'No,' I said comfortably. 'I'm useless.'

He did not contradict me.

'We haven't spoken any Portuguese,' I said as we sat at tea.

'My dear Wilmet, I'm afraid that after one lesson you would hardly be up to the kind of conversation I should like to have with you,' he smiled.

'I hope I may be one day,' I said. 'I have enjoyed this afternoon so much — seeing the furniture depository and walking by the river. All those rooms of furniture — just think!'

'We'll build in sonnets pretty rooms,' said Piers strangely. 'And now I really should call in at the press to see if anything has come in for me.'

'Might something have come in this afternoon?'

'Today,' said Piers. 'I haven't been in all day, I'm afraid.'

'Should you have been?'

'Certainly I should.'

'Then why haven't you?'

'Wilmet, when you work for your living — and I hope you may never have to — you find that there are some days when you can hardly bear to do your work, and others when you definitely cannot bear to. This has been one of those days. I woke up this morning knowing that I couldn't bear it, so I didn't go.'

I hardly knew what to say. Neither sympathy nor reproach seemed quite what was called for. I found myself thinking that if he hadn't been at work at all he really had no excuse for being so late for lunch. I also felt that I had not done very well by distracting him when he might have gone to work in the afternoon. But then I had not known the circumstances. Perhaps I had helped to make him a little happier by my company and that might be something.

'Will you come in?' he said, as we approached the press.

'Yes, I'm rather curious to see where you work.'

'Or don't work!'

We went up a dark narrow flight of stairs, and Piers led me into a mean little room where a middle-aged man and an elderly woman sat reading with green-shaded lights pulled low over their tables. Long strips of galley proof were festooned over chairs and tables, and some had slipped on to the floor. I noticed an untouched cup of tea, now cold and grey-scummed, on the windowsill.

'Ah, Mr Longridge, we are honoured.' The elderly lady spoke without looking up from her work.

Obviously this could not be the colleague with whom Piers shared a flat. Nor did it seem likely that it was the middle-aged man, who was muttering to himself, taking no notice of us.

'We were wondering if we should send out a search party,' said the woman, whom Piers had introduced as Miss Limpsett. 'Your tea was poured out and ready at a quarter to eleven and still you did not come. Mr Towers began to do some of your work, but of course he could not manage the Portuguese.' She took off her spectacles and rubbed her eyes. 'I have been reading Greek all day — really, I am quite tired. And I have got a nice chop for my supper. I think I shall go home.'

I saw that she also had a popular woman's magazine in her basket, and was glad to think of her escaping into a world of romance after her dreary day at the press.

Piers picked up a bundle of proofs. 'I shall take these home with me. I do sometimes work at home,' he added when we were out of the room. 'Miss Limpsett and Mr Towers are not the most stimulating of companions.'

'Have you always done this work?' I asked.

'Nobody has *always* done it. Mr Towers was once a clergyman and had a preparatory school. Miss Limpsett looked after her old father, a considerable scholar, until he died. Then it was discovered that all his years of tyranny had given her the means of earning some kind of living. I mean better than she could have earned as a servant or companion. Now she gets her own back by raising obscure queries which drive the authors into a frenzy. But the printers' readers must assert themselves somehow.'

I felt depressed by what I had seen, and wished I could have gone straight home after tea. I did not like to think of Piers working in such surroundings.

'I imagine the person you share your flat with wasn't either of those two,' I said, with an attempt at laughter.

'No, it certainly wasn't,' said Piers.

'I must go home,' I said. 'Thank you for the afternoon.'

'I'm glad you enjoyed it,' he said without much interest. He seemed now to be distant and withdrawn, and I felt I should not extend an invitation to dinner or suggest any future meeting.

'Here is a taxi coming,' I said. 'I think I'll take it. The rush hour will have started, won't it?'

'Yes, and the pubs will be open.'

The taxi took me away, and my last glimpse of Piers was of him standing on the edge of the pavement with the bundle of proofs in his hand.

When I got home Sybil greeted me in an unusual way.

'*Falo, falas, fala, falamos, falais, falam,*' she recited. 'I suppose you will have learnt more than that this afternoon.'

'I don't know,' I said, for now that it was all over I hardly knew how to describe my lunch and afternoon with Piers. I felt that I could tell Sybil about the furniture depository — she would like that — but not about the confusion of pleasure, sadness, uneasiness and expectation that the day seemed to have left behind.

CHAPTER SIX

NOVEMBER came upon us with all its usual fogs and dreariness, the approach of winter and the shortening days bringing a corresponding depression of spirits. I saw nothing more of Piers except in his capacity as a teacher of Portuguese. He made no special effort to talk to me after the classes, and pride prevented me from joining the group which crowded round him asking what seemed the most silly and obvious questions. We went through all the tedious beginnings of learning a language, with everything in the present tense and the personnel peculiar to grammar books — the father, the mother, the uncle, the aunt, the professor, the dog, the blackboard, the pencil, the pen. Occasionally, when he was in a good mood, Piers would digress and tell us about Portuguese wines or the odd things Brazilians said when they spoke the language. I had not expected that the cosiness of the afternoon by the river would be repeated, and it was no doubt just as well that it should not be, but I found myself wondering whether Piers did not sometimes want to see me again as he had apparently enjoyed my company on that occasion. I had really no idea what he did in his spare time, apart from drinking, or who his friends were, and although I planned to ask him to dinner to meet Rodney and have a pleasant civilized evening, the weeks went by and I did nothing about it.

One morning I received a card from the blood transfusion centre asking me to attend a session the following week. I had quite forgotten that I had filled in a form which Mary Beamish had given me some time ago, but now the idea of giving blood seemed exciting and I looked forward to the experience like a kind of treat. On the day I was to go, Mary rang up and said that she would come with me. It was too soon after her last session for her to give blood, but she had thought I might feel strange, not having been before.

We were to attend the afternoon session and Sybil made me eat a particularly large lunch. She seemed to think that it would enrich my blood and make it all the more valuable to some dying person.

'I was very much afraid I shouldn't be able to get away,' Mary chattered as we met at the bus stop. 'Mother was in one of her restless moods, but eventually I got Miss Prideaux to come and sit with her so she'll be all right till I get back. In fact, Miss Prideaux very kindly promised to give her her tea so I really needn't hurry back. I've got them some crumpets, and Mother always likes those.'

I saw old Mrs Beamish with the butter running down her chin, licking her fingers.

'Here we are,' said Mary brightly, 'this is where we get off.'

The hospital was next door to a church and the blood donor's centre was in the crypt. We went down some steps and along a passage whose walls were adorned with eighteenth-century memorial tablets. It seemed fitting that we should be going into a kind of charnel house to give our blood, but the room we entered was all bustling efficiency, lit with strip lighting and hygienically clean. Only the patches of damp on the greenish distempered walls gave any hint that we were in a crypt. Several people were lying on beds, others sat on chairs clasping bottles which bore different coloured labels. Two men in white coats sat at a table receiving the donors as they came in, and joking as they made out cards and took drops of blood from pricks in our fingers.

As we waited I studied the people round me, who were of all types and ages, trying to decide whether they all had some air of nobility in common. I came to the conclusion that while some were young, the majority were of the burden-bearing type, middle-aged and tired-looking, the sort of people who would take on yet another load in addition to all the others they already bore.

Soon my turn came and I found myself lying on one of the beds while a nurse rolled up my sleeve and fixed a kind of tourniquet on my left arm. Then a disconcertingly young looking doctor pricked me with a needle, fixed a tube and told me to squeeze the block of wood I was holding. I lay back and stared at the ceiling preparing to meditate until the right amount of blood should have gone out of me.

But suddenly there was a disturbance at the door. Raising my head a little I saw that a tall rather mad-looking woman in a bushy fur coat and red hat was arguing with the men in white coats.

'I really cannot wait in the queue. I am Miss Daunt,' I heard her say in a loud ringing tone. 'My blood is Rhesus *negative*, the most valuable kind. I have a letter from the Regional Director.' She seemed to fumble with a paper, then raised her voice. '*This precious blood*,' she read, 'that is the phrase used. And you expect me to wait here behind all these people! Why somebody might be dying for want of my blood while I sat here waiting! How would you feel if *that* were to happen?'

I did not hear the men's answers, if indeed they gave any — I supposed they might have a kind of professional indifference to death — but Miss Daunt apparently gained her point and soon appeared on the bed next to mine, flinging off her coat with a gesture and baring her arm triumphantly.

'This precious blood,' she murmured, and began muttering to herself, first about her blood and then about irrelevant things which I could only half hear — a quarrel with somebody about a broken milk bottle and what they had said to each other. It seemed like a 'stream of consciousness' novel, but I was relieved when she stopped talking for I had been afraid that she might address me. Virginia Woolf might have brought something away from the experience, I thought; perhaps writers always do this, from situations that merely shock and embarrass ordinary people. And after all, Miss Daunt was probably only a little odd. Nevertheless I was glad when I was lying down in another room,

78

drinking rather too sweet tea. I was sure that Miss Daunt would have refused indignantly had she been asked if she wanted to lie down after she had given her blood.

'Now you mustn't rush away too soon as it's your first time,' said Mary fussily.

'Not like you did that morning at the Settlement,' I reminded her.

'I feel quite dashing having the afternoon off,' said Mary. 'Are you doing anything afterwards?'

'Well, I don't know really,' I said cautiously, wondering what she was about to suggest.

'I was just wondering if you would like to come and help me to choose a dress,' Mary went on. 'I really do need a new one, you know — a sort of wool dress suitable for parish evening occasions.'

'A sort of wool dress suitable for parish evening occasions' — I turned the depressing description over in my mind. Poor Mary, was that really all the social life she had? I supposed that it must be.

'Mother was saying that my blue is so shabby that I must get something else.' She mentioned the name of an old-established but fashionable shop where her mother had an account, so we made our way there. I was surprised, knowing the shop, that Mary did not appear better dressed.

'I usually go to the sales,' she added, explaining what I wanted to know. 'They have some very good reductions, but I suppose I shall have to pay more now.'

Obviously, then, it was Mary and people like her who bought the trying electric blue or dingy olive green dress which had been reduced because nobody could wear it. And she probably gave the money she saved to the church or some charitable organization. And I bought as many clothes as I wanted in all the most becoming styles and colours, gave a little money to the church and none at all to charitable organizations. The contrast was an uncomfortable one and I did not wish to dwell on it. It was

79

better when we were engulfed in the perfumed air and soft carpets of the shop, and Mary, like a schoolgirl being taken out for a half holiday, was excitedly calling my attention to the various counters.

'What lovely scarves! The colours are so pretty now, aren't they? And all these beads and jewels — it's like Aladdin's cave, isn't it!' she chattered. 'But I suppose dresses will be upstairs, so we'd better not waste time down here.'

We entered the 'gown salon', which was rather empty at this time of the afternoon; acres of grey carpet seemed to stretch in front of us. A black-gowned saleswoman advanced upon us and addressed her offer of help to me.

'Well, it's really I who want to be helped,' said Mary in her open way. 'I just want an everyday wool dress in blue or green, nothing too elegant.'

'Have you ever considered black?' I asked when the saleswoman had gone away to get some dresses. 'I think it would suit you.'

'Do you?' asked Mary doubtfully. 'I've never worn it, except when Father died. Mother doesn't consider it suitable for girls. I mean,' she smiled, 'she didn't when I *was* a girl — so I've nearly always had blue or green.'

She tried a few dresses which fitted quite well but were uninteresting. Then I asked the saleswoman to bring something in black. I wondered why I was taking all this trouble over Mary Beamish, for when one came to think of it what did it matter what she wore? She might just as well buy a dress as much like her old blue as possible, for all the difference it would make to her life.

But when the black dress was brought it fitted best of all, and the plain bodice and full pleated skirt were very becoming.

'The neckline is rather severe,' said Mary critically. 'Still, I suppose it would do for church functions.'

'Well, madam, it would be just the thing for anything like that,' said the saleswoman, smiling ingratiatingly. 'Clergymen do wear such a lot of black, don't they?'

This aspect of the situation had not occurred to either of us, and we could not help laughing at it.

'And you could always dress up the neckline with pearls,' I said enthusiastically, like a fashion magazine.

'Yes, I have the string Father gave me on my twenty-first birthday,' said Mary.

'Oh, not English gentlewoman real pearls,' I said. 'I mean artificial ones like we saw downstairs — two or three strings at least — perhaps pink ones, they would give you a kind of glow.'

'Do I want to have that?' Mary asked with a smile.

'Surely all women want it,' I said, wondering if this were true.

'Of course, I don't use make-up, except for a little powder,' said Mary. 'I never have, really. I suppose it would improve me.'

I made a noncommittal answer.

'I think it would only make me feel awkward if I started to use it now,' Mary went on, 'and I don't know what Mother would say.'

She decided to take the black dress away with her, and I also persuaded her to buy a necklace to go with it — a double row of pearls with the faintest tinge of pink in them.

'I don't know when I shall wear them,' she laughed.

We turned into a side street where I knew of a good place to have tea, a favourite haunt of shopping women. It was already crowded but we managed to find a small table to ourselves, sitting on a narrow green banquette wedged against the silver-striped walls.

'This place is really for women, isn't it,' whispered Mary, pointing out a rather uncomfortable-looking husband with his wife's parcels piled on his knee. 'That poor man looks so miserable.'

At that moment a young clergyman with an elderly woman, presumably his mother, came in. The two men looked at each other as specimens in a zoo might, each commiserating with the other in his unhappy situation.

'I suppose very few men are free to come out to tea in the

middle of the afternoon,' I remarked, 'and they let themselves be led by their women. But clergymen must have quite a lot of free time in the day — what do they do with it all, I wonder? Certainly one doesn't see great droves of them having tea in this sort of place. Perhaps they go to the pictures?'

'They aren't really free,' said Mary seriously. 'They have to visit in the parish, you know. Father Bode does a great deal of visiting in the afternoons. He told me that if he does it in the evenings he finds that people are looking at the television and don't like to be interrupted.'

'Does Father Ransome do much visiting?' I asked.

'I don't think he has yet,' said Mary. 'But he spends a lot of time at the clergy house so we don't see him very much.'

I thought I detected some confusion in her manner. She had seemed to hesitate, as if wanting to tell me something but not quite being able to bring it out.

I suggested another cup of tea, and after we had started to drink it I began to ask her more about Father Ransome, hoping for the revelation of some interesting personal details about him.

'He's always very friendly,' she said evasively. 'We sometimes ask him to coffee in the evenings.'

'Are his rooms self-contained?' I asked.

'No, but there is a bathroom up there, and a gas ring in his sitting-room. I went up one day and had a cup of tea with him,' she said shyly.

I wondered what Mrs Beamish had thought of that.

'Mother had gone out to tea with Miss Dove and Mrs Pollard — they came to fetch her in their car,' Mary explained quickly.

'And was it fun — I mean, did you like having tea with him?' I asked.

'Yes, he was very interesting — telling me about his experiences in the East End and in North Kensington,' said Mary seriously. Then her face reddened and she brought out in a kind of rush, 'He asked me to call him Marius, but I don't feel I can, somehow.'

'Why not?' I said lightly enough, though I was conscious of a feeling of annoyance at her revelation. 'Did he just ask you without any warning, as it were?'

'Yes, it was when I was going downstairs. I suppose I said, "Well, Father, thank you for the tea", or words to that effect, and then he asked me to call him Marius.'

'I think calling him Father is a bit much,' I said.

'But it is what he is, Wilmet, even though he is younger than Father Thames and Father Bode. Marius is such a peculiar name for a man though, isn't it. And then my own name being Mary — I suppose I got confused and thought it would sound silly if I asked him to call me Mary.'

I thought she was making rather too much of the matter, but I did begin to wonder whether it was because of Marius that she had bought the new dress, even though her mother had said she needed one. He was handsome and charming, what more natural than that she should be a little in love or at least interested in him? It was, after all, a classic situation. I wondered if it had occurred to Father Thames that this might happen when he had accepted the Beamishes' offer of accommodation for Father Ransome. I supposed it hardly could have done.

'Isn't it sad, the winter coming,' said Mary, after we had been silent for a moment, both looking out of the window at the darkened sky.

'Yes, though I've almost got used to it now,' I said, 'and have begun to accept the more comfortable aspects like fires and warm clothes.'

'The end of summer is really worse — late September, perhaps,' Mary went on. 'Do you know that poem:

> There is a wind where the rose was;
> Cold rain where sweet grass was ...'

she quoted in a low clear voice, looking at me rather intently.

I felt horribly embarrassed. I remembered the poem and a later line about 'tears, tears, where my heart was', and although I did not imagine it could have any personal significance for Mary, I felt I could not bear to be invited to a womanly sharing of confidences. I looked at her dispassionately and saw almost with dislike her shining eager face, her friendship offered to me. What was I doing sitting here with somebody who was so very much not my kind of person? It was my own fault for getting involved with St Luke's, I told myself unreasonably.

'Yes, it's a good poem,' I said abruptly.

'I'm afraid I read rather a lot of poetry,' Mary went on, 'it's a kind of indulgence of mine.'

The afternoon seemed to be ending in confusion and embarrassment. I could not bear to think that she might have read my own favourite poems, and my one idea now was to escape from her as quickly as I could.

'I really prefer reading novels,' I said, putting on my gloves, 'and that's much more of an indulgence.'

'Oh, I don't know. There are some very worth while novels after all,' she said doubtfully.

I knew that she would mention some heavy foreign translations or historical works, and of course she did.

'I like the frivolous witty kind one can skim through in an afternoon,' I persisted.

Mary smiled in an irritating way. 'Goodness, look at the time!' she said. 'I must be getting home. Thank you so much for helping me to choose the dress, Wilmet. I should never have got such a nice one by myself.'

When we got outside I made some excuse about wanting to go into a shop before it closed and she went on the bus without me. I turned into a sweet shop that made special truffles I liked and bought half a pound, thinking rather defiantly of Mary as I did so. I was unable to decide what it was that I found so irritating about her goodness; it could not be only that she was such a contrast to myself and made me feel guilty and useless. Then I began to examine the paradox of good and wicked people: why the wicked were often nicer. I was still pondering about the unpleasant character of the wise virgins in the parable when I found that I was nearly home without realizing it, and that a tall dark figure was coming rather hesitantly towards me. I saw that it was Father Ransome.

'Good evening,' I called out. 'I don't suppose you'll remember me, but I'm one of your parishioners — Wilmet Forsyth.'

'But of course I remember you — you were at the "social evening",' — he picked out the words as if putting them into quotation marks — 'and I've seen you in church.'

'Were you coming to call?' I asked.

'Well, I was thinking I might. Father Thames is anxious that people who don't actually live in the parish shouldn't feel neglected because he isn't able to get round much himself, so he gave me a list of addresses to work through.'

'That doesn't sound much of a pleasure, but I suppose it must be a chore, really,' I laughed.

'I've really been quite lucky,' Father Ransome said. 'I've had three teas this afternoon, but it's getting rather late for tea now.'

'And you don't quite like to assume that people will have gin or sherry to offer?'

'Well, they might not have, or there might be just that half inch left in the decanter which can be more of an embarrassment than if there were nothing at all.'

I was a little surprised at his tone, which seemed not to reflect his experiences in the East End or North Kensington. Perhaps — though I had not heard this — he had private means, and was used to life's little comforts.

'I hope you will come and drink sherry with me, then,' I said. 'I think our decanter will not embarrass you.'

The prospect of a conversation with him was quite pleasing. Rodney would not yet be back from the Ministry, and Sybil had gone to a lecture on Roman Britain with Professor Root.

'Do you always get refreshment of some kind when you go visiting?' I asked, when we were settled in the drawing-room by the fire.

'Usually, but not often as good as this.' He held his sherry glass up to the light.

'My husband and mother-in-law are agnostics,' I said rather flatly. 'So I suppose that might be a good reason for the clergy to visit this house.'

'I don't think much can be done about that by visiting,' he said comfortably. 'The main purpose of visiting is to keep in touch with the faithful and regain the lapsed. Professed agnostics require rather different treatment.'

I wondered if he would be capable of giving it.

'Ought you not to be at Evensong?' I asked, seeing him leaning over towards the fire and warming his hands at it.

'No, it's Bode's turn tonight.' He glanced at his watch. 'I mustn't stay too long, though. We are dining rather unfashionably early tonight.'

'Have the study groups on South India started then? Father Thames suggested I might like to go to them.'

'Oh, he is always talking about them but nothing ever seems to come of it. No, Bode and I are going out with Coleman and some of the servers to see the Crazy Gang.'

I expressed my astonishment. 'What an odd thing to be going to!'

'Well, it's the servers' choice and it's their outing, but it does seem to create a rather dangerous precedent, doesn't it?'

'Yes indeed, when you think of the things the Crazy Gang get up to. But Mr Coleman is so reliable, I'm sure you couldn't have a better master of ceremonies.'

'Yes, Bill Coleman is a good chap,' said Father Ransome in more curately style.

'Bill? I thought his name was Walter.'

'It may be, but he's always called Bill.'

'He looks the kind of person who would be. Will Mr Bason be going with you?'

'I think *not*! He and Coleman had words one Sunday and there is still some coolness between them.'

86

'What happened?'

'We were short of a server and Bason said he would help us out as he knew what to do, but unfortunately he was too zealous and put on Coleman's cassock by mistake and was rather uncooperative when it was pointed out to him.'

'Do they all have their own cassocks, then?'

'Most of them do, and Coleman had his specially made for him at an ecclesiastical tailor's, so you can imagine that he was rather annoyed.'

'It all seems rather trivial,' I said.

'I know — but it's the trivial things that matter, isn't it? Anyway, Coleman now takes his cassock home with him and brings it every Sunday in a little suitcase, so there can be no mistake.' Father Ransome laughed and stood up to go.

'I hope Mr Bason gives you good meals,' I said.

'Indeed yes, he's an excellent cook. I make my own breakfast, as you may have heard,' he smiled, 'so I particularly appreciate the meals I get at the clergy house.'

'I went shopping with Mary Beamish this afternoon,' I said, curious to see whether he would make any remark about her.

'Ah yes, Mary is a fine person,' he said thoughtfully.

I did not quite know what to make of this. I should not myself have felt particularly flattered at being so described, but then it was inconceivable that anyone should describe me in this way. And what other way *was* there to describe poor Mary. A fine person....

When he had gone I found myself picturing him and Father Bode and the servers all doubled up with laughter at the antics of the Crazy Gang. I hoped it would not come into my mind the next time I saw them in church.

CHAPTER SEVEN

SOME time before Christmas, Rodney and I had arranged to have lunch with Rowena and Harry. It was to be a sort of get-together to talk over old times — perhaps a substitute for the meeting Harry had been going to arrange with me, which was probably a good thing. But in the end the children developed mumps and Rodney was cluttered up with conferences and meetings — in themselves a kind of mumps — so that Harry and I had our tête-à-tête luncheon after all.

We met at a rather masculine sort of restaurant, famed for its meat, where great joints were wheeled up to the table for one's choice and approval. This ritual seemed to take the place of the ordeal by fire which the more foreign restaurants went in for, where every dish apparently had to submit itself to being heated up in the leaping flames while the patrons looked nervously on. When the joint came to us I found myself turning aside with a kind of womanly delicacy, hardly able to look it in the face, for there was something almost indecent about the sight of meat in such abundance. All the same it was very splendid beef and I found myself eating it with enjoyment, even relish.

'Do you remember the Fleet Club in Nápoli?' asked Harry rather sentimentally.

'All those fried eggs on top of steaks and everything, regardless, it seemed!' I said. 'Was there *anything* that couldn't have a couple of fried eggs on top of it?'

'No, they thought it was what the English and Americans wanted, and I think they were right. Even *your* eyes lit up at the sight of all those eggs. You were so gay and sweet.'

'I'm not now,' I said quickly, confident of being contradicted and yet in a way not wanting to be.

'A little less gay, perhaps, but even more appealing. Now

there's a kind of sadness about you that wasn't there before. As if life hadn't turned out quite as you'd hoped it would?' he added tentatively.

'Well, does it ever — *quite?*'

'Heavens, no!' said Harry heartily. 'But there can be — there often are — things one can do about it.'

I said nothing but went on admiring my meat, occasionally eating a mouthful.

'You know, I did want to have lunch alone with you, Wilmet,' he said earnestly. 'I should like us to have fun together — I believe we could.'

'Do you think so?' I said rather coldly. Then I suddenly thought — why, it's only old Harry Grinners, whom you've known for ten years, no need to treat him with such chilly detachment! 'Endless good lunches with lots of lovely meat?' I said more gaily. 'Is that the idea?'

'Darling, you will have your joke — that's the surprising and tantalizing thing about you.'

From then on he became more obviously flirtatious in a heavy Edwardian style and we enjoyed ourselves very much. I wondered if all the men in the restaurant who happened to be lunching with women were also flirting with them. Then I wondered about Rodney, presumably lunching in the canteen at the Ministry. Did he flirt with the typists, or was such behaviour only possible with women of the same grade as himself — those rather formidable women whom Sybil and I had once discussed, who got out of the train at St James's Park with briefcases? But they would rate a better meal than the Ministry canteen could offer. There are, of course, restaurants, I said to myself, and the idea seemed highly entertaining. Did I mind — did Rowena mind — did any of us mind? After all, it made no difference to our fundamental relationships — or did it? What would Father Thames have said, or Father Bode, or Father Ransome? Could unmarried clergymen really understand these things except in an academic way?

'How is your new vicar getting on?' I asked suddenly.

'The new vicar!' Harry seemed a little startled. 'Oh, not too badly. He's going to have Midnight Mass this Christmas, which is a new thing for us. Rather a good idea, I think.'

'But I thought you were all against these Romish practices?'

'Well so I am, but this seems rather nice, going to church at night, you know. There's something — well — rather *nice* about it,' he mumbled, looking down at his plate. 'You feel more in the mood, somehow. I think I shall give it a trial.'

I reflected on the difficulties which must beset a priest going to a country parish and trying to establish a coherent system of worship.

'I suppose he hears confessions?' I asked rather naughtily.

'Heavens, don't talk about *that*!' Harry was almost purple in the face. 'He preached a sermon about it. Disgraceful! Some people walked out.'

'Poor Father Lester,' I said.

'We might go to the theatre some time,' said Harry. 'Or how about dinner and dancing somewhere? You used to like dancing.'

The meal ended on this note, but he went meekly enough back to Mincing Lane and I to Regent Street to do some Christmas shopping. It was pleasant to think that we might go dancing, for Rodney had never liked it, but somehow I didn't think we ever would.

That same evening we were sitting in the drawing-room before dinner when the telephone rang. We were expecting guests — Rodney's colleague James Cash and his wife Hilary — and I imagined the call would be from them, perhaps warning us that they might be late, for it was a foggy evening. But when Rodney came back into the room he said, 'It's for you, dear.'

'Really? Who is it?'

'I'm afraid I didn't ask. Cultured male voice.'

'Oh.' I turned over the possibilities in my mind, but they did not range farther than the clergy, and I could not imagine why any of them should want to telephone me.

'Wilmet, is that you?'

'Yes,' I said, not recognizing the voice.

'I want you to come and spend the evening with me.'

I had certainly not expected Piers. Though, when one came to think of it, he was the most likely person to ring up at a time when one would either be having dinner or be just about to.

'Piers!' I exclaimed. 'But what a surprise! How are you?'

'Rather depressed. I should like you to come and spend the evening with me — didn't you hear what I said?'

'Yes, but it's quite impossible, I'm afraid.'

'Why?'

'We're expecting people to dinner.'

'Oh, you *would* be! Can't you leave them? Pretend you've got to go and visit a sick relative or something?'

'You know I can't. But I'm sorry you're depressed. What can I do to cheer you up?'

'I've told you.'

'Yes, but what else? Why don't you come and have dinner with us one evening before Christmas — that would be nice?'

'Would it?'

'Well, you'd get a good dinner — I could promise you that. Do say you'll come.'

'I'm afraid my plans are rather uncertain over Christmas, thank you. Perhaps we could meet in the New Year.' His voice sounded bored.

'What will you do now, then?' I couldn't resist asking.

'What do you suppose? I wanted to see you and you won't come.'

'It isn't that I *won't*,' I began. But then, feeling that the unsatisfactory conversation should be brought to an end, I added, 'But I'm very sorry — I should have liked to come.'

'Never mind,' his voice sounded a little warmer. 'It will just have to be one of those nice things that didn't happen.'

I wished him a happy Christmas and put back the receiver. I

felt a kind of glow as I went back into the drawing-room to meet the raised questioning faces of Sybil and Rodney. Naturally they did not ask who I had been talking to.

'I've refilled your glass,' Rodney said.

'Is that a car stopping outside,' Sybil asked.

'They will come in a taxi, I imagine,' said Rodney.

'It was Piers Longridge,' I said. 'Such an odd time to telephone.'

'Did you speak in Portuguese?' asked Sybil in her dry tone.

The front doorbell rang and Rodney got up quickly. 'That will be James and Hilary,' he said. 'I'll go to the door.'

A minute later James and Hilary Cash entered the room — he apologizing for their lateness, she rather desperately trying to do something to her hair. Rodney would not have realized that women need a little more than just having their coats taken off them in the hall.

'Why, Rodney!' I said, in the most irritatingly wifely way. 'Didn't you take Hilary upstairs?'

'Well, we were so late that I really thought I shouldn't waste any time titivating,' said Hilary in a hearty tone, and it occurred to me that she did not really much mind what she looked like. The gesture of tidying her hair was just something she thought she ought to do. She was blonde and healthy-looking, a Scandinavian type, in contrast to James's greying Celtic appearance.

Dinner ran its course in the way that such meals often do, the men tending to talk shop while the women had a rather uneasy conversation among themselves about domestic matters and Hilary's new baby. Sometimes there was a little cross-talk on matters considered to be of universal interest. Towards the end of the meal Sybil and Hilary discovered a common interest in social work and I found myself left to my own thoughts which naturally enough turned to Piers Longridge. I began trying to picture his evening. I supposed he would be alone in his flat, his colleague or girl friend or whoever he lived with being out for the evening or perhaps already away for the Christmas holidays. I tried to visualize the flat itself — in the Holland Park area but rather too near the Goldhawk Road, he had said. It might be in a large shabby house, perhaps not even properly self-contained. There would be a row of bells with old cards and bits of paper indicating the occupants; some of the bells would probably be out of order. Inside there would be a narrow hall with a Victorian hatstand, prams and bicycles perhaps, and a smell of cooking. Going up the stairs one might meet one of the other occupants of the house, a young man coming out of the bathroom, an old woman peering out of a door. One would be filled with apprehension as one climbed farther. I took a mouthful of cheese soufflé, a dish at which Rhoda excelled. Perhaps I was overdoing the squalor of Piers's environment. He could live in a block of new flats and the stairs one climbed might be of concrete and smell only of dust. Or there might even be a lift. I made a kind of New Year resolution to find out some time. Anyway, he had probably gone round to the pub by now, where he might sit morosely in a corner or join in conversation with the regulars; he would be known there and perhaps liked — he might even make jokes....

'Thank goodness another Christmas at the Ministry is over!' said Rodney. 'That is always something to be got through.'

'You have a kind of party, don't you?' said Hilary.

'Yes, there's tea and Christmas cake and everyone stands round in a circle, pressing back against the filing cabinets and seeming to be struck dumb.'

'The women exchange presents,' said James. 'Thank goodness *we* don't have that embarrassment. The woman who works in my room had a supply of small emergency gifts in case anyone should give her a present unexpectedly.'

'I suppose men don't exchange handkerchiefs or sticks of shaving soap wrapped in gay Christmas paper?' asked Sybil.

'Not among themselves,' said Rodney, 'but the women aren't above giving us presents.'

93

'Aren't above!' said Sybil indignantly. 'What a way of putting it! You don't deserve to get any presents at all.'

Christmas always makes me feel rather sad. 'The children's time,' people say in cosy sentimental tones, and I suppose we all remember the childish excitements, the waking up in the dark on Christmas morning, the mysterious bulging stocking or the shrouded shapes at the foot of the bed. But now one can foresee only too clearly the pattern of grown up Christmases for the rest of one's life. Sybil had invited Professor Root to stay with us this year, so I supposed we should be treated to the kind of dry conversation he and Sybil enjoyed together — the dispassionate discussion of the significance of the festival, the Christian taking-over of pagan symbols and all the rest of it. Rodney would listen politely and when the time came for me to go to Midnight Mass he would take me in the car and come to fetch me afterwards.

But in the meantime there was the excitement, which I still felt, of the Christmas post arriving two or three times a day in the week before Christmas Day. The usual cards from Rodney's colleagues and from families we all of us knew flopped through the letterbox. Every available flat surface was soon cluttered up with arty agnostic angels and cherubs, stylized cats, dogs and birds in brilliant colours, old prints and homemade lino cuts, and the personal snapshot cards — husband and wife on the beach at St Tropez, or the children and the dog in the garden at home. We received very few of the ironically named 'religious' cards, and those that we did were not of a high artistic standard, and the verses though sincere were often embarrassingly bad. I imagined people buying them in the religious bookshops, not liking to push because of the holy forbearing atmosphere of the place. Indeed, I had been in one myself and had allowed a little woman in a religious habit to take my turn, my first feeling of annoyance giving way to admiration and envy of her lack of worldly knowledge in this respect.

Father Thames's card was a safe choice in good taste, a reproduction of an Italian primitive, the sad lopsided faces giving it a modern look as if it had been painted by Modigliani or somebody of that school. I could not expect to receive cards from Father Bode and Father Ransome, but I amused myself by imagining what theirs would be like. Father Bode might send a small highly coloured holy card of an eastern scene with a flowery verse, I thought, but Father Ransome's choice was more difficult to guess. It might almost be the arty agnostic angel type of card, I felt, remembering our conversation when we had drunk sherry together. It annoyed me to think that Mary Beamish would probably know just what it was.

Parcels were usually kept to be opened on Christmas Day, the little ceremony seeming to give a point to the day which it might not otherwise have had. I recognized the usual presents from relatives and women friends which arrived by post, and put them away in the cupboard in the morning room. Rowena and I always sent each other some extravagantly feminine thing, which we might probably have bought for ourselves anyway, only in a rather exaggerated form. I noticed that this year her parcel was even larger than usual. I had to include the children's presents with hers, but I did not usually do anything about Harry. This year, however, I had an obscure feeling that I ought to put in something for him, so I bought some white handkerchiefs of a goodness and dullness that could neither please too much nor offend in any way. When I had done all the necessary shopping I began to think about the unnecessary. Should I get some little thing for Piers? I wondered. But what? A book or some gloves or a bottle of whisky? Certainly he would not send me anything, probably not even a card. Nevertheless, I watched the post eagerly for a sign of something in an unfamiliar hand. But nothing came, nor did I send him anything, and by the time it was Christmas Eve I had almost given up looking.

In the afternoon we were listening to the carols and lessons from King's College Chapel, which always make me cry, so that I was glad to slip out of the room when I heard the post come. There were some more cards and two little parcels — one from

Sybil's optician and the other addressed to me in block capitals. It was small and square and looked almost as if it might contain jewellery. Could it be a surprise from Rodney? I wondered. But no, he would give his present to me personally on Christmas Day, as he always did. I turned the box over in my hands and examined the writing, but it told me nothing. Impulsively I slipped the string over the corner and tore open the paper. I saw a small cardboard box, and now I did not hesitate to open this too. It was filled with shavings; but when I had pushed these aside I found nestling among them another little box, heart shaped and made of enamel, Regency or early Victorian, prettily decorated. Something was written on the lid. I moved underneath the light and read the inscription.

> If you will not when you may
> When you will you shall have nay.

For a moment I was struck with bewilderment, trying to puzzle out what the words meant. Then I remembered my telephone conversation with Piers and was filled with an agitation that was half painful and half pleasurable. When I went back into the drawing-room I felt like the heroine of a Victorian novel, for I had thrust the little box into the pocket of my dress so as to hide it, and my fingers were nervously feeling it, tracing out the inscription on the lid. Who but Piers could have thought of such a thing, and what did he mean by it? I kept asking myself.

CHAPTER EIGHT

D INNER on Christmas Eve was enlivened not only by my agitated speculations about the little box but by a note which arrived by hand for Rodney.

'Read this, darling,' he said, pushing it across the table to me. 'It came this evening. What should we do?'

'Do?' I murmured, my eyes on the letter. 'Let me see what it says.'

It read:

Dear Forsyth,

It would give me much pleasure if you and your wife would take tea with me one day at the clergy house. Boxing Day would suit me very well, if convenient for you, and I suppose four o'clock or thereabouts is the most civilized hour to suggest. I do hope you will be able to come.

Yours very sincerely,
WILFRED J. BASON

'Fancy his name being Wilfred!' I exclaimed when I had finished reading. 'And does he always call you Forsyth, like that?'

'He seems to now, though I can't remember that he ever did at the Ministry. Still, things were rather different there. Should we go?'

'I should love to,' I said, full of curiosity. 'And Boxing Day is always so dreary anyway. Do you think the poor man is lonely? He evidently isn't going away for Christmas, but I suppose he could hardly leave the clergy at a time like this.'

'Perhaps he has no relatives or friends to go to,' said Sybil, making her statement sound like a sociological observation rather than the kind of remark to bring tears to the eyes.

'I've been meaning to ask him here,' said Rodney guiltily,

'but somehow I've never got round to it yet. I suppose we should go to tea with him, then. I'll telephone him. I suppose the clergy house *has* a telephone? In touch with the infinite, no doubt, but an ordinary worldly one too?'

'Goodness, yes! There's even one in the vestry. People are always ringing up to ask Father Thames to luncheon or Father Bode to high tea.'

'All right, then. I'll say we'll be delighted.'

'I wonder if he's *really* without relatives?' I said. 'He strikes one as the kind of person who would have a mother.'

'Well, everybody has or had a mother,' said Sybil. 'But I see just what you mean. No doubt you will find out when you go to tea with him.'

The hours between dinner and Midnight Mass seemed very long and I began to feel sleepy. I wondered whether Harry and Rowena had decided to give it a trial at their village church and hoped that poor Father Lester would have a good congregation. Then of course I wondered, though I tried not to, what Piers would be doing, whether he would be going to church — and, if so, where. He might even come to our church, it was not so very far away and he had told me that he did not frequent any particular one. *Could* it have been Piers who had sent the little box? I could think of nobody else who would have been likely to. The circumstances fitted so well and it was just the kind of unusual and imaginative thing he might do. It was tantalizing not to be able to see him and find out and even to follow up its implications, whatever they might be, for I could not know his mood when he had sent it. I could only think that he must have been walking in some street where there were antique shops — not, somehow, the Goldhawk Road — and had seen the box in a window and thought it would be just right for me, being the kind of thing I liked and the words so appropriate to my refusal or inability to spend an evening with him. Of course it was all a joke, really, but it gave me a pleasant feeling of being remembered in a rather special way.

Rodney took me to church in the car and deposited me in the porch. After he had driven away I suddenly wished I had tried to persuade him to stay for the service, but it was too late then. People were crowding in and the church already looked full. The crib had been put up at the west end; the brightly coloured plaster figures, put away from last year, had been taken out and washed or dusted; the straw, the flowers and the lights arranged by some devoted hand. Other devoted hands had decorated the church with lilies, white chrysanthemums and holly, and I wished that I might have had a share in it. Father Thames in his cassock was standing at the back of the church as if to encourage the many strangers who would be coming to the service. He nodded and smiled vaguely as I passed him.

I usually sat in the same pew as Mary Beamish and her mother; but as I made my way towards it I noticed that there was something not quite right about it, for at the end nearest the chancel, instead of the bulky shape of old Mrs Beamish and the drab self-effacing Mary, I saw only Miss Prideaux and another elderly lady and beyond them some distance away the ex-housekeeper at the clergy house, Mrs Greenhill. A kind of rustling sound, like dry autumn leaves in the wind, seemed to be coming from the elderly ladies, sitting in their yellowish-brown fur coats, a little upright as they were slightly uneasy at being there. I could not at first decide whether the rustling sound came from their natural age and brittleness or whether they were whispering together about something. As I passed them to get to my seat Miss Prideaux whispered, 'Mrs Beamish and Mary aren't coming to-night. I'm afraid Mrs Beamish isn't very well.'

'Oh dear, I'm sorry,' I whispered back inadequately.

'I expect it will be the end,' said Miss Prideaux in a confident tone.

'Not really?' I said, hardly knowing whether to believe her or not.

I knelt down to say a prayer, and when I had sat up again I found Mrs Greenhill, on my other side, lying in wait as it were.

'Mrs Beamish had a nasty turn this afternoon,' she said.

'Oh dear,' I said again. 'What's the matter?'

'Heart,' said Mrs. Greenhill, pursing her thin lips together. 'And you know what *that* means.'

I did not really know for I had always been vague about Mrs Beamish's health, supposing that she was not really ill at all but just old and difficult. I sat thinking of Mary, wondering how she was feeling, until my thoughts wandered and I began speculating on the nature of Miss Prideaux's fur coat. It seemed to be of such a very strange kind of fur, not cat or rabbit or any of the more expensive varieties, but something one couldn't put a name to. Wolf, perhaps, or some strange bushy animal shot long ago in those Imperial Balkan forests.

The service began and was both beautiful and exhausting because there were so many people, and it was after half past one before we had finished. Getting out of church was slow, and there was a crowd in the porch exchanging greetings with the clergy and with each other. I noticed Mr Coleman, rather ostentatiously still wearing his cassock over which he had flung a duffle coat; and then I remembered that of course he had to take it home with him now after the unfortunate incident Father Ransome had told me about. He was with two of the servers — the thurifer, who worked in a garage, and another who taught in a secondary modern school.

'Ooh, Bill, look how you've parked the car!' I heard the latter say in a shrill mean voice — made so, I supposed, by his years of teaching and constantly having to say, 'Now, boys!' in just that sort of tone.

'Ah, Mrs Forsyth, I'm delighted that you and your husband are able to take tea with me on Boxing Day,' said Mr Bason coming up to me. 'That's really tomorrow, isn't it — today being Christmas Day now? Let me wish you both the compliments of the season — and to your husband's mother, too,' he added with what seemed a comic effect.

I thanked him and returned the greeting.

'And now I must rush away,' he said. 'They'll be wanting some kind of a snack after this, and who can say they haven't earned it!' He flung out this last remark in a challenging way. 'Father Thames was hearing confessions up to eight o'clock,' he added in a lower voice. 'I had to put dinner back half an hour, but luckily it was only a fish pie.'

A crowd, mostly of women, had collected round the three priests, and I heard one say to Father Ransome almost gloatingly, 'Father, you must be *so tired*. And then there is the seven o'clock Low Mass and the eight o'clock, and then the High Mass at eleven ... I simply don't know *how* you're going to manage.'

Father Ransome gave her his charming weary smile. 'Don't worry,' he said. 'I'll get my feet up this afternoon.'

The lady turned away, perhaps disconcerted by his flippancy.

I had been wanting to talk to him about Mrs Beamish and Mary, and took this opportunity to ask him about them.

'Poor Mary,' I said. 'This must be a time of great anxiety for her.'

He looked at me for a moment, still with the charming weary smile as if I were another of his sympathizers, then appeared to realize what I had said.

'Yes, I'm afraid Mrs Beamish is gravely ill. She took a turn for the worse this evening.'

'Oh, I'm sorry. I wonder if there's anything I can do for Mary?'

'She will be glad of your sympathy at a time like this,' he said in a formal clergyman's way.

I felt rather chilled, for I had not meant anything so indefinite as that. I suppose I had imagined myself busy in a practical way — cooking meals or running errands, even being what people call a tower of strength.

'Do you think I should call or telephone?' I asked. 'You will have later news of the situation than anybody else.'

'They have two nurses there,' said Father Ransome, 'but I'm sure Mary would be glad of *your* company.' He smiled, a charming almost intimate smile.

I turned away from him. His charm seemed out of place, even shocking, at such a time. I wished I had been talking to Father Bode, with his eager toothy smile and weak kindly eyes magnified behind his thick glasses, or even to Father Thames, querulous and complaining, but with a presence fitting to serious occasions.

I saw that Rodney had arrived in the car and was looking for me among the crowd of people, so I said something indefinite to Father Ransome and moved away. It was obviously no use ringing Mary up at half past one in the morning, however anxious I was to be helpful.

'Supposing Ella Beamish dies,' said Sybil as we were eating our breakfast later on Christmas morning, 'and she very well may. I wonder what Mary will do then?'

'She will be quite free,' I said, 'and she'll have money, too. It will be wonderful for her, really.'

'Darling, should you say things like that?' Rodney asked. 'Won't she be quite lost without her mother, a good religious young woman like that?'

'She'll miss her of course, but she'll be able to lead her own life — travel and all that sort of thing.'

'Travel?' echoed Rodney. 'I find that hard to visualize, somehow. Will she go and stay with friends in the south of France, or join a jolly party going to the Italian lakes, or what? What *do* lone women suddenly presented with money and freedom do?'

'She might come with us to Portugal,' said Sybil practically. 'But of course that wouldn't be immediately. And what *are* we talking about!' she exclaimed suddenly. 'Poor Ella Beamish is still with us, as far as we know.'

'I suppose there is a good deal of money there,' Rodney continued. 'Old Beamish was in the city, wasn't he? And there are two sons doing pretty well, I believe.'

'Yes — Gerald and William,' I said. 'They're both a good deal older than Mary. I expect she'll get most of her mother's money. Oh dear, here we are *still* talking as if she were going to die. I really think I might telephone Mary now and ask if there's anything I can do. Ten o'clock in the morning seems quite a suitable time.'

Mary herself answered the telephone and was obviously glad to hear from me, but she assured me that there was really nothing I could do at the moment. Her mother was very ill, but they had two excellent nurses. 'And Marius has been such a comfort,' she added.

Marius? I thought, and then realized that she must mean Father Ransome. I wondered in what way he was being a comfort — in practical ways, or simply by the exercise of his charm? Then it occurred to me that he probably would not use his charm on Mary, whom he regarded as a fine person — that, presumably, was reserved for people like me who were less fine, the kind of women who would expect it. The idea depressed me, as did my own sophistication and inability to accept even a pleasant smile from a clergyman at its face value.

'Well, she seems to be about the same,' I said to Sybil. 'I suppose Father Thames will be praying for her at Mass this morning.'

'I never know what it is that Christians expect or want when they pray for the sick,' said Sybil. 'Obviously death is greatly to be desired for believers, and yet they never quite like to pray for that — at least not publicly.'

'Mother, you can hardly know what is done, when you never go to church,' Rodney reminded her.

'But one hears what goes on,' said Sybil. 'And Arnold has told me a good deal, you know. He frequently has to attend funeral and memorial services in an official capacity.'

I remembered then that Professor Root was to take Christmas dinner with us, and the thought depressed me rather. Nevertheless when the time came and I saw the interesting-looking little parcel he had brought for me I felt more warmly towards him, and began to look forward to the time when we should open our presents.

The little parcel turned out to be a charming early Victorian mourning brooch, a lock of auburn hair delicately framed in gold. I was delighted with it.

'I hope you are not superstitious — and perhaps some relic connected with death is not the happiest of thoughts for this time. But I believed it was the kind of thing you might like, and certainly it seems to be appropriate to your own style of beauty, which, if I may say so, is happily not quite of this age,' said Professor Root, flushing a little as he hurried over these last words.

We had all been drinking champagne, otherwise I suppose he would not have had the courage to say what he did. I was touched by his compliment and the tears came into my eyes.

'I think it's charming,' I said, 'and just the kind of thing I like best.'

I was curious to see what his present for Sybil would be, for she was in some ways so very unfeminine that I always found it difficult to know what to get for her. But Professor Root's choice of a warm mohair stole seemed brilliant, and Sybil was obviously very pleased with it. I tried to imagine Professor Root going into a shop and buying it, but this was difficult and I concluded that his sister or housekeeper must have chosen it for him.

I had given books to Sybil and Professor Root, and a wallet to Rodney. His present to me was always money, but there was generally some small token as well; and this year he had bought me a pair of pearl earrings in a pretty unobtrusive setting unlike so much of the vulgar modern jewellery which I dislike.

'Darling, I hope you don't think *real* pearls vulgar,' he said teasingly, 'but I thought you needed something for those innumerable parish occasions you seem to be attending lately.'

'They're lovely,' I said, feeling for some obscure reason that I hardly deserved them. 'Do you think they will be suitable for tea with Mr Bason tomorrow?'

'Not unless he asks us to stay on for sherry,' said Rodney, 'and that hardly seems likely. Good heavens — is that what Rowena gave you!' he exclaimed, taking up a prettily packed box containing two bottles. '*Moon Drops* — what an earth can those be? — and *White Sable* — what extraordinary things even reasonably intelligent women will put on their faces. What results do you expect to achieve? One hardly likes to conjecture from these rather odd names!'

'They just help to preserve our beauty,' I said lightly, gathering up the pieces of Christmas wrapping paper which littered the carpet.

'There's another little parcel you seem to have forgotten,' said Sybil, pointing to a little soft square package wrapped in holly paper.

'Oh dear, it's two handkerchiefs from Mary,' I said, 'and I didn't give her anything. We've never exhanged presents before.'

'It seems suitable that Mary should be the more blessed one, giving rather than receiving,' said Sybil drily. 'But never mind, you may very well be able to make it up to her in the future.'

'I do hope so,' I said. But I was really thinking of that other present for which I had as yet made no return — the little box with its provocative inscription. I was not at all sure how I was supposed to make it up to Piers.

CHAPTER NINE

'I THINK we had better be five or ten minutes late for tea, don't you?' said Rodney the next day.

We were settled comfortably with books in front of the fire, and I could tell that he did not really want to turn out on a cold afternoon.

'Yes,' I agreed, 'but not more. I feel Mr Bason is the kind of person who might take umbrage easily, and we don't want to make it look as if we had forgotten his invitation or that we thought it didn't matter.'

'Should we go in the car?'

'Well, that *is* making rather a business of it, don't you think? After all it's only a quarter of an hour's walk — less really.'

We set out at ten to four, Rodney grumbling a little; but my step was eager, for I had not seen inside the clergy house before. I wondered whether we should meet Father Thames on the stairs, or hear Father Bode practising a sermon behind closed doors.

As we came up to the clergy house I saw the notice about not ringing unless on *urgent* business. But there was hardly time to consider whether we should ring or not, for the moment we set foot on the doorstep I noticed a curtain at a ground floor window being flicked aside and heard footsteps within. Evidently Mr Bason had been watching for our arrival in a rather Cranfordian way.

The door was flung open.

'Ah, just on the dot,' he called out.

'I think we are just a *little* late, aren't we?' said Rodney, consulting his watch. 'We didn't leave home till nearly four.'

'Well, perhaps you are fashionably late by just a minute or two,' Mr Bason agreed. 'Now do come in.'

I entered eagerly, looking about me with interest and curiosity.

The hall was quite large, with a parquet floor not as well polished as it might have been. The paint was green and the walls cream, but both were dingy looking. Against one wall stood a massive oak chest flanked on either side by chairs with high carved backs. There was a large umbrella and hat stand of Victorian type, suitably hung with birettas, clerical mackintoshes and other dark garments that might have been cassocks. One or two pictures hung on the walls and were of the kind I always think of as oleographs, though I have never been sure exactly what oleographs are. They were of vaguely holy subjects — buildings and people in ancient dress — and there was also a brightly coloured reproduction of the Sistine Madonna in a gilt frame.

'The dining-room and parish meeting-room aren't particularly interesting, but you might like to see the room Mrs Greenhill had,' said Mr Bason, opening a door leading off the hall.

'But how dark it is!' I exclaimed. 'And right up against the church wall. I should think it *would* be damp. Father Thames said it was a storeroom, didn't he?'

'A repository for old copies of Crockford,' said Rodney, poking at one with his umbrella. 'I always thought you could sell them.'

'Perhaps he likes to keep them for a special reason,' I said, opening a volume. I saw that against some entries Father Thames had made his own notes. '† d. 1952.' I noticed against one, 'St Alphege, Harvist Road, N.W.6. ? 1941' against another, while a third had simply been crossed out altogether in heavy ink lines.

'Well, Bason, I hope you have a better room than this,' said Rodney.

'Yes — mine is really delightful. I thought you might like to have just a peep at some of the other rooms too,' Mr Bason called over his shoulder as we mounted the stairs. 'Everyone is out at the moment. Father Thames is having tea with Sir Denbigh Grote. Father Bode has gone to the pictures.'

'Do you think we should?' asked Rodney doubtfully.

I am afraid that I made no protest though I also felt that it was perhaps not quite the thing. Still, as Mr Bason was our host it seemed only polite to accept the programme he offered.

'Father Thames loves showing people over the house,' he went on.

'To emphasize how few rooms there are?' I suggested, remembering that this had been his defence for not having Father Ransome to live at the clergy house.

Mr Bason burst into a peal of laughter. 'There's plenty of room really, you know. Now this is the oratory — quite charming don't you think? I really don't know what it was built for, originally.'

'It could have been the nursery,' I said. 'We know that the first incumbent had five children.'

'It would hardly have had that stained glass window,' Rodney objected. 'I think it was a bathroom.'

We paused in the doorway, silent for a moment as if in recognition of the sacred purpose for which the room was now used.

'Now,' said Mr Bason moving us on like a guide. 'I think we might take the merest *peep* into Father Thames's study. I expect you would like to see that.'

He had already opened the door before we could express any opinion and I crept forward rather guiltily as if expecting some kind of retribution to fall on me.

The first impression was of a rather crowded museum, for there seemed to be a great many objects arranged in glass-fronted cabinets and on the mantelpiece. The room was dominated by an enormous desk of some dark rich-looking wood. This rather surprised me, for I had not hitherto had the impression that Father Thames was the scholarly type of clergyman; though, on thinking it over, I supposed that every parish priest must have a large desk, if only to answer his correspondence and prepare his sermons. Books I had expected to see, and there were certainly a great many including some well bound sets of the English poets, and Dante and Goethe. I wondered whether in his youth Father Thames had been one of those preachers who adorn their sermons with quotations, like a certain Archdeacon Hoccleve who had been a distant cousin of my mother's and who even sometimes took as his text a phrase from one of our greater English poets. Such sermons seemed to have gone out of fashion, for all we got from Father Thames now was ten minutes' rather dry teaching on such topics as 'The Significance of Evensong', or little nagging perorations about why we ought to go to confession. No doubt the modern way was better, but I could not help regretting the passing of the old.

'He seems to have some nice objects,' said Rodney. 'A whole cabinet full of Dresden, and that Fabergé egg is particularly charming, don't you think?'

'Yes, delightful,' I agreed. 'But what on earth is *this*?'

We were looking at a piece of statuary which stood on a little table in a corner. It was of a young boy, the features blunted with wear and age, but very pleasing none the less.

'He brought that back from Italy, he told me,' said Mr Bason. 'Apparently it was dug up somewhere near Siena, I think he said — he was staying with friends at the time in their villa. He brought it back in the hope of being able to put it somewhere in the church, but when he got it home it didn't seem suitable.'

'Yes, it has a very pagan look,' I agreed. 'I can't quite see it in a church here, though it might look well in a Roman church abroad.'

'Yes, in one of those rather dark side chapels,' said Rodney.

We left the room and passed another door, which I assumed must be Father Thames's bedroom. I was glad that Mr Bason was showing enough delicacy to draw the line somewhere — I really had been beginning to wonder whether he would show us quite everything.

As we ascended to the second floor I noticed that the thick red stair carpet gave way to an inferior kind of drugget, and that the walls were hung with old faded sepia groups of the kind one sees in junk shops or at jumble sales. I scanned them eagerly, and was rewarded by seeing a young Father Thames in a rowing group, and again at an even earlier stage with three women who might have been elder sisters or young aunts having tea on a lawn by a large monkey-puzzle tree.

'Now we must get Wilmet away from brooding over these old photographs,' said Rodney. 'She gets very melancholy over things like that.'

'I hadn't realized he was a rowing man. It all seems such a long time ago, doesn't it — from that to this, whatever it may have been or is now,' I said thoughtfully. 'One can see it all — that tall splendid figure, the enthusiastic spectators on the tow-path ...'

'Come, darling,' said Rodney, taking my arm. 'We are to see Father Bode's study now.'

'Well, there's nothing to see really,' said Mr Bason, flinging open the door with a gesture of contempt. 'He hasn't got any nice things of his own.'

'No, I can see that,' I said, for the room we were now looking at was quite disconcertingly bare, and such personal touches as I noticed were of the simplest and cheapest — a lampshade decorated with an ugly pattern of orange leaves, an old greenish-brown rug on the worn beige linoleum in front of the gas fire, a pipe rack made in fretwork, and a Goss china jar full of paper spills. On the table, for there was no desk, stood a framed photograph of a church — perhaps the one he had attended as a boy or served his first curacy at, I decided.

'Of course he hasn't Father Thames's artistic tastes,' said Mr Bason, perhaps unnecessarily.

'Or his private means,' added Rodney in a dry tone.

'And *this* is the guest room!'

We now found ourselves on the threshold of a room of quite startling austerity. An iron bedstead covered with a white honey-comb quilt, a yellow deal chest of drawers, a washstand and a strip of worn carpet, was all it contained. There was also, how-ever, an ugly ornate crucifix on the wall and a pile of green-covered Penguin thrillers on the chest.

'Do you have many guests?' I asked doubtfully.

'No. The room seems to be used only in an emergency,' said Mr Bason. 'If somebody misses the last bus or train, or is stranded for any reason. Most of the visiting priests who come to preach seem to be from near-by churches, don't they?'

'I suppose Father Ransome could have had this room,' I said disloyally. 'He could have brought his own things — I daresay he has some, and after being in the East End and North Kensington he should be us. to austere living.'

'Yes, I suppose it could have been arranged,' Mr Bason agreed. 'But he and Father Thames are in some ways too much alike — they would have vied with each other.'

I smiled at the quaintness of the expression and imagined the two priests feverishly amassing Fabergé objects and Dresden china. I had not, of course, seen Father Ransome's rooms at the Beamishes', but from what I had seen of him I guessed that Mr Bason would not be far wrong.

'And now we are to see your room,' I said, feeling that some such remark was expected of me, but my 'But this is charming!' came perhaps a little too soon — almost before I could really have taken in the rather chintzy prettiness of the room we were now entering.

'Mother made these covers,' said Mr Bason, 'and I always like to have fresh flowers in the room.' He indicated a jar of white chrysanthemums and a red cyclamen in a pot. 'I'm afraid I must have beautiful things around me. I'm like Father Thames in that,' he added complacently.

Tea was already laid on a low table in front of the gas fire, and Mr Bason busied himself with the kettle on a gas ring in the hearth.

'Did your mother make this lace tablecloth?' I asked.

'Yes, she is always doing crochet,' he said. 'She can't get about much now, but her eyes are still very good.'

'It's beautifully fine work,' I said, picking up a corner of the cloth to examine it.

'How different people's mothers are,' said Rodney. 'It's

difficult to imagine mine doing any kind of fancywork.' He flinched a little over the last word as if he had not really meant to say it, but it had come out regardless, as words appropriate to situations sometimes do.

'I am assuming that you both like Earl Grey,' said Mr Bason, his hand poised over the tea caddy, 'though I have Lapsang if you would prefer it.'

We both murmured appreciatively. The tea was made and we started to eat little sandwiches made of gentleman's relish and crab-meat.

'Goodness, this is a bit different from tea at the Ministry, isn't it, Bason?' said Rodney in a robust tone.

'Yes — I suppose people still queue up with their mugs for that dreadful brew they used to call tea. How one ever endured it I don't know! And the *atmosphere* of that place.' Mr Bason glanced round the room complacently, or it seemed that he did, and he would certainly have been justified in calling attention to the difference between his chintzy elegance and the starkly utilitarian setting of the Ministry.

'I'm afraid you weren't very happy there,' said Rodney, perhaps resenting Mr Bason's air of superiority. 'You are lucky to have found your niche, as they say.'

'Well, my talents — such as they are — are rather out of the ordinary, perhaps. Now, Mrs Forsyth, do try some of my sponge. I think you will find it very light.'

It was certainly an exquisite cake, and I was just complimenting Mr Bason upon it when the telephone was heard ringing in a near-by room.

'Oh bother, I wonder who that is,' said Mr Bason. 'I suppose I must answer it.'

'It might be something urgent,' said Rodney, 'I suppose people do telephone the clergy about things like that — matters of life and death.'

'Yes, of course,' Mr Bason's face brightened. 'I'll take the call in Bode's study.'

Rodney and I sat together in an awkward silence, as people do when their host or hostess is called from the room.

'A lovely tea,' I said stiffly. 'Do you think he made these meringues too? I think I shall try one.'

'Yes, he would like us to help ourselves, I'm sure. I suppose that is his mother in the photograph?'

Rodney took down a silver frame from the mantelpiece and we examined the photograph of an elderly woman with Mr Bason's egg-shaped face and a mass of white hair.

'He's being a long time,' I said uneasily. 'I hope nothing has happened to his mother.'

'Darling, you're too imaginative,' said Rodney soothingly. 'That kind of dreadful thing *could* happen in life—indeed it does, but we'd rather it happened in fiction. But he seems to be coming back—we shall soon know.'

We could hardly help glancing up expectantly as Mr Bason came back into the room, for he was obviously the kind of person who would not keep things to himself. His demeanour seemed to be a mixture of pleased self-importance and distress with a hint of exasperation, if such a thing can be imagined. We waited for him to speak.

'Oh dear,' he said, '*that* was Ransome.'

I noted that he had dropped the 'Father', as also when he had said 'Bode's room', and wondered why.

'It's poor old Mrs Beamish,' he went on. 'She's gone.'

'You mean she's dead?' asked Rodney.

'Yes, dead — passed on or over.' Mr Bason giggled nervously. 'On Boxing Day, in the middle of tea, and all the clergy out— it does seem ...' he began pouring water into the teapot to hide his confusion. I have often noticed that preoccupation with tea-pots is a good way of covering embarrassment.

'Poor Mary!' I exclaimed. 'Do you think we should go to her? Would there be anything one could do?'

'Well, Father Ransome is with her,' said Rodney, 'and I suppose there will be nurses and that kind of thing.'

'Yes, one would only be in the way if one rushed in now. Could we order some flowers, darling, or something? — I mean for Mary, just to show that we are thinking of her?'

'You could have these chrysanthemums,' said Mr Bason, taking the dripping bunch out of the vase. 'They were only bought on Christmas Eve, so they're really quite fresh.'

The whole affair now seemed to be turning into something ludicrous, and I was glad when Rodney attempted to take control by pointing out that there was nothing any of us could do at the moment and that we had much better finish our tea.

'Yes, how right you are,' said Mr Bason. 'It was really rather upsetting though, hearing the news like that — one always wonders who will be the next to go. Now, Mrs Forsyth, what did you think of my meringues?'

'So you did make them yourself — they were delicious.'

'Everything is homemade here — I mean the cakes.' He paused and then went on quickly. 'Now Ransome will be ringing up Father Thames to tell him the sad news, and Sir Denbigh will be upset too — they are both elderly men and will be wondering if their own time is near.'

'Do you think people do wonder that when they hear someone is dead?' asked Rodney. 'I think old people feel a kind of triumph at having outlived a contemporary or a younger person, and then there's the natural personal sorrow and regret at losing a friend.'

'There won't be much of *that*, judging by all accounts,' said Mr Bason waspishly. 'Everyone says she was an old terror and treated poor Miss Beamish shamefully.'

'Oh, I don't think it was quite as bad as that,' I protested. 'I think she was selfish, as some old people are, but Mary was devoted to her mother.'

'Well, blood *is* thicker than water, isn't it? Now what about another cup?' asked Mr Bason brightly. 'I think I can manage one.'

We allowed our cups to be refilled, but conversation had become disjointed and it was obvious and perhaps fitting that a kind of gloom should have been cast over the tea party by the news of Mrs Beamish's death.

'Now do take these flowers,' said Mr Bason as we stood up to go. 'I can easily put some paper round them for you.'

'Well, thank you very much — but I think we shall be able to get some,' I said quickly. 'It would be such a pity to spoil your arrangement.'

'Yes, it's most kind of you, but I've just remembered that my mother had some sent to her which would do very well,' added Rodney.

I wondered if the thought had occurred to him, as it had to me, that Mr Bason might wish to be associated with us in the sending of the flowers. I saw the surprising card that might accompany them:

With love and deepest sympathy from Wilmet and Rodney Forsyth and Wilfred J. Bason

Down in the hall we lingered by the hat stand where Rodney had left his umbrella.

'What a lot of cassocks!' I exclaimed. 'Do the clergy like to have one in every place in case of emergency, like keeping a plastic mackintosh at the office as Rodney does?'

'One of those is mine, as a matter of fact,' said Mr Bason.

'Oh?' I said innocently. 'Don't you keep it in the choir vestry, or wherever the servers keep theirs?'

'That isn't always very satisfactory,' said Mr Bason stiffly. 'Mistakes have been known to occur, and although some would think nothing of it others don't take that line.'

'Mr Coleman has rather a nice cassock,' I couldn't resist saying. 'I noticed it one day when he was putting out the candles after Mass. It seemed to be a rather fine silky material.'

'He had his specially made!' said Mr Bason his voice going rather shrill. 'He *would*, of course! Not that it's anything special really, that cassock of his — there isn't all that much difference between it and the others.'

'Well, Bason, thank you for an excellent tea,' said Rodney. 'I shall be able to tell them at the Ministry that you are happily settled.'

He stood on the steps and waved goodbye to us, for all the world as if it were his own house.

When we had got a safe distance away, we both burst out laughing.

'What was all that about the cassocks?' Rodney asked. 'I didn't quite get the point.'

I told him of the unpleasantness between Mr Bason and Mr Coleman.

'What a fuss! Why does contact with the church seem to make people so petty!' he exclaimed.

'People are petty everywhere about small things,' I retorted. 'Wouldn't you be annoyed if somebody used your special teacup at the Ministry?'

'Nobody *could* use it — I keep it in my locked drawer.'

'There you are then! And Mr Coleman's cassock *is* a particularly nice one, whatever Mr Bason may say. Isn't he an odd sort of man — I can imagine he wouldn't do very well in the civil service. I really think it was brilliant of us to get him into the clergy house.'

'Yes, a fortunate combination of circumstances, wasn't it? I was a bit doubtful about going through all those rooms, though — do you suppose everyone who visits him is given a conducted tour?'

'They could hardly be if the clergy were there,' I pointed out. 'I must admit that I found it fascinating. We didn't see the bedrooms or bathrooms, though — so not *quite* everything was revealed.'

'We should have been quite justified in asking to see the bathroom if we had needed it,' said Rodney.

'What a pity — I didn't think of that. I might have done if it hadn't been for the interruption. Oh dear, what about poor Mary? Should we send those flowers or shall I just write a little note?'

'I think perhaps a little note would be the best thing,' said Rodney.

I began to wish even more that I had sent Mary something for Christmas, but there was nothing I could do about that now. I resolved to be as helpful as I could to her in the future, and with this in mind sat down at my desk to compose a letter of condolence. I struggled even longer than is usual with such letters, for it was so difficult to imagine anyone really regretting the loss of old Mrs Beamish.

CHAPTER TEN

'I SUPPOSE I *could* take the afternoon off,' said Rodney rather doubtfully. 'I really think I shall have to. I couldn't let my wife go to a funeral alone, could I?'

'Of course you could,' I said. 'There will be people there that I know, and Mary wants me to go to the flat afterwards to help her with the relations.'

'When I was young,' said Sybil, 'women didn't go to funerals, for some reason or other it wasn't customary. Perhaps one can see why. Women nearly always outlive men, and I suppose it may have been a kind of subconscious jealousy — the men wouldn't want to have the women standing there in the cemetery, triumphant at having outlived them. You go along, Wilmet, and be a comfort to Mary. I will come with you to the church out of respect for poor Ella,' she declared surprisingly. 'Then Rodney need not worry.'

'No, I should really find it difficult to take time off *now*,' he said, with that air of mysterious importance which I have noticed sometimes in men, and especially women, who work in offices or ministries.

I did not expect to enjoy the funeral, though I felt a certain satisfaction in doing my duty. The little crowd of people — and it did seem to be such a very little crowd — in unrelieved black, the coffin standing in the chancel, the cold bleak day at the end of the old year with as yet no promise of the new, all combined to depress me to the point of tears. Sybil beside me seemed stoical and comforting. Not believing in an after life must simplify things, but the flat finality of such a creed was surely not to be borne where people one loved were concerned. I could of course be rather more detached about Ella Beamish, and was even able to notice who exactly had come to mourn her.

In the front pew I saw Mary, rather small and fragile beside her brothers, Gerald and William — large prosperous looking men, one of whom was accompanied by his wife, swathed in silver fox furs. Behind them sat Miss Prideaux and Sir Denbigh Grote and a few other elderly people, contemporaries or even friends of the dead woman. Some younger people, presumably family connections, were massed together on the opposite side of the aisle. Behind, at a respectful distance, I noticed Mrs Greenhill. I believed that she was the kind of person who would appreciate a good funeral, and I wondered if she came to all those that took place in the church. She was with her friend Mrs Spooner, and I imagined them perhaps comparing notes afterwards. Sitting exactly opposite to me was Mr Bason. I caught his eye as he came in, and for one moment it looked almost as if he were going to wave to me. As it was he gave me a kind of conspiratorial nod, as if our having been together when Father Ransome telephoned the news of Mrs Beamish's death had made a bond between us.

Father Thames and Father Bode were officiating at the Requiem Mass. I could not help wondering what Father Ransome was doing. His position must be rather delicate now, for he could hardly go on living in the flat alone with Mary. Perhaps he was even now looking for lodgings. Then it occurred to me that this particular day was his day off, so he might have been doing practically anything — walking in the park or round the shops, even wallowing in Cinerama, perhaps.

The coffin was to go from the church for burial at Kensal Green, accompanied only by the men, so that we women found ourselves in an awkward little group, waiting for the cars which were to take us the short distance from the church to the Beamishes' flat. Cynthia, the sister-in-law in the silver foxes, had her own little car and invited me to drive back with her and Miss Prideaux.

Comment after a funeral is much more difficult than after a wedding. The easy social expressions of pleasure and praise are inappropriate, and I felt that even a remark about the beauty of some of the floral tributes would be out of place. So we sat in silence, except for Cynthia's brusque comments on the state of the motor car.

'She's got cold standing here,' she said, 'though I did put a rug over her.'

Miss Prideaux murmured anxiously when the pressing of the self-starter failed to have any effect; but soon all was well and in no time at all we were at the flat, making our way into the vast high-ceilinged drawing-room, cluttered with heavy furniture — the kind of sofas and armchairs which engulfed a person of normal size in their brocaded depths, and the little tables covered with knick-knacks and photographs.

Mary was already in the room making us welcome.

'I think a cup of tea would be best, don't you?' she said anxiously. 'There is sherry, of course; Gerald and William thought ...'

We reassured her that tea was what we all wanted and she went into the kitchen to put the kettle on. I followed her.

'Oh, Wilmet, I'm so *glad* you're here,' she said. 'Mrs Brock asked if she should come to see to the tea and everything, but I thought I'd be glad to have something to do. William and Gerald can pour out the sherry when they come back from the cemetery. Do you think we should have the silver teapot?'

'How many are we?'

'Well, there's you and Cynthia and Miss Prideaux and me — that's four, isn't it? — yes, I think the silver teapot, though it isn't a very good pourer.'

'Are these the cups here?' I asked.

'Yes, Mrs Brock put everything ready. There's this Dundee cake — oh, and some bread and butter covered up in the larder. There's some Christmas cake too. I thought the men might like that with sherry. Wouldn't Mrs Forsyth have liked to come back to tea? I saw her with you when you came out of church.'

'No, Sybil just wanted to come to the church, thank you very much.'

'She doesn't usually come to church, does she?' Mary asked.

'No — she doesn't believe in anything, you know. But having known your mother so long she felt she'd like to be there.'

'It was good of her. Could you carry in this tray, Wilmet? I hope the fire's going well in the drawing-room—poor Miss Prideaux does feel the cold so terribly.'

'Where is Father Ransome?' I asked rather bluntly.

'He has had to move his things this afternoon. You see, he couldn't very well stay here under the circumstances.'

'No, I suppose not. Where has he gone then?'

'To the guest room at the clergy house for the moment.'

'Goodness,' I exclaimed, 'I wonder how he'll like that!' The memory of its austerity was still fresh in my mind.

'I suppose he will be reasonably comfortable. Then he'll get lodgings somewhere else.'

Our conversation had to be broken off at this point, for we began to carry the tea things into the drawing-room and the next few moments were occupied in getting everybody comfortably settled with tea and something to eat.

'I thought Oswald looked *very* tired,' said Miss Prideaux in a high piping voice.

'Oh, Father Thames,' I said. 'Yes, he did look tired.'

'He never spares himself,' said Miss Prideaux.

I reflected that perhaps one did not really expect clergymen to spare themselves, but did not voice my thought.

'Yes, the older generation is like that,' said Cynthia ingratiatingly. 'I'm afraid we have a lot to live up to.'

'And Sir Denbigh *insisted* on going to Kensal Green,' said Miss Prideaux. 'Luckily he has that good thick overcoat.'

'The one with the fur collar?' I asked, just for something to say.

'Yes. He had it when he was in Warsaw — of course he would need it there. It has a fur lining too.'

'Really?' said Cynthia, and we all murmured in approval. It

was obviously right that retired diplomats should have fur-lined overcoats.

'Will Father Ransome be staying here?' asked Miss Prideaux, accepting another cup of tea from Mary.

'No – I was telling Wilmet just now. He has moved his things to the guest room at the clergy house for the time being. I suppose lodgings will be found for him somewhere.'

'He might stay with Julian and Winifred Malory in Pimlico,' suggested Miss Prideaux. 'They have a flat in the vicarage. I believe there's a deaconess in it at the moment, but I've no doubt she could be got rid of.'

I was a little surprised at the strength, almost violence, of her language, and wondered if it had anything to do with her long sojourn in European countries where people were more easily 'got rid of' than in England.

'Is that far from here?' asked Cynthia in a disinterested tone, one hand stroking her silver fox stole which she had placed beside her on the sofa.

'Well, it is Victoria really,' said Miss Prideaux. 'He could come on a bus or on the Circle line from Victoria. The trains start running very early, I believe.'

'But he could hardly be here in time for a seven o'clock Mass, could he?' asked Mary a little anxiously.

'It would certainly be quite a long way to come fasting,' observed Miss Prideaux, folding a piece of bread and butter and taking a bite.

'Perhaps he could get a dispensation,' I said.

'I expect some nearer lodgings will be found for him,' said Mary. 'Apparently Father Ransome does know of a vicar in the Holland Park area who might be able to take him – a contemporary of his at college, I believe.'

'That does sound more satisfactory,' said Cynthia.

Mary looked up at the little clock on the mantelpiece of whose ticking we had all become rather conscious. 'I expect the men will be here soon,' she said.

I think we were all relieved when they came into the room, the Beamish brothers rubbing their hands, Sir Denbigh merely looking pinched with cold.

'I wondered whether the parsons might like to come back too,' said Gerald Beamish, 'but apparently they had another — er— funeral after this. Bad show in this weather.' He held up a decanter and turned to Sir Denbigh. 'This is quite a decent Amontillado, or would you prefer something with more body? Or there is tea, of course.'

'Is it China tea?' asked Sir Denbigh.

'Well no, I think it's just the usual tea we always have,' said Mary apologetically, 'but I can make some fresh.'

'Please do not trouble, Miss Beamish,' said Sir Denbigh. 'I really prefer Indian tea that has stood for a while — stewed, I believe one calls it.'

'Why did you put that rug over the car?' William Beamish asked his wife Cynthia. 'It's quite unnecessary, and it might get stolen. You never know in London.'

I had heard that they came from Leamington and wondered whether people were more honest there.

Cynthia replied with wifely sharpness. 'She was cold when we came out of church — it was a pity I didn't cover her up then. And that rug is such an old one, anyway.'

'I'm afraid people are very dishonest nowadays,' said Miss Prideaux complacently.

The conversation continued on the same agonizing level of unreality, which must, I thought, have been a great strain for Mary. But it became easier when Miss Prideaux left, taking Sir Denbigh with her as it were. Now that only the family were left the talk became more personal and to the point.

'What is happening to Mother's clothes and things?' asked Cynthia brusquely. 'I suppose you'll send most of them to charity?'

'Yes, I had thought one of the distressed gentlefolks' associations would be glad of them,' said Mary. 'But there are some furs that I shan't want myself, so I wondered if you would like to have them?'

'Let me see,' said Cynthia thoughtfully, 'there was quite a good summer ermine cape, if I remember rightly, or was it only squirrel?'

'I don't really know,' said Mary unhappily, 'but do have it if you would like it.'

'Well, I'll think it over and let you know,' said Cynthia, getting up from the sofa and gathering her silver foxes to her bosom. 'I really think we ought to be getting on our way, you know. William isn't too happy about driving in the dark, are you, dear?'

William muttered something.

'Gerald is staying for a while, isn't he, so you won't be alone?' Cynthia asked perfunctorily. 'That's good, then.'

I imagined them driving back to Leamington, perhaps bickering about the car or speculating on the details of Mrs Beamish's will if they did not know them already.

'I suppose you'll give up this flat and get a smaller one?' I said to Mary when we were alone together.

'Yes, of course I shan't live here. I've never really liked rooms this size. Shall we go into my room — it's easier to talk there, somehow.'

Mary's room looked out on to a quiet back street and one could see the spire of St Luke's in the far distance. The atmosphere was very different from the heavy formality of old Mrs Beamish's drawing-room. Mary still kept the painted furniture which she must have had as a girl, and the bookshelves were full of childish books; the only grown-up ones I noticed were a few novels by well-known women writers and some anthologies of poetry. On one wall hung the popular picture of a shepherd boy asleep on a hill, and on the little table by the bed there was a photograph of an Aberdeen terrier in a passe-partout frame.

The bed was strewn with black clothing of various kinds.

Mary apologized for the confusion, and drew up a basket chair for me to sit down by the gas fire.

'It really is a mess,' she said, 'but I've been going through my clothes. I found it helped to have something definite to do.'

'Shall you wear black?' I asked. 'I hadn't realized that people wore mourning very much these days.' I could remember my own mother mourning her father's death in black, then grey, and finally mauve; she had had a lilac summer coat which seemed much too pretty to be mourning.

Mary seemed confused for a moment. 'Well, it isn't exactly for mourning,' she said. 'I'm going to spend some time with the sisters at St Hildelith's; I don't know if I told you, probably not, because of course I couldn't while Mother was still alive.'

A look of horror must have shown itself on my face, for she said quickly, 'Oh Wilmet, don't look so shocked – it's something I've always wanted to do.'

I remembered our glib plans for Mary – foreign travel and leading her own life – this seemed to me to be exchanging one kind of imprisonment for another even worse, for although I had learned to accept the idea of the religious life for a few people it seemed terrible to contemplate when applied to oneself or anybody one knew at all well.

'You don't mean that you're going to be a nun?' I asked naively.

'Well, of course I don't know how things will work out, but I'm going to test my vocation. It may very well be that I can do more good out in the world – I mean,' she smiled, 'in so far as I can do any good anywhere.'

'And you have to wear black clothes there?' I said, rather at a loss.

'Yes, to begin with. I have one black skirt and a cardigan, and of course the dress I bought when you helped me to choose it, but somehow I'm not sure whether that will be suitable.'

'I don't know – it's quite plain, and as you obviously *won't* be dressing it up with masses of pink pearls I should think it might do very well.'

Mary smiled. 'I've still got the pink pearl necklace,' she said, 'and I shan't ever have worn it. I was wondering if I could have this blue dress dyed black — do you think it would take well?'

'I hate wearing dyed clothes, and of course dyeing does show up the worn bits, if there are any,' I began, before I realized that wearing clothes one hated with worn bits showing on them might not be so inappropriate for the life Mary was proposing to lead. 'Has Father Ransome advised you at all?' I asked quickly. 'I don't mean about clothes, of course.'

Mary laughed. 'Poor Marius, he has found it all rather overwhelming, and then having to turn out and find somewhere else to live hasn't made it any easier for him.'

I was indignant, for it sounded very much as if he had turned out to be a broken reed.

'But it's his job to be helpful in circumstances like these,' I protested. 'He shouldn't find it overwhelming.'

Mary smiled in her rather irritating way. 'Well, he's only young, after all,' she said, 'and of course he has been very kind. But Father Bode has really been the best.'

'Better than Father Thames?'

'Yes. Father Thames is old himself and doesn't quite realize the personal upheaval of it all. I mean, so many of his friends must have died and I suppose he is prepared to go himself quite soon. Father Bode is full of *practical* sympathy.'

I was interested in this classification of the clergy as comforters in bereavement, and we were still discussing it when I got up to go.

I had said goodbye to Mary and was outside on the pavement when her brother Gerald came running after me..

'Oh, Mrs — er — !' he called out. 'I'm so sorry I didn't catch your name, but you seem to be a great friend of Mary's.'

'Is there anything I can do for her?' I asked. 'One does feel so useless at times like these.'

'It's about this nunnery business,' he blurted out. 'She seems

126

so set on it. Can't you do something to talk her out of it? I feel she might listen to you.'

'But if it's what she really wants to do, have we any right to try to talk her out of it?'

'It isn't as if she wouldn't be comfortably off now — and she could make her home with us if she felt lonely. She knows that. What on earth will people *say*?' he groaned.

'I don't suppose people will say much. After all, it isn't such a *very* unusual thing to do.'

'We have never had anything like it in *our* family before,' said Gerald, seeming to draw himself up to his full height.

'Perhaps not. But is it as bad as having a murder in the family, or even a divorce?'

He seemed doubtful. 'But what is the *reason*?' he persisted. 'Some love affair gone wrong, do you think? Somehow I've never associated Mary with that kind of thing. You don't think this curate fellow — ?' he said suddenly.

'You mean Father Ransome?' I asked in astonishment. 'But he is a celibate. I hardly think there could be anything in that, or that Mary would have considered it for a moment.'

'He's not bad looking,' said Gerald dispassionately.

'That's hardly the point,' I said impatiently, for it was cold standing about. 'Anyway, people don't go into convents these days because of love affairs gone wrong. They usually have more positive reasons.'

We parted in a mood of slight mutual antagonism, and in my anxiety to take Mary's part against her stupid pompous brother I had quite forgotten the dismay I had felt on first hearing her news.

CHAPTER ELEVEN

MARY spent the first weeks of the New Year disposing of some of her mother's effects and putting the furniture into store—into that splendid building by the river which Piers and I had observed on our autumnal walk. I imagined Mrs Beamish's brocaded sofa and armchairs, and the heavy mahogany chests and wardrobes incarcerated in those great echoing rooms, and wondered if they would ever emerge again. It seemed that they, too, like their owner, were renouncing the world and might almost have protested when the remover's men came to take them away. If we went that way again I could say to Piers, 'I know some furniture in there'; but the chance of ever doing that seemed as remote as summer seems from the middle of winter.

Mary's brother William and his wife Cynthia had invited her to go to Madeira with them in February, and uncongenial though the company might have been I thought it would be a good thing for her. But she decided that she did not want to go away, and so on a bleak January day she entered the convent, which was a branch house of the one in the parish and in another part of London.

Father Ransome had found lodgings with the vicar of a near-by parish — the old college contemporary, in fact — who lived alone in a large vicarage. It was certainly not so convenient as the Beamishes' flat had been, and once, at an early weekday Mass, he was late and looked very much as if he hadn't had time to shave. I remembered an article I had once read in the *Church Times* which declared that nothing but the failure of a priest's alarm clock could excuse such a thing. It had come as a shock to me to realize that the alarm clocks of priests could be fallible, mortal almost. I was glad that *I* did not often have to be woken by such barbarous means.

There was no doubt that Father Ransome had his following in the parish. His good looks amply compensated for his short-comings in the pulpit — for he was an uninspired preacher — and young girls could be seen struggling to suppress their giggles when we sang such lines as

> And when earthly things are past
> Bring our ransomed souls at last ...

in the best known of the Epiphany hymns.

In the middle of January the Portuguese classes started again. I had been looking forward to them as an opportunity to see Piers, and almost wished that Sybil were not quite so indefatig-able in her attendance so that I might have a chance of talking to him alone after the class.

The first evening we discovered that our classroom had been changed, and we were directed by mistake to one where teaching was already in progress.

'You must not use the verb *desejar* if you are just wanting a glass of water or a piece of chocolate,' said the teacher, who was a lively young Brazilian. 'It is too *strong*. *Desejar* means to *desire*....' He looked despairingly at his class as if wondering whether they were capable of experiencing such a strong emo-tion. Then his glance lighted on Sybil and me, standing in the doorway clutching our umbrellas and books.

'We want Mr Longridge's class,' I said stupidly. 'He doesn't seem to be here.'

'No, he isn't,' said the teacher. 'But why don't you come and join *this* class? We are always laughing but we learn a lot.'

We backed out of the doorway rather foolishly. I felt that he and his class had been laughing at us, and was also resentful because they seemed to be more advanced than we were. Piers had never told us about *desejar*.

'That sounds a lively class,' said Sybil. 'I sometimes feel it's a pity that Piers is so *moody*. Ah, there is Mrs Marble going into a door at the end of the corridor — that must be the right room.'

We found that it was and greeted our classmates with a rather marked lack of enthusiasm. Some of the commercial gentlemen were absent — perhaps they really had been sent to Pernambuco. There was no sign of Piers.

'You'd think he could be punctual at the *first* class,' grumbled Mrs Marble. 'I was in two minds whether to come this term or not. I don't feel I learnt very much last term, and then, well, not having a Christmas party — that wasn't very nice, was it? When I did Spanish we had a party at the end of every term. We all contributed three and sixpence, and bought food and coffee and drinks — nothing alcoholic, of course — they wouldn't allow wines and spirits to be drunk in the college. You can understand that, really —'

'It can't have been much of a party, then,' said Piers in his most languid tone. 'Not really a party at all.' He walked past us to his desk and began to open his books.

Mrs Marble looked annoyed but said nothing.

The lesson started. We were to learn the subjunctive, and I found myself wondering whether I could take so kindly to the Portuguese now that I realized how often they seemed to use it. It seemed as if there were going to be a great many things I couldn't possibly say. Piers was in one of his provocative moods and hardly looked at me during the lesson. It seemed as if he were paying me out for not having spent that evening with him before Christmas. I kept thinking about the little box and its strange inscription, so much so that I did badly when I was asked to translate, and he made a sarcastic remark about people who didn't listen to what he said.

I was very annoyed and reluctant to follow Sybil over to him when the class was at an end. To my surprise she asked him to dine with us one evening in the following week when Harry and Rowena were coming. I think I was even more surprised when he accepted with every appearance of delight.

'I should tell you that your sister and brother-in-law are

130

coming,' Sybil added. 'I feel it is hardly fair to bring families together without warning.'

'That was thoughtful of you,' said Piers. 'We aren't always on the best of terms, but Christmas usually improves family relationships — at least temporarily, don't you think?'

'You went there for Christmas?' I couldn't resist asking.

'No, Wilmet,' he looked at me for the first time, 'I was in London.'

'Not alone, I hope?' said Sybil rather drily.

'No, I wasn't alone.'

'Were there festivities at the press on Christmas Eve? Great drinkings and all that?' I asked.

'There *was* drinking, but not there.'

'Which church did you go to?'

'Unfortunately I didn't manage to get to any church.'

'But surely at *Christmas* —' I protested. 'There were so many services.'

'Not between three and five in the afternoon, which was the only time I really felt capable of attending one,' said Piers defiantly.

'Were you drunk *all* the time?' asked Sybil in an interested tone. 'I do hope we shall be able to supply your wants when you dine with us next week. There will be gin and sherry, wine with the meal of course, and possibly liqueurs. Later, I suppose, there will be whisky for the men. My son will see to all that.'

'I'm sure it will be delightful,' said Piers. 'I was really only trying to shock Wilmet, you know.'

We began to laugh and all parted in a good humour.

'Poor Piers, he is frustrated and unloved,' I said, feeling strangely cosy as the words came out. 'That's why he does these silly things. He needs taking care of.'

'I thought he was only joking,' said Sybil. 'And of course young men do like to show off.'

'He isn't as young as all that,' I protested. 'I do hope he will arrive sober on Wednesday.'

'It isn't really a thing to joke about,' said Sybil seriously. 'I have seen so much of the other side of it in my work. It can bring about great unhappiness.'

'It seems to be the other way round in the people we know,' I said. 'I mean drinking is the result of unhappiness rather than the cause.'

'Then Piers is unhappy?' said Sybil thoughtfully. 'No more than many people of his age, I imagine. And it will pass, you know.'

Her pronouncement seemed to emphasize what I usually forgot — that there were nearly forty years between us. I suppose by the time one is seventy one can say confidently and from personal experience that things will pass. At thirty one is still living experimentally, guessing that they will yet almost hoping that they will not.

Nevertheless Piers did come to the dinner party sober and in a neat dark suit. What was more, he was the first to arrive and we were able to have some conversation before the others came. But it was disappointingly general and I could not bring myself to mention his Christmas present to me, although I was conscious of it lying between us, drawing us together or separating us — I could not decide which.

Rowena came into the hall, looking radiant in a red coat with a high fur collar framing her face. She kissed me and Piers, and then flung her arms around Rodney who looked delighted. Harry retaliated by kissing me on the cheek.

'All this show of affection,' said Piers rather fretfully. 'Is this what's expected at a dinner party? I'm so unused to going into society these days. If only I'd known, I could have kissed Wilmet. Did you expect it? Were you disappointed when I didn't?' he asked, smiling at me.

To my chagrin I felt myself blushing and saying in a silly awkward way, 'Of course not, I didn't think of it — I mean, one doesn't ...' failing entirely to carry off the occasion with the lightness appropriate to it.

'Wilmet is rather cool and unapproachable,' said Harry, 'or she gives that impression. Very fetching it is, too.'

I felt still more embarrassed and annoyed, and drank up the remains of my sherry quickly.

Rodney and Harry went into a corner and began talking about old army acquaintances whom they had seen lately. Piers and Rowena and I were left together.

'Well dear, had a good day at the press?' asked Rowena.

'Much as usual,' said Piers. 'One doesn't have *good* days. I amused myself by raising a number of irritating Portuguese orthographical queries which are practically insoluble. My colleague was doing some articles about Africa and seemed to be enjoying himself. I expect several people will be cursing the printers' readers and their queries before the week is out.'

'Darling, it seems such a *nasty* job,' said Rowena in a distressed tone. 'It seems to bring out the worst in you.'

'Do forgive my lateness,' said Sybil, hurrying into the room. 'But I've been having trouble with the table.'

There were murmurs of interest, curiosity and concern.

'You know how a hostess is supposed to have a last minute look at the table to see that all is well? I went into the dining-room and found that Rhoda had thrown away my table decoration — she thought it was dead!'

'Oh dear, what did you do?' asked Rowena.

'I had to get it back out of the dustbin. You see, strictly speaking, it *was* dead. I'd been making an arrangement of dried leaves and branches that I'd seen in Wilmet's *Daily Telegraph*. I was rather proud of it. Come in and see — I think I've put it together again quite successfully.'

We took our places in the dining-room and examined the table decoration with interest. I saw at once that it was not quite what the woman in the *Telegraph* had meant. The components were a little *too* dead, and the arrangement carelessly haphazard rather than artistically casual. Dear Sybil, with her lack of any natural artistic sense, had somehow missed the point.

'Really, Mother, I don't blame Rhoda,' said Rodney. 'People will think we can't even afford a few late chrysanthemums.'

'We've been having lectures on flower arrangement at the Women's Institute,' said Rowena. 'I discovered that I've been doing mine wrong for years. My arrangements, which I always thought so pretty, had no interesting focal point! Now I'm so humiliated and discouraged that I feel I'd rather have nothing at all or just plants in pots that arrange themselves.'

'It's a pity when everything becomes so scientific,' said Rodney. 'I like to think of young girls at home arranging flowers according to the light of nature.'

'Waiting desperately for husbands,' said Piers.

'And instead they're all in the civil service and have learnt to arrange flowers according to the latest methods,' said Rowena.

'Do you have some pretty young things in your office, old boy?' Harry asked Rodney.

'It's not the same as Mincing Lane,' Rowena broke in. 'Women in the civil service are beautiful rather than pretty, I always imagine — isn't that so, Rodney?'

Rodney seemed to have no ready answer.

'What about that splendid Miss Hitchens?' Sybil prompted.

'Yes, she's certainly very capable and a good sort, but she's not much to look at. Besides, she wears — ' he hesitated and we waited in almost breathless anticipation.

'Go *on*, Rodney,' said Rowena eagerly. 'What *can* you be going to say?'

'Well, sort of thick stockings — cotton or something, would they be? She goes to play golf sometimes straight from work — I suppose that's why,' Rodney added, as if feeling that he had been unchivalrous.

'Intellectual women are seldom attractive,' said Piers. 'The combination of beauty with brains is to me unnatural and therefore rather repellent.'

'That's an old-fashioned idea,' said Rowena. 'Nowadays

134

women seem to have everything — I suppose men find that frightening.'

'Not always,' said Rodney. 'Miss Hitchens has a friend who's most attractive and intelligent too — she brought her to lunch in the canteen one day. A Miss Bates,' he added solemnly.

'Miss Bates?' I laughed. 'Hasn't she a christian name?'

'Yes, it's Prudence, I believe. She works for Grampian, the economist. Eleanor Hitchens tells me that she was engaged to a Member of Parliament but broke it off.'

'Now what does that tell us?' asked Sybil. 'That she was too beautiful to be an M.P.'s wife or that he was too stupid to be the husband of an intelligent woman? Was he Tory or Labour? — perhaps it would be invidious to speculate. And now,' she went on, 'I have a surprise for you. Does anybody remember what day this is?'

'Tomorrow is Ash Wednesday,' said Piers rather surprisingly, 'so today must be Shrove Tuesday. I hope the surprise is pancakes.'

'You're quite right, it is,' said Sybil. 'Pancakes should be thin enough to read a love letter through, they say. Now who can put it to the test?'

Rodney drew a piece of paper with cyclostyling on it from his pocket. 'A bit of a report I've been working on — not confidential, of course — that should do quite well.'

'Oh, Noddy!' exclaimed Sybil. 'Can nobody do better?'

'I think I can,' said Piers. He produced what was undoubtedly a letter, written on lined paper in very blue ink, in a round childish looking hand. I tried hard to read some of it, but without success.

'Was that *really* a love letter that Piers brought out?' I asked Rowena, when we had retired to my bedroom for a moment after dinner. 'It looked rather an uneducated sort of handwriting.'

'Wilmet, darling! Surely the writing of love letters isn't a monopoly of the educated, is it?' said Rowena, who was sitting at my dressing table trying out my bottles of scent. 'Anyway your guess is as good as mine. I suppose one knows less about the affairs of one's near relations than one does about anyone else's.'

'I've often wondered who he shares his flat with,' I said, 'though of course I've never asked him outright.'

'He did share it with a friend who worked with him, but I've never met him and for all I know they may have quarrelled. People who share flats do seem to quarrel, don't they? Piers is *always* chopping and changing.'

'Do you usually like his friends?'

'I haven't met many of them. They aren't usually our type.'

I could imagine this. 'I suppose he has led his own life,' I said tritely.

'Well, of course.' Rowena took up another of my scent bottles and dabbed some on the nape of her neck. 'I shall smell simply marvellous,' she said. 'Do you think Rodney will be impressed? It seems a waste just for Harry.'

'Rodney doesn't notice particularly,' I said in a complacent wife's tone, 'but he may if it's you, of course.'

'Wilmet —' Rowena began looking at herself intently in the glass, smoothing her eyebrows with a finger.

'Yes?' I asked, rather puzzled.

'You weren't *annoyed* about Harry's Christmas present, were you?'

'Annoyed?' I echoed, even more puzzled.

'You didn't mention it — that's why I wondered.'

'But what was it? I don't think I can have had it — I do hope it didn't go astray?'

'Oh, I *hope* not!' Rowena turned round to face me. 'It was a rather pretty little box, just the kind of thing you like — Regency or something — and it had an inscription on the lid.'

'I know,' I said. "If you will not when you may, when you will you shall have nay." I *did* get it and thought it charming, but I couldn't imagine who it was from,' I added quickly.

'Harry thought you'd guess.'

'Did he tell you about it?'

'Well, not exactly. I think he meant to do it secretly, but I happened to see it, so of course he had to tell me then,' Rowena laughed. 'Men aren't nearly so good at secrets as women, are they? I do think you might have guessed, though — surely you knew Harry had a bit of a thing about you?'

I felt so deflated and stupid that I could hardly bring myself to answer. *Harry* had sent the little box. The revelation disappointed and sickened me out of all proportion. I could only be thankful that I had been spared the humiliation of making some coy allusion to it when I was with Piers.

'I knew Harry liked me,' I brought out at last. 'He took me to lunch at Simpson's.'

'You lucky thing! Really, I'm quite jealous,' Rowena laughed. 'All that wonderful meat. He never takes me there. You did like the box, didn't you?'

'I simply loved it,' I said enthusiastically. 'And I shall go and tell Harry at once.'

We linked arms and went down to join the men. I reflected what a splendid and wonderful thing the friendship of really nice women was. It could surely be said that Rowena and I were fortunate in each other.

'*Harry!*' I burst out in my most extravagant tone, 'so it was *you* who sent me that delicious little box? And I never guessed!'

'Glad you liked it,' said Harry, mumbling rather. 'Saw it in a shop in Jermyn Street — thought it was the kind of thing you'd like.'

'What box is this?' asked Rodney.

'A sweet little box Harry sent me at Christmas.'

'I didn't know Harry had sent you anything,' persisted Rodney.

'No, darling, Wilmet didn't either,' said Rowena in her sweet voice. 'Neither did I. It was an anonymous gift — so much more fun than the other kind.'

'Do we all take *black* coffee?' Sybil broke in.

'I should imagine so,' said Piers. 'And perhaps with brandy, too.'

The evening went on with everybody being rather bright and drinking a little more than they should — almost like young people, I thought sadly. Sybil brought out some knitting.

'Mother, I haven't seen you knit for years,' said Rodney.

I had seen the wool when she bought it, a rather becoming shade of green. She intended to knit a pullover for Professor Root.

'It's a lovely green,' said Rowena.

'Yes, there is green in Arnold's eyes,' said Sybil surprisingly.

'Nobody ever knits for me,' said Piers, glancing at me.

I turned my head away. I was angry with him and yet it was not his fault. He would never know.

'I don't like knitting,' I said.

'No, I despise women who are always knitting,' said Sybil. 'But it can be a useful occupation — the kind of thing one can do when talking.'

'I wonder if women brought their knitting when Oscar Wilde talked,' said Piers.

'I daresay not,' said Sybil calmly, 'but that doesn't mean they wouldn't have liked to.'

Before the guests went I thanked Harry again for the box, and later, when we were upstairs, I showed it to Rodney. He read the inscription aloud in his most civil servantish voice, I thought.

'A bit subtle for old Harry,' he commented.

'Yes, it sounds almost as if he were inviting me to have an affair with him, doesn't it?' I said.

'An affair? Old Harry Grinners? Oh, darling, *really* —'

'Well, I don't think it's all *that* funny.'

'No, I daresay Rowena does have a good deal to put up with,' said Rodney complacently.

'Don't all married women?'

Rodney looked rather confused. 'You didn't display the box with your other Christmas presents,' he said. 'I suppose you were embarrassed.'

'Yes, that was it. And I hardly know what to do with it now.'

'Well, what do women do with things like that? Keep pins in them, I suppose.'

'Yes, pins — that's what I'll keep in it.'

But I never really use pins, I thought resentfully, as I got into bed. Rodney had already put out his light and turned over as if about to go to sleep. I was about to do the same when I realized that it was Ash Wednesday tomorrow, the beginning of Lent. Obviously the little box full of pins was intended to be some kind of a penance.

CHAPTER TWELVE

'WAS it *you* who telephoned the clergy house yesterday evening?' asked Mr Bason, hurrying to my side as I left the lunchtime service on Ash Wednesday. I had been unable to get up for the quarter to seven or even the eight o'clock services, and was thankful that Father Thames provided this later opportunity for fulfilling one's religious obligations. There had been a good many strangers in the congregation, but I had not noticed Piers among them.

'It sounded rather like your voice,' Mr Bason went on.

'No, it couldn't have been me,' I said. 'Why did you think it might be?'

'Oh I don't know, and I see now that it couldn't have been you. This lady was asking for the times for the Imposition of Ashes, and you already knew the times, of course. She had a deep very cultured voice.'

A deep very cultured voice asking the times for the Imposition of Ashes — I wondered if I should have liked to think of myself like that. It seemed an ideal to aim at for Lent. I felt in a way that I had already fallen short by not being that woman.

'The services have been *very* well attended today,' said Mr Bason rather unctuously. 'One does feel that is a good thing.'

Surely he couldn't have attended more than one? I thought, and then it occurred to me that his domestic duties at the clergy house would be lighter than usual today. Meals would be fewer and less elaborate.

'I suppose you haven't much cooking to do today?' I said rather chattily.

'No, the poor things don't eat much on Ash Wednesday, of course, but they'll be having a meal this evening.' His eyes brightened and he took a piece of paper out of his pocket.

I saw that it was covered with what looked like a list, written in purple ink in a large bold hand. For one wild moment I thought it must be a Lenten laundry list — the purple ink, of course, representing the liturgical colour. Naturally it was not that but something very nearly as good — a list of menus which Mr Bason had compiled for the clergy house during that solemn season.

'Just a few suitable dishes that occurred to me,' he explained. 'I've been carrying the list round with me in case anything strikes me.'

'Like a poet jotting down felicitous lines and images,' I suggested.

'Exactly, Mrs Forsyth. And what poetry there *is* in cooking! Poor Mrs Greenhill hadn't an idea beyond boiled cod or macaroni cheese for Lent. I hope to do a good deal better than that. Do you know one thing I propose to give them?' he asked. 'If I can get it, that is.'

'You seem to have such good ideas,' I said. 'I'm sure it must be something unusual.'

'It is — fried octopus! What do you think of *that*?' he asked triumphantly.

'It's certainly most original, but I doubt whether Father Bode would like it,' I hazarded.

'Oh, *Bode*!' said Mr Bason contemptuously. 'I've no doubt he was perfectly satisfied with Mrs Greenhill's cod. Then I thought I might give them scampi sometimes — with garlic butter, of course — and even escargots, not to mention all the delicious ways there are of doing quite ordinary fish.'

'I wonder whether they ought to eat anything actually *delicious* during Lent,' I said. 'I suppose the idea of fasting is that one should eat only enough to sustain life.'

Mr Bason laughed merrily, as if my ideas were too naive or old-fashioned to be taken seriously, and we parted on this note.

A few days later I happened to get into conversation with Father Thames on my way out of church after one of the Lenten services. I found myself remembering Mr Bason's menus and wondering if perhaps this very evening octopus was to be eaten at the clergy house, but I felt it was beyond my province to ask. We had been subjected—that seemed to be the only way to describe it—to an address of great dullness, and they were all to be given by the same man, Father Edwin Sainsbury, with whom Father Ransome was now lodging. He was one of those preachers who, on coming to the end of what they have to say, find it impossible to stop. Sentence after sentence seemed as if it must be the last but still he went on. I felt as if I had been wrapped round and round in a cocoon of wordiness, like a great suffocating eiderdown. I hardly knew what comment to make to Father Thames when I found myself beside him.

Luckily he spoke first. 'It was good of Father Sainsbury to take poor Father Ransome in, wasn't it?' he remarked. 'But of course he has plenty of room. Now this will surprise you—that vicarage has eight bedrooms! Eight bedrooms—just think of that! And he has no curate.'

'Is he married?' I asked in a rather social way, feeling that the question was a little unsuitable.

'Not that I know of,' said Father Thames rather oddly, for it seemed unlikely that a fellow priest would have any reason, or indeed be able, to conceal a wife. 'Between ourselves, you know,' Father Thames's tone became suddenly confidential, 'I'm not at all sure how long Father Sainsbury will be with us.'

I was at a loss—was he expected to die or become a missionary, or just get another living? I wondered.

'I suppose you read that letter of his in the *Church Times* last week?'

'The one about—' I began, hoping that Father Thames would prompt me.

'South India—exactly. He is taking an extreme view, and I am rather afraid that he may influence Ransome.'

'I suppose they would naturally discuss it a good deal, living in the same house.'

'Yes, they might very well—and before we know where we

are we may have to be looking for another assistant priest.' He sighed heavily. 'And you know how difficult they are to come by these days.'

'You mean that Father Sainsbury and Father Ransome might become Roman Catholics?' I said simply. 'Because they disapprove of the attitude we are taking towards the Church of South India?' I said 'we' but I was lamentably ignorant on the subject myself. I remembered the study groups Father Thames had mentioned. Perhaps he was now of the opinion that they would be too dangerous and send half his congregation over to Rome.

'Ransome is not very stable,' mused Father Thames, as if talking to himself, 'but of course he is young.'

'I do hope Mr Bason is being satisfactory?' I said, changing to what I felt might be a safer subject.

'He is a great treasure. I am most thankful for what you did for us there. We have had some most unusual dishes, I can assure you. Now this will amaze you — what do you think he gave us last night?'

'Octopus?' I suggested, laughing.

'Exactly! You thought of the most unlikely thing and that was it. Octopus fried in batter — delicious! Mrs Greenhill would never have thought of that.'

'No, I don't suppose so. It reminds one of Italy, doesn't it?'

'Ah yes, how it does!' Father Thames shivered and drew his cloak more closely around him. He seemed about to exchange some Italian reminiscence with me, but evidently guessed that our memories of that country might be slightly different and thought better of it.

'*A rivederci!*' I said boldly, and he responded with a wave of the hand, then walked up the steps of the clergy house, perhaps to brood in his study among his beautiful objects. Picking up his Fabergé egg he might well forget his anxiety over Father Ransome's instability in the contemplation of its elaborate — though to my mind rather vulgar — beauty.

It was certainly worrying for all of us if Father Sainsbury had leanings towards Rome which might eventually be the means of taking Father Ransome from us. I began to look out for him anxiously every day to see if I could detect any subtle change in him; and I was decidedly relieved when Miss Prideaux telephoned to ask me to tea with her, adding as a kind of bait, 'Father Ransome has promised to look in for a moment.'

I was not sure whether it was Father Ransome himself or Miss Prideaux who had suggested that it might be only a moment, for when I arrived he was comfortably installed by the fire and seemed to have been there for some time.

Miss Prideaux was saying how nice it was for him to be lodging with an old college friend. 'There is much pleasure to be had in discussing old times, I always think,' she said.

And *what* times, I thought, for in her case they were the past glories of the Austro-Hungarian regime and life with a noble Italian family — hardly to be compared with the petty gossip and intrigue of a theological college. I had always thought of them like this since hearing of one where the principal was reputed to creep around in carpet slippers listening at doors, but it was probably unfair to generalize.

'Yes, we do a good deal of reminiscing,' said Father Ransome. 'It's always interesting to see how one's contemporaries have done.'

'I suppose you have theological discussions as well,' I said.

Father Ransome looked a little embarrassed, or it seemed to me that he did. 'Yes, we do occasionally,' he said, 'though it's surprising how little time one really has for things like that, and how much time is taken up with trivial domestic things. This morning, for instance, I discovered that the rain was coming through a corner of my bedroom ceiling, and we spent most of breakfast talking about that.'

Miss Prideaux made clucking sounds of distress. 'I should hardly call that a trivial thing,' she said. 'I hope it hasn't been too uncomfortable for you.'

'Well, a rather large piece of plaster fell down from the ceiling, but I've been able to move my bed to the other side of the room,' said Father Ransome modestly. 'But I suppose a little discomfort does one no harm, especially in Lent.'

'I'm sure the early fathers didn't envisage anything like *that*,' said Miss Prideaux indignantly. 'After all, a cave in the desert wouldn't have *that* kind of danger.'

'No, I suppose it was wild animals rather than falling plaster,' I said. 'One hardly knows which would be worse.'

'I think I prefer the more civilized forms of discomfort,' said Father Ransome smiling.

'I had a letter from Mary Beamish a few days ago,' said Miss Prideaux, as if mention of discomfort had reminded her of the convent. 'She was getting her letter-writing done before Lent. She didn't say very much about herself. The letter was mostly questions about various people and activities in the parish. I have a feeling she misses the *worldly* things, you know.'

I could not help smiling at the idea of Mary's harmless, indeed praiseworthy, activities in the parish being regarded as worldly, and yet I supposed that they were. It was all a matter of comparison. I too had had a letter from her of a similar kind. I could hear her eager voice in the questions she asked: Had I been to the Settlement with Sybil lately? How was Mr Bason getting on at the clergy house? Had the study groups on South India started yet? Who was giving the Tuesday evening Lenten addresses this year? She did not mention Marius Ransome, and this omission made me suspect that they had perhaps written to each other. I wondered if he would mention that he had heard from her, but he did not. We left Miss Prideaux's tea party together, and I tried to lead the subject back to Mary by asking him whether he thought she would stay at the convent for always.

'I couldn't really say. I believe that she intended to when she first went there. She is a fine person,' he said uncertainly.

I felt impatient with him for having so little to say about her and for using a phrase in which he had already described her once before. Then I began to wonder whether it was the only thing he ever said about women, the only compliment he knew.

'She could do a great deal of good in the world now that she has her mother's money,' I said. 'I should have thought that might have appealed to her.'

'Yes, one can do good with money, of course,' said Father Ransome. 'Did you know that Mrs Beamish had left *me* a legacy?'

'No, I didn't,' I said, rather taken aback.

'Yes — five hundred pounds. An awkward amount really.'

'How do you mean, awkward?'

'Well, had it been five *thousand* pounds one might have done some rather spectacular good with it. As it is there is the temptation to do good only to oneself.'

'I'm sure she must have meant it just for you to use as you wanted,' I said. The picture had come into my mind of old Mrs Beamish altering or adding a codicil to her will, surely almost on her deathbed, for Father Ransome had been with them such a short time before she died. It was like a scene in a Victorian novel. 'Did she leave legacies to all the clergy?' I asked.

'She left Father Thames a pair of Georgian silver wine-coasters which he had always admired — I don't know about Father Bode. He is always so much better than the rest of us that one feels he was not left anything — to distinguish him, as it were.' Father Ransome smiled rather ruefully.

'Won't you come and have a glass of sherry with us?' I asked, as we approached the house.

'Thank you very much, but I've given up drinking for Lent,' he said, not looking at me.

'So the clergy *do* give up things?' I said lightly. 'They are always urging us to, so I'm glad to know that they practise what they preach.'

There was a rather uncomfortable silence and I felt that my remark had perhaps been cheap and frivolous.

'We have to try to, sometimes,' he said at last, 'otherwise we shouldn't be able to preach at all, and think what a loss *that* would be.'

I was reassured to find him back in his usual form.

'All these abstinences and fastings are rather difficult for lay people to remember,' I said. 'I always find them very muddling. I suppose one could always ask the clergy when in doubt.'

'Of course,' he agreed, 'or write to our favourite church newspaper. "Is there any liturgical objection to eating hot cross buns on Maundy Thursday?" you might ask.'

'And whatever would the answer to that be?'

He looked at me solemnly, then said in a prim tone, 'We *know* of none, though we should *not* care to do so ourselves.'

I parted from him laughing and turning over in my mind the rather surprising news that Mrs Beamish had left him a legacy in her will.

CHAPTER THIRTEEN

WE had a hard winter that year. February and March were cruel months — not in the poet's way perhaps, but bad enough for most of us. Only Rodney seemed to enjoy himself, lagging pipes, unfreezing the tank and dealing with a neighbour's burst pipe in the middle of the night. I began to wonder if I really knew the man I had married, for I had not hitherto suspected these talents. Like writers to the cheaper daily papers who urged us to think of the old-age pensioners, I could not help thinking of Mary in her presumably cold convent, and Miss Prideaux and Sir Denbigh with so little on their old bones to keep them warm. I am afraid I did not worry overmuch about Father Ransome and his leaking ceiling, nor even about the possibility of his going over to Rome. I somehow felt that the cold weather might discourage doubts, or at least temporarily suspend intellectual activity, like food preserved by freezing. Father Thames took to his bed with influenza in Holy Week and Father Bode battled gallantly with the exacting services of that solemn season. It was not until Holy Saturday, when the flame from Bill Coleman's cigarette lighter efficiently kindled the New Fire of Easter in the dark church, that any feeling of hope rose in me. The lights revealed a bough of golden forsythia decorating the font, and life seemed to stretch out before me new and exciting.

April was balmy and delicious, and cruel in the way the poet did mean, mingling memory and desire. The memory was of other springs, the desire unformulated, unrecognized almost, pushed away because there seemed to be no place for it in the life I had chosen for myself.

One day Rowena and I met to have a cosy women's shopping lunch together. She had come up to town to buy new clothes for the children, but when I met her in our favourite restaurant she admitted that she had spent the whole morning buying things for herself and nothing for the children at all.

'And this afternoon we're having our hair done,' I reminded her, for we were going together to my hairdresser who was to create elegant new hairstyles for us.

'Oh this weather,' Rowena sighed, pulling off her pale yellow gloves. 'It makes one so unsettled. One ought to be in *Venice* with a *lover*!'

'Of course,' I agreed. 'Whom would you choose?'

There was a pause, then we both burst out simultaneously, 'Rocky Napier!' and dissolved into helpless giggles.

'We say this so glibly,' Rowena pointed out, 'and yet we're both so respectable. Neither of us has had a lover, or is ever likely to. The idea has got translated into something remote, even comfortable, now. Like morning coffee with a woman friend in a country town — none of the uncertain rapture and agony of those Rocky Napier days!'

I suddenly felt that I wanted to break out of the mould of respectability into which Rowena had cast me and say, 'Speak for yourself!'

'Even this restaurant,' Rowena went on, 'in spite of its gay Italian paintings round the walls, has an air of Eastbourne about it. Look at the curtains — cream net and cretonne with a Jacobean design — *that* brings one down to earth all right! Perhaps it's just as well. But sometimes, you know, I envy really *wicked* women, or even despised spinsters — they at least can have their dreams.'

'And can't we?' I asked.

'Not really,' said Rowena, 'or if we do, we know that there's absolutely no hope of their coming true. Whereas the despised spinster still has the chance of meeting somebody — perhaps a young man who will love her for her money, or an old one to whom she can be a comfort in his declining years. At least she's *free*!'

We were eating spaghetti. Rowena managed hers clumsily and began to giggle. 'As a matter of fact,' she went on, 'I do feel wonderfully free at this moment — my wicked selfish shopping, a good lunch with drinks and the prospect of a new hairstyle this afternoon. I almost feel as if I had cast off Harry and the children for good. And he may be feeling the same, for all I know.'

'I shouldn't think so,' I said, but then, remembering our winter luncheon together, I wondered if perhaps Rowena wasn't right. Surely on that occasion he had cast off Rowena and the children for a little while? I believed it was a thing men did quite easily. I felt a sudden prick of annoyance that the lovely spring weather had not inspired him to ask me out again. Perhaps he had felt something of the anticlimax of the little box, for, with Rowena and Rodney knowing all about it, it did seem to be that.

'He's so fond of you, Wilmet,' Rowena said, as if reading my thoughts. 'I know it sounds dreary put like that, a man's wife telling another woman that her husband is so fond of her, but he really is.'

I wanted to ask if Piers was fond of me too, but didn't like to.

'And Rodney is fond of *you*,' I said feebly.

'Oh, but hardly in the way that Harry is fond of *you*,' said Rowena rather too quickly, so that I now knew what I had often suspected — that she considered Rodney rather dull and unlikely to break out as Harry might.

'At last she has arrived,' I said in a low voice, for earlier we had commented on an attractive looking young man sitting alone at a corner table, obviously expecting somebody.

The girl was not beautiful but there was a kind of glow about her. She wore a black dress, and round her wrist she had twined a string of beads, rose-coloured and translucent like some delicious sweet. The young man stood up as she came to the table and she held out her hands towards him.

'They're going to drink a whole bottle of claret,' said Rowena in a low rather sad voice. 'What will they do afterwards? Walk in the park?'

'I hope neither of them has an office to go back to,' I said, thinking of Piers and an occasion, so long ago it now seemed, when he had not returned to his.

'They might go to an art exhibition,' Rowena went on. 'Really *modern* art is extraordinarily sympathetic when you're in love and have eaten and drunk well. I once...well, it was a long time ago, and now I suppose I'm just as ignorant and prejudiced as most women of my age and background. To think that I could once have looked at a Picasso, or even *worse*, with love and sympathy,' she sighed extravagantly.

'You'd think that *we* had been drinking a whole bottle of claret instead of a modest half carafe of *rosé*,' I said. 'We mustn't be too long over our coffee or Monsieur Jacques will be angry.'

Monsieur Jacques was no less tyrannical and no more French than most hairdressers. In moments of stress and anger his Midland accent became more pronounced and I liked him the better for it, imagining the provincial boy making good in London and how proud his mother must be of him. I pictured her as a cosy grey-haired little woman, far beyond the range of any of her son's elaborate coiffures.

'Really we are at our lowest ebb here,' said Rowena, as we sat side by side in the big room under the driers, turning the glossy pages of expensive magazines. 'Do you think we should have our nails done while we're about it? Several of our companions seem to be having red claws made. I long to ask if their husbands really like that colour, or if they just do it to keep up their tottering morale.'

'I wonder why it is that one can never read a serious book at the hairdresser's?' I asked. 'Does the actual haircutting and shampooing do something to one's brain — shrivel it in some way?'

'You mean you'd like to think of yourself reading Proust or a book about archaeology?' Rowena asked. 'Yes, it's a strange thing. Here we sit capable only of turning the pages of these magazines, reading snippets about the Royal Family or looking at pictures of clothes and society goings-on — not even reading the stories. *Sunday Evening*, by Catherine Oliphant,' she read out. 'It begins rather well with a young man and girl holding hands in a Greek restaurant, watched by the man's former mistress — unknown to them, of course.'

'But what a far-fetched situation,' I protested. 'As if it would happen like that! Still, it must be dreadful to have to write fiction. Do you suppose Catherine Oliphant drew it from her own experience of life?'

Rowena laughed. 'I should hardly think so! She's probably an elderly spinster living in a boarding-house in Eastbourne — or she may even be a man. One never knows.'

'Jennifer, take the pins out of these madames!' hissed Monsieur Jacques, patting our heads rather too hard. 'They are dry.'

When we emerged — for that is surely the word — from Monsieur Jacques' establishment, we were both rather red in the face from the heat of the driers but otherwise more elegant than when we had gone in.

'After we've had a cup of tea shall we go and see Piers?' Rowena suggested.

'You mean at the press?'

'Yes, pay him a surprise visit. I'm sure he'd be amused.'

'Do you think so?' I asked doubtfully. 'It's so very dingy there. I think we'd be rather out of place.'

But Rowena would not be put off and we were soon on our way.

'It *is* sordid, isn't it?' she said as we climbed the dusty stairs. 'I can't imagine what made Piers take a job here. Perhaps the hours are easy — I can't believe the pay is very good.'

Rowena went boldly forward and knocked on a door. 'Is *this* where he generally is?' she whispered. 'I can't quite remember — anyway, somebody will be able to tell us.'

A sharp female voice bade us come in, and we entered the room where Piers had taken me before. A woman, whom I remembered as Miss Limpsett, was sitting alone at a table.

We hesitated, almost drew back, but it was too late for that.

I experienced the embarrassment, guilt almost, that an elegant soignée young woman may, if she has a nice nature, feel when confronted with another who is none of these things. Miss Limpsett was older, uglier and more untidy than I had remembered. She had obviously had a hard and tiring day, for her grey hair was awry as if she had been running her fingers through it, and there was ink on her fingers. Her face was haggard, and it occurred to me that it was not only this day which had been hard and tiring, but all days and even life itself.

'Yes?' she barked, gathering up a long slippery bundle of galley proofs and seeming to clasp them to her bosom.

'We're looking for my brother, Piers Longridge,' Rowena explained in a rather faltering tone.

'He's not here today,' said Miss Limpsett, 'nor is Mr Towers.'

The galleys finally eluded her clutch and slithered to the floor. I hurried to pick them up.

'Oh don't bother,' she said ungraciously.

'He isn't here,' Rowena repeated. 'I hope he isn't ill?'

'That isn't usually the reason for his absences,' said Miss Limpsett rather sourly. 'As a matter of fact he hasn't been here all this week. He may even have left, for all I know.'

'Oh *dear*.' Rowena looked worried. 'Well, I'll telephone him,' she said, backing out of the room. 'So sorry to have disturbed you.'

My eyes, which had been searching round the room for personal touches, came to rest on a vase of pussy-willows, all golden and fluffy, on top of a filing cabinet. I supposed that Miss Limpsett must have put them there, and the idea seemed almost unbearably pathetic. Had she gathered them in the country one fine week end? I wondered. Or bought them at a florist's, perhaps having to skimp on her already meagre lunch to be able to do so?

I confided my thoughts to Rowena as we hurried away down the dark stairs.

'Oh, Wilmet, you're much too sentimental,' she said. 'She's a perfectly grisly woman. It's just as likely that Piers or Mr what's it bought the pussy-willows.'

'That seems even worse, somehow — *men* buying flowers to brighten a dusty office. But, Rowena, she said Piers hadn't been in all this week and that he may even have left. Oughtn't we to find out, or something?'

'Well, I must get a taxi to Waterloo if I'm to catch my train,' said Rowena looking at her watch.

'You don't feel like going to call on Piers at his flat?' I suggested tentatively.

'No, Wilmet. Piers is not the kind of person one drops in on unexpectedly, and in any case I must get this train.'

'I suppose we could telephone?'

'Yes, you do that. I really haven't time.'

'I don't think I've got the number,' I said. 'And it probably won't be under his name in the book, will it?'

'No, but I have it.'

Rowena handed me her diary, and I took down the telephone number and the address, which did not convey much to me.

'What a lovely day it's been,' said Rowena, 'and it's still a lovely evening. The kind of day when a wife hopes her husband may bring her back some exciting present.'

It was true that Rodney did occasionally buy me an unexpected present, but never just because it happened to be a lovely day. He might have been passing an antique shop and noticed something in the window that he thought I would like, or have seen something I had once expressed a wish for. There was always a good reason.

Nevertheless, when I got home I saw that there was a large bouquet of flowers on the chest in the hall. Remembering the little box at Christmas I approached it cautiously, my mind a blank.

Now who can be sending me these lovely roses? I wondered, unable to suppress entirely a feeling of excitement as I looked for the card that would tell me. It probably wouldn't be Rodney or Harry and it certainly wouldn't be Piers, so there remained the possibility of some unknown or forgotten admirer.

The little envelope was addressed to Mrs Forsyth, but when I took out the card it said 'To Sybil', followed by some words in Greek which I could not understand. I put it back quickly, feeling annoyed and disappointed. Why should anyone send flowers to Sybil? I wondered. It wasn't her birthday and she was hardly the kind of person who invited these spontaneous tributes of admiration.

I took the box into the drawing-room and waited impatiently for her to come back from her committee meeting at the Settlement. The evening post had brought a letter from Mary Beamish. She wrote in a curious disjointed way, so that I began to wonder if spring had penetrated even the walls of the convent. The gist of the letter was that she wanted me to go and visit her. 'I've had such an odd letter from Marius and should like to talk to you,' she wrote. I was pondering over what she could possibly mean when Sybil came in, looking rather harassed.

'Oh dear,' she said, sitting down heavily in an armchair, 'the old people are *still* being difficult about that fish dinner. Poor Miss Holmes is at her wits' end. Though,' Sybil added drily, 'the extent of her wits is somewhat limited.'

'Why not give them fried octopus?' I suggested. 'Like Mr Bason does at the clergy house. By the way, these flowers came for you.'

'For me? How nice. Is there a card with them?'

'I think so,' I said casually, turning away while she read it.

'Why, they're from Arnold,' she laughed. 'Two dozen of these beautiful hothouse roses — so extravagant! It was a joke we had, and he has underlined it with a little classical quotation'.

She did not tell me what the quotation was and I felt slightly hurt, though I realized that there was no reason why I should.

Sybil arranged the flowers in a heavy cut glass vase, rather badly.

'I shall have to get on with his pullover at this rate,' she said, settling down with her knitting. 'I'm only half way up the back, but I've promised it shall be ready by the autumn.'

'You'll have plenty of time if he doesn't expect it till then,' I said.

It was really rather sweet that Professor Root should have sent Sybil the flowers, I decided, but when Rodney came in and had not brought *me* any unexpected little gift I began to feel restless and dissatisfied. During dinner I made up my mind that I would telephone Piers, and when the meal was over I told Sybil and Rodney what I intended to do.

'He wasn't at the press when Rowena and I called there this afternoon, and she was rather worried,' I explained, not quite truthfully.

'I hope he isn't ill,' said Sybil. 'There's been a good deal of spring flu about lately. Lady Nollard is down with it and wasn't at the Settlement this afternoon.'

I smiled at the idea of Lady Nollard and Piers having anything in common. It seemed so unlikely.

I went into the morning room and took from my bag the old envelope on which I had written Piers's number. I dialled it and heard the ringing tone, a harsh and rusty sound as if the whole house were empty. I imagined the room dismantled of all furniture, the telephone crouching on the floor alone, ringing unheeded.

I was quite startled when I heard a click and a guarded 'Hello?'

'I wanted to speak to Mr Longridge,' I said, rather flustered.

'I'm afraid he isn't here right now.'

It was a flat quiet voice, slightly common, though not American in spite of the phrase it had used.

'Oh, I see. Is he away then?'

There was a slight pause, then the voice said, 'Well, not exactly, but he isn't here now. Could I give him a message?'

I said lamely, 'Well, perhaps you'd just tell him that Mrs Forsyth rang up, would you?'

'Yes, Mrs Forsyth,' said the voice respectfully. 'I'll certainly tell him you called.'

I hung up the receiver with a feeling of bewilderment. I wished now that I had asked the name of the person who had answered me. As it was I could only speculate on who it might have been. Piers's colleague, with whom he shared the flat? That seemed unlikely. The voice did not sound right, though I could not have said exactly why. Then it occurred to me that the flat was not self-contained and that the telephone was a communal one which rang in the hall downstairs. In that case anyone might have answered it, some other person living in the house or the land-lady's son. Having settled that point I began to ponder on the information I had been given. He wasn't here 'right now', but he wasn't away — 'not exactly' had been the phrase. What did that mean? I wondered. That he was there but did not wish to be disturbed? That he had a hangover — in the evening? It was all rather unsatisfactory and disturbing. I could only hope that Piers himself, if he ever received my message, would get into touch with me and set my mind at rest.

CHAPTER FOURTEEN

I NEVER knew whether Piers had received my message, for nearly a fortnight went by before I heard anything of him; and when he did telephone it might just as easily have been a spontaneous impulse that had prompted him.

'We said we'd have lunch together in May,' he declared, 'and now is the time. Can it be soon — tomorrow, or the next day even?'

I did not remember any arrangement to have lunch together in May, but I was learning to take Piers as I found him so did not argue the point.

'Tomorrow would be lovely,' I said. 'Shall we meet in the same place as before?'

'No. I'm afraid it must be somewhere nearer my work this time. I'm being rather drearily conscientious at the moment. Also, I haven't any money.'

'Oh,' I said, wondering how I was expected to react. Perhaps I could offer to pay my share as girls were sometimes advised to do in magazines? 'Where shall we meet then?'

He named a restaurant in Fleet Street which was unfamiliar to me.

'I suppose I shall find it,' I said doubtfully.

'You will see hordes of workers pouring into it, so you'll hardly be able to miss it.'

It did not sound at all my kind of place and I pictured myself waiting there, for Piers was sure to be late, while the city workers streamed past me. It happened that I was to go and see Mary Beamish that afternoon and it was rather difficult to know how to dress for two such different occasions. I naturally wanted to look my best to meet Piers, but I felt that some restraint was desirable for the convent parlour. Then it occurred to me that being in the world I should be expected to look worldly, perhaps even flashy, so there need not be any difficulty of choice after all. Of course in the end I wore a black suit with a pretty little spring hat and pale gloves.

To my surprise Piers was already waiting when I reached the restaurant. He looked very handsome, I thought. His fair hair was windswept and there was an air of sparkle and boyishness about him which was unusual. When he saw me he came forward eagerly. The restaurant did not seem to be the kind where people were coming forward eagerly; most of its occupants were business men reading newspapers or talking shop together, or lone women reading novels or just eating and looking blankly in front of them. It was not the kind of place I was used to being taken to, but my pleasure at seeing Piers looking so well made me forget my surroundings and I was very ready to forgive him for not having chosen somewhere a little more worthy of the occasion.

'There is a table in the corner,' he said. 'I know this waitress, and she's kept it for us.'

Perhaps this is his life as it really is, I thought, threading my way among the crowded tables; he comes to places like this every day. My first feeling of disappointment now gave way to one of pleasure that he should consider me the kind of person who could fit into his ordinary routine in this way. It seemed to mark an advance in our relationship.

'We could have some beer, if you like,' he said, 'though you look much too elegant for anything so low.'

'I'll have just what you have,' I said happily.

'How sweet you are! Would you even have sausage toad if I ordered it?'

'I daresay,' I said doubtfully. 'I know what it is.'

'She knows what it is!' he laughed. 'But the roast veal will probably be better.'

'You're in a good mood today,' I said.

'I hope I always am with you,' he said smiling at me.

'Well, you do vary,' I said boldly. 'I'd say you were a moody person.'

'I'm a Gemini, a mercurial temperament, and I collect car numbers. It was sweet of you to come today.'

'I was quite surprised when you telephoned. I was beginning to think you hadn't got my message.'

'What message?'

'Didn't you know Rowena and I called to see you at the press?'

'Yes, Miss Limpsett told me.'

'We were a bit worried especially when she said you might have left.'

'Yes, I did actually give in my notice, but they *begged* me to reconsider it — think how gratifying that was!'

'I'm glad they did that,' I said. 'But I rang up your flat that same evening. Rowena had given me the number. I don't know who answered the telephone, but he said he would tell you. I thought at first it was your colleague, but then I decided it couldn't be — the voice didn't sound right.'

'Why — what kind of a voice was it?'

'It's hard to say, really —' I hesitated. 'It was, well ...'

'Not quite *our* kind of voice — is that what you don't quite like to say?' Piers smiled.

'Yes, not a colleague's voice.'

'You and your ideas of what a colleague would sound like!' said Piers indulgently.

'Isn't your flat self-contained then?'

'No, there are other people in the house.'

'I was afraid you might have been ill — I do hope you weren't.' I had decided not to probe further by asking what was meant by 'not exactly', when I had asked if Piers was away. I felt that I might learn more by a tactful silence.

'As a matter of fact I was recovering from a hangover,' he said, 'so I *was* ill, in a way.'

'I see,' I said. 'That explains everything.'

'I didn't feel like talking to anyone at that moment, not even *you*, Wilmet.'

'Well, you're all right now, that's the main thing.'

'Yes, life isn't quite as grim as it was. Do you think you would like to eat Devonshire tart, whatever that may be? I suspect it may be the same as Leicester tart which we have on Mondays, Wednesdays and Fridays.'

'I'll eat whatever you suggest,' I said, 'as long as it isn't a pink blancmange.'

'And now, why weren't *you* at Portuguese these last two weeks?' said Piers accusingly. 'Were *you* ill or something?'

'No,' I said. 'I felt a kind of despair as one always does at some stage of trying to learn something. And I got so tired of hearing Mrs Marble talking to you in her ninety per cent Spanish.'

'I'm with you there. But why do you want to learn, anyway?'

'It was Sybil's idea — you know how she is. And I thought it might be good for me to have some occupation.'

'Haven't you enough occupation? That's what I like about you — your air of leisure and elegance. Don't be any different or think that you must be. You can always do church work if you want a worthy occupation.'

'I do feel I'm making a little progress there,' I said. 'The last time I saw Father Thames, he was even confiding his fears about Father Ransome to me.'

'What fears?'

'He's afraid that Father Ransome may go over to Rome because the clergyman with whom he lodges is leaning in that direction.'

'He needn't worry,' said Piers. 'From what you've told me of Father Ransome he doesn't sound the kind of young man to do anything as definite as that.'

'No, but how can one be sure what goes on in a person's head?' I said, before I realized that I was thinking not only of Father Ransome but of Piers as well.

'It's better not to speculate,' said Piers lightly. 'I'm afraid we shan't have time for any extraordinary expeditions as we did the last time we lunched together. I must be back by half past two.'

'Ah, the furniture depository,' I sighed. 'Did I tell you that poor Mary Beamish's furniture is stored there now? I'm going to see her at the convent this afternoon.'

'How will you get there? In a taxi?'

'No. I shall take a train from Temple Station.'

'I thought you never travelled in such an ordinary and sordid way, but it's all the better because we shall be able to walk through the Temple together.'

'Are you turning over a new leaf?' I asked, as we walked down Middle Temple Lane. 'All this having to be back punctually?'

'Not exactly. But I'm finding it easier to work at the moment, so I may as well take advantage of being in a good mood. Later, when the bad weather comes or I'm otherwise depressed, I shall slip back again, I've no doubt.'

'Piers', I said impulsively, 'I hate to think of you being depressed. If only I could help you in some way!'

He smiled at me and was silent for a moment, then he said, 'Oh, but you do.'

I could think of nothing to say, and perhaps nothing was needed. I was in the kind of exalted mood when all one's sensibilities seem to be sharpened, and I thought I had never seen anything so beautiful as the black persian cat crouching in a bed of double pink and white tulips on the side of the path where we were walking. Then we went down some steps and I noticed a fig tree, now putting forth its new leaves among the old dark green fruits which had never properly ripened.

'I suppose figs never *do* ripen properly in England,' I said, feeling that I was making conversation but not minding.

'No, Wilmet, I don't believe they ever do,' said Piers in the same formal tone that I had used. 'The sun isn't hot enough.'

'They would ripen in a conservatory, no doubt,' I went on.

'No doubt,' he echoed, mocking me.

We were nearly at Temple Station now, and a desperate feeling came over me that we mustn't end up just by talking about figs.

'Piers,' I said, 'if there *was* ever anything I could do —'

'You're very sweet,' he said. 'I'll buy you a ticket.'

I got into the train in a kind of daze. As it lurched on from station to station I gave myself up to a happy dream in which I went to look after Piers when he was ill or depressed or just had a hangover. And yet, had that been what I meant when I had made my offer to him? Not an offer, exactly. But if not an offer, then what? I felt that Piers really needed me as few people did. Certainly not Rodney, I told myself, justifying my foolish indulgence. Piers needed love and understanding, perhaps already he was happier because of knowing me. When I had reached this conclusion I felt contented and peaceful, and leaned back in my seat, smiling to myself. What should I do next? I wondered; but even as I wondered I realized that I couldn't do anything. I must just wait and see what happened.

The directions Mary had given me were easy to follow and I soon found myself approaching a large ugly red house which stood well back from the road. The bell was of the kind that may easily come away in your hand when you pull it, and I was relieved that it did not.

A nun with steel-rimmed spectacles, and the pale lips and eyes that I always find so sinister, opened the door and smiled at me in a guarded remote sort of way. I felt that she could see right into my mind and knew all that I had been thinking about Piers. I could imagine her turning the whole thing over, coldly and dispassionately. But when she spoke her smile seemed warmer, and she said in a pleasant friendly voice, 'Would you wait in here, please? What a lovely day it's been, hasn't it?'

She led me along a corridor and into a kind of waiting-room. I was reminded a little of the clergy house, for there was the same bareness and lack of comfort, though everything was more highly polished. There was a vase of lilac on the table, and a copy of the *Church Times* which I began to read, turning first to the advertisements. I was just pondering over an offer of hospitality

163

from an elderly widow to a curate ('must be of gentle birth and education') and wondering how many would dare to measure themselves up to that standard, when Mary came quickly into the room and almost ran up to me, her face beaming.

'Oh dear,' she smiled, 'I'm so excited at seeing you that I quite forgot about moving quietly. Wilmet, it's *lovely* to see you, and how *pretty* you look! It's so nice to see some smart clothes after these.' She indicated the old black dress and stockings she was wearing.

'I expected you to be wearing a habit,' I said.

'Not yet, and I don't suppose I ever shall now.'

I looked around anxiously, for her tone had been rather loud and eager, and I was afraid that somebody might have heard.

'We could walk in the garden if you'd like to,' Mary went on, 'it would be easier to talk there.'

She took me through a side door and along a narrow path shaded with lilac bushes. I continued to look around anxiously, though I told myself that it was absurd to have this suspicious Protestant attitude towards convents. Nevertheless I was careful to keep my voice low when I saw a group of nuns walking across the lawn.

'Haven't you been happy here?' I asked, when we had got some way into a little shrubbery. 'You sound as if you weren't going to stay much longer.'

'It isn't that I haven't been happy, Wilmet, it's been a wonderful experience, but I've been feeling more and more that it isn't the right kind of life for *me* — or I should say that I'm not the right kind of person for *it* — that's what I mean really.'

'Well, it's a good thing to find that out now,' I said rather feebly, at a loss for suitable words. It was the kind of thing people said when one broke off an engagement, perhaps the only thing that could be said. I felt that in this case I ought to have produced something better.

'Of course in a way it's humiliating to have to admit it,' Mary went on.

164

I did not say that humiliation was supposed to be good for people, feeling somehow that she would say it; and of course she did, though in the humblest way.

'I suppose it was arrogant of me to think that I should ever be good enough to live this kind of life, but after Mother died it did seem ...' she broke off in distress.

'Poor Mary, nobody could say that you were arrogant,' I said, 'and I'm sure there are lots of things you could do just as well out in the world. I always have thought so. And now,' I went on, taking as it were a real headlong plunge into the world, 'what's all this about Marius Ransome and the odd letter you mentioned?'

'Yes, poor Marius. I'm rather worried about him.'

'Father Thames seems to be too. Is it about the friend he's lodging with, and his leanings towards Rome?'

'Yes, that's what it is.'

I was silent in respectful tribute to a woman who could really worry about such things. All the same, bringing Mary down to my own level for a moment, I wondered if this was really all.

'He's written me several letters, all so full of doubts and questionings. He seemed to think that I could help him to resolve them. It may sound an odd thing to say, but I feel he *needs* me in some way — my advice, of course — though that sounds very conceited I know, and obviously nothing *I* could say would make any difference.' She hesitated and looked up at me appealingly.

'I know just what you mean,' I said, 'and I think men *do* need women in that way, for our advice and strength which is sometimes greater than theirs.' I was thinking that Mary was a little bit human after all, and what a strange coincidence it was that we should both at this moment be in rather similar positions. In some curious way Piers needed me, and Marius needed her. Perhaps it made a little bond of happiness between us, for everybody wants to be needed, women especially. For a moment a wild idea came into my mind that Marius and Mary — the names sounded odd and yet right together — might marry, but I dismissed it almost before it had time to show itself, for obviously if he went over to Rome he would want to go on being a priest and therefore couldn't marry anybody. And even if he stayed where he was and decided to marry, he would choose somebody younger and more attractive than Mary. Besides, women did not come out of convents to marry people — it would be a complete reversal of the old procedure. All the same I wondered if it ever *had* been done.

'This friend of his — Edwin Sainsbury — seems to have a great influence on him,' Mary went on. 'I don't suppose I could counteract that. Anyway, it wouldn't be because of Marius that I'd come back into the world, as people say,' she smiled apologetically. 'I wrote to Father Bode, and he's been so kind and helpful. He knows somebody who runs a house for retreats and he thinks I might be able to get a job there as a kind of housekeeper.'

'That sounds an excellent idea,' I said. 'Where is it?'

'I'm not sure exactly, but somewhere near London — on the Green Line bus route, Father Bode said.'

I smiled as I imagined busloads of retreatants whirling through the countryside, and wondered if the retreat house would have a special stop which the conductor would distinguish by some witticism.

'I suppose I ought to be going,' I said.

'Oh Wilmet, and we've talked about my affairs all the time,' said Mary penitently.

'But that's what I came for,' I said. 'And in any case I really haven't got much news. How long will it be before you're back with us again?'

'I hope it will be before Corpus Christi,' said Mary. 'I always love the service at St Luke's, with all the candles and flowers and the procession. Shall we go to it together?'

'That would be nice,' I said. 'But where will you stay when you come out? Not in the guest room of the clergy house, I imagine!'

Mary laughed. 'No, not quite that. I think Mollie Holmes could give me a room at the Settlement.'

'But that's miles away. You must come and stay with us for a bit until you decide what you're going to do,' I said impulsively, wondering even as I spoke if I should regret my rash invitation, and what Sybil and Rodney would say.

'That would be *lovely*, Wilmet — how very kind of you! And in the meantime, if you can do anything to help or advise poor Marius —'

'I'm afraid I shan't be likely to have the opportunity,' I said, 'and even if I did I'm sure my opinion wouldn't carry any weight. I don't suppose Father Sainsbury will *really* take the plunge, anyway,' I added reassuringly.

But later on in the train, when I had nearly finished reading my evening paper, my eye was caught by a small paragraph tucked away at the bottom of a column. It was headed VICAR QUITS ANGLICANS. I wanted to exclaim out loud but I restrained myself, for obviously it would interest few if any of my fellow passengers to learn that the Reverend Edwin Sainsbury, vicar of St Lawrence's, Holland Park, had announced his intention of being received into the Church of Rome because he considered that the attitude of the Anglican Church towards the Church of South India no longer entitled it to be regarded as a part of the Catholic Church.

It was perhaps arrogant of me to feel that I was the only person in the carriage to whom the news meant anything; and looking around me I realized that I was probably mistaken, for the man sitting next to me, I now noticed, was reading the *Tablet*. I drew away from him with a kind of superstitious dread, and when I got out it seemed that his beady black eyes, suitably peering through a pair of pince-nez, were following me. I almost ran off the platform. The day had somehow been too full.

CHAPTER FIFTEEN

'I SHAN'T be in to dinner this evening,' Rodney announced rather self-consciously one morning a few days later.

'Why, darling, are you working late at the Ministry?' I said in a silly teasing way.

'That's the idea,' he said, not looking up from *The Times*.

'Then poor Wilmet will be all by herself,' said Sybil, 'because I shall be out too. My annual dinner and theatre with Violet,' she explained.

Violet was an old school friend of Sybil's and they had this kind of ritual meeting every year. It always seemed slightly incongruous to me and I think to Sybil, too, but she kept it up religiously.

'But I *like* being by myself,' I protested. 'I shan't mind at all.'

All sorts of wild ideas began to rush through my head, the foremost of which was that I could ask Piers to come and dine with me; failing that, I might have a talk with Marius Ransome, who had not yet, as far as I could see, shown any signs of following his friend over to Rome. His demeanour at Mass on Sunday morning had been very much as usual; he had even preached the sermon, but that gave no clue, for he was a poor preacher and the limping platitudes which poured from his lips had been on something so entirely untopical that I could not even remember the subject of the sermon now. Then it came to me — something about visiting the fatherless and widows in their affliction, and trying to be kind to coloured people in various unspecified ways. There was certainly no indication here as to what his spiritual doubts might be. And of course, thinking it over, I could hardly ask him to spend an evening with me alone. Perhaps I could not ask Piers either. It was for him to make the next move. Having been married young and not having experienced any unsuccessful love affairs before that time, I had never had to take the initiative myself. All the same, I wanted to see Piers so much that I wondered whether I might not telephone him some time during the evening to suggest that we had a drink together, or that he dropped in for coffee.

Then a brilliant idea came to me. I would do a little detective work, and go and see where he lived. I would walk casually past the house and have a good look at it. I could pretend I was on my way to somewhere else — I should have to work out the details — so that if by any chance he should see me I should not be at a loss. The idea of a summer evening walk with an objective seemed most attractive, like the trolley bus rides which I never took.

Rhoda brought me my dinner on a tray in the drawing-room — cold consommé, a fricassee of chicken and some fruit. I drank a glass of Chablis and looked at maps, planning which way I should go. Some of the country would be familiar to me, but Piers seemed to live in a dark wasteland beyond Shepherd's Bush and I could only guess at what that might be like. There was something a little frightening about setting out alone in the evening on such an expedition. It was very warm and the sky had clouded over, as if thunder might be coming. The leaves on the trees in the square, still newly green, seemed to have darkened and looked heavy and menacing. I stood at the window, my coffee cup in my hand, wondering what I should do.

As I looked out I saw a grey car, which I recognized as Mr Coleman's Husky, coming slowly towards the house and stopping opposite the door. After a moment Mr Coleman himself got out, slammed the door and locked it, examined what seemed to be a scratch above the back wheel, tapped out his pipe on the heel of his shoe and walked slowly across the road, looking up at the house with a worried expression on his face.

What on earth can *he* want, calling at this odd time? I wondered. It must be some church business, something connected with the servers, but *what*? I was unable to think of any likely explanation and waited for the front door bell to ring, patting my hair nervously and dabbing powder on my nose. I half expected that the bell would not ring, but it did, and I hurried down to answer it myself before Rhoda could come grumbling up from the basement. I felt almost excited as I opened the door.

'Good evening, Mrs Forsyth,' said Mr Coleman, looking at me with his serious blue eyes. 'Is Mr Forsyth in? I wonder if I could see him for a minute?'

'I'm afraid he's out,' I said. 'Would you like to leave a message?'

'Well, it's a bit awkward really. I wanted to consult him about something.'

'To consult him?' I was very puzzled and inquisitive by now. 'Won't you come in? I don't know whether I could help, could I?'

'Thank you, Mrs Forsyth. I feel I ought to tell somebody, and perhaps you would tell Mr Forsyth when he comes in.'

Whatever could he have to tell Rodney? I wondered, as we went upstairs. I tried to remember where Mr Coleman worked. I had heard that he was a chartered accountant, but I could not see what possible connection he could have with Rodney's Ministry. And if it were a business matter he would hardly feel inclined to tell me about it.

'Would you like some coffee?' I asked, seeing that the tray was still on the little table by the window.

'No thanks.' He stood awkwardly in the middle of the room until I invited him to sit down.

'Do smoke your pipe if you'd like to,' I said, though I cannot bear the smell of pipe smoke myself.

He refused, but took out a packet of cigarettes and offered me one which I accepted, thinking that it might make the situation easier. This is the lighter that kindled the New Fire in the dark church at Easter, I thought irrelevantly, as he gave me a light. Yet perhaps it was not so irrelevant, for I could not believe that Mr Coleman would be here unless on some matter connected with the church. Perhaps he had come to ask Rodney if he would like to be a server? I smiled at the idea of it.

170

'You must think it funny, me coming here like this to see Mr Forsyth when I don't really know him,' Mr Coleman began, 'but I thought it was the best thing under the circumstances. I believe he got Bason the job at the clergy house, so he probably knows something about him.'

'Yes, he does know him of course. Mr Bason used to work in the same department at the Ministry,' I said, wondering what was coming next, 'and when he was looking for a job and it happened that Father Thames wanted a housekeeper I mentioned it to my husband. At least, I can't remember exactly how it came about — I think he told me about Mr Bason first.'

'So he got the sack then, did he?' asked Mr Coleman bluntly.

'Well, I don't think it was exactly that. Mr Bason wasn't suitable for the Ministry job and didn't really like it. In fact, I think he'd been looking for a domestic post. But has something happened to Mr Bason?' I asked, unable to restrain my curiosity any longer.

'Not happened, exactly. It's only that he's pinched the vicar's egg, and I don't quite know what I ought to do.'

'*What* did you say he's done?' I asked, hardly able to believe that I could have heard aright.

'Pinched the vicar's egg,' repeated Mr Coleman doggedly.

'But *what* egg?'

'That egg he has on the mantelpiece in his study.'

'Oh, *that* egg!' At last I understood. 'The *Fabergé* egg.'

'I don't know what you call it. It's a kind of coloured Easter egg — a fancy thing with jewels in it, quite valuable, so they tell me.'

'Yes, it was made by the Russian court goldsmith.'

'Russian?' He looked at me with the suspicion that many a good Englishman shows when the words Russian or Russia are spoken.

'Yes, in the days of the Czars.'

'Oh, I see.' He seemed relieved. 'Then it's an antique thing?'

'Well, almost — and rather valuable, as you say.'

171

'Amazing what some people will spend their money on, isn't it?' said Mr Coleman.

'It's all according to one's tastes,' I said, wondering whether I myself would prefer a Fabergé egg or a Husky, and not being absolutely sure. 'But how do *you* know that Mr Bason has taken it?' I felt I could hardly say pinched.

'He showed it to me.'

'But when?'

'After Mass yesterday morning. He had it in the pocket of his cassock.'

'Good heavens!' I wanted to laugh but knew that I must not. 'Tell me what happened.'

'Well, it was like this. I had rather a lot on my mind yesterday. To begin with I was worried about the Husky.'

'The Husky? Oh, of course — your car.'

'A friend of mine had scraped it against a wall when he was reversing and I was wondering if I'd have to have the whole side resprayed — you know, Mrs Forsyth, your thoughts can wander even in the Sanctuary, and we're all human, after all.'

'Oh, *yes*!' I agreed.

'I don't know if you noticed' — he smiled for a moment — 'but Bob nearly forgot to remove the Paschal Candle and I didn't spot it for some time. Just imagine, me not noticing a thing like that!'

'I'm afraid I never remember exactly when it should be removed,' I said. 'I always think it looks so pretty there with the flowers round it that I wish it could stay.'

'But that would be liturgically incorrect, Mrs Forsyth,' he said seriously. 'It should be removed after the Gospel on Ascension Day. Luckily I don't think many people *did* notice. But Bason did, you bet!'

'Did he say something to you then?'

'Yes, he was a bit sarcastic afterwards in the vestry. He passed some remark — I can't remember exactly what he said, but I was just taking off my cassock and then he said something about that.'

'About your cassock?'

'Yes. He once put it on by mistake, and ever since then he can't seem to leave the subject alone. He's really childish about it.'

'But what did he say?'

'Oh, something about mine being a good material but look what he had in *his* pocket — just like a kid. Then he took the egg out of his pocket and tossed it up in the air and caught it, and then put it back again.'

'What an extraordinary thing!' I exclaimed, turning my head away and fumbling in my bag for a handkerchief, for again I was overcome by a most unfortunate desire to laugh, feeling that the scene described by Mr Coleman had something comic about it. 'But how did he get hold of the egg?' I went on. 'Are you sure he — er — stole it?'

'He took it off the mantelpiece. He told me so.'

'And Father Thames didn't know about it? No, obviously not. What did you say?'

'I was a bit taken aback, naturally. I think I said, "Father Thames's egg! Where did you get it from?" or something like that. And he just laughed.'

'You didn't say anything about it to anyone?'

'Well, not really. At least, I mentioned it to a friend — he's a school teacher, you see, and has had experience of juvenile delinquency — but I didn't tell any of the clergy. I was a bit flustered really, what with the Paschal Candle and everything, and by the time I'd finished putting things away Bason had gone.'

'Perhaps he's put the egg back by now. He may just have borrowed it because he liked the look of it. And of course Whitsuntide is nearly here — I should think he'll be sure to put it back by then.' I was thinking that if he made his Whitsuntide confession he would have to mention it, and I was reminded of those old-fashioned manuals of self-examination with their lists of questions which often included 'Have I stolen anything?' Many an Anglo-Catholic gentlewoman has no doubt been surprised or even shocked at having to ask herself this. I had always imagined that such questions were intended for working lads in the great East End and dockside parishes which had seen the beginning of the Catholic revival in the nineteenth century. I now realized that my imaginings had been too narrow.

'He may have done it for a lark,' said Mr Coleman doubtfully. 'He's an odd sort of chap. Do you think Mr Forsyth could have a talk to him?'

'But first we should have to know if the egg was still missing, shouldn't we?' I suggested. 'I suppose somebody could sneak into the clergy house and see?' I liked to imagine myself doing this, but did not quite see how it was to be managed.

'Yes, but with all that junk the vicar has in his study it wouldn't be all that easy to see if the egg was there or not.' Mr Coleman gave a short laugh. 'I often think when he asks people to bring stuff for a jumble sale that he could do worse than clear out some of his own junk in that study.'

'Good heavens — a Fabergé egg at a jumble sale!' I exclaimed. 'That *would* be something.'

'And he's going to Italy again for his holidays this year,' said Mr Coleman in a meaningful tone.

'To stay with friends near Siena, I believe.'

'No doubt he'll pick up a few more broken statues and old pictures there,' said Mr Coleman sarcastically.

It struck me as odd that one who played such an important part in the elaborate services we had should appear to be so totally unappreciative of beauty.

'Don't you like the statues we have in church?' I asked in curiosity.

'Oh yes, Mrs Forsyth, but they're bright and new. The ladies keep them dusted and cleaned. Poor Mrs Greenhill used to have a job keeping Father Thames's study clean though — she often said so. Well, Mrs Forsyth, I don't know what's best to be done, but I've got it off my chest, anyway. This business of the egg's been worrying me, I don't mind telling you — that and the Husky. I'll be taking it to the garage tomorrow.'

'I do hope it will be all right,' I said vaguely. 'And thank you for coming to see me — we shall just have to see how things go. I think it quite possible that Mr Bason may return the egg before it is missed.'

From the window I saw Mr Coleman cross the square, light up his pipe and get into his car. Its clean-cut lines were probably his ideal of beauty, which made me wonder why he had not chosen the simple austerity of a Nonconformist service as his form of worship. No doubt upbringing had something to do with it, and there was no accounting for tastes, as he himself might well have said.

It was now much too late to set out on the little excursion I had planned. The visit to Piers's territory would have to wait for another time; perhaps a fine afternoon when he was unlikely to be at home would be best. Now I could only wait rather impatiently for Sybil or Rodney to come home. They, with their greater experience of what is known as the seamy side of life, would no doubt be able to decide what was the best course of action to follow. Sybil's work at the Settlement, and Rodney's at the Ministry and with his men in the Army, had equipped them better than my sheltered years at home and my brief spell of gaiety serving my country in the Wrens. I began to be ashamed of my lack of experience — I had not had a lover before I married, I had no children, I wasn't even asked to clean the brasses or arrange the flowers in church. But I had done something to make Piers happy and that compensated for everything. I sat in the dusk thinking about him, and was surprised thus by Sybil returning from the theatre.

'Such a silly play! Just the kind to go to with an old school friend, a real *woman*'s evening,' she said, flinging her old moleskin cape down on the sofa. 'But how the audience loved it! How they roared with laughter when the vicar entered through the french windows at the back of the stage.'

'Was it funny, then?' I asked.

'The vicar's entry? Not particularly. He just stood there,

holding his hat in his hands and blinking through his spectacles. He reminded me a little of your Father Bode, but it brought the house down.'

'And he's such a good man. I think it's all wrong, making the clergy appear comic.'

'I wonder — would they have laughed so much had he been wearing a cassock and biretta? Perhaps not. Have you had an interesting evening, dear?' Sybil peered at me rather closely. 'You looked a little sad sitting there in the gloaming.'

'I've had a rather strange evening. Mr Coleman called with an odd story about Mr Bason. He wanted to see Rodney really, so perhaps I'd better wait until he comes in, then I shan't have to tell it twice.'

'Noddy was out to dinner, wasn't he? 'said Sybil. 'Did you know where he was going?'

'Just some friend from the Ministry — James Cash, perhaps,' I said vaguely. 'I don't suppose he'll be very late.'

'Isn't that his key in the lock now?' said Sybil. 'The sound a wife is said to love above all others?' she added in a dry questioning tone.

I ran downstairs feeling a little confused. Rodney stood in the hall, hesitating, as if he could not decide whether to come up or not. I thought he had probably been drinking a little more than he should and did not feel quite equal to facing the steely glances of his wife and his mother.

'Come on, darling,' I said, running towards him. 'I've got something to tell you.'

He put his arm around my shoulders and we went like that upstairs into the drawing-room.

'Now,' said Sybil, looking up from her knitting, 'we can hear this odd story about Mr Bason. Wilmet has been waiting for you to come in.'

'About Bason?' asked Rodney. 'Has he put arsenic in the soup, or what?'

'No, it isn't a joke,' I said, and began to tell the story of the egg as Mr Coleman had told it to me. I felt it lost something in the telling but the effect on Rodney was none the less striking.

'Oh my God!' he exclaimed. 'So he's up to his tricks again. I was afraid he might do something of the kind.'

'Why — has it happened before?'

'Yes. That was why he left the Ministry, really — though of course he wasn't suited to the work, as you know.'

'He took something there, you mean?'

'Yes.'

'But what would there be to take at the Ministry?' asked Sybil. 'A wire basket, a box file, somebody's teacup — or was it money?'

'No — it was actually a little jade Buddha.'

'Good heavens!' I laughed. 'What an unlikely object. Where did he find it?'

'It was on the desk of one of the principals — a woman,' Rodney added.

'You seem to imply that a man wouldn't have such a thing on his desk,' said Sybil, 'and it does seem as if only a woman would realize that civil service decisions need the wisdom of the East.'

'Perhaps she just thought it was a pleasing object,' I suggested.

'And yet,' Sybil went on, 'is the wisdom of the East quite what is wanted in government departments today? I'm reminded of that Chinese saying, "If you have two loaves, sell one and buy a lily" — it's not *practical*, of course, but its ministerial interpretation might be interesting.'

'I don't think that was a saying of the Buddha,' said Rodney. 'But we're getting off the point. If Bason has really stolen — taken — this Fabergé egg, it's a serious matter. I wondered whether I ought to mention his weakness to Father Thames before he engaged him, but I thought it was perhaps hardly fair on Bason. And I must say,' he added, indignation coming into his voice, 'it didn't occur to me that there would be much temptation of *that* kind in a clergy house.'

'Would there be any other?' asked Sybil thoughtfully. 'Any

177

other kind of temptation, I mean? You sound almost as if you thought there might be.'

'Goodness, Mother, why must you always take one so literally,' said Rodney irritably. 'You know what I meant — I thought it unlikely that there would be any objets d'art of the kind Bason fancies lying around in a house full of celibate priests.'

'I don't see that celibacy has anything to do with it,' persisted Sybil obstinately.

'Anyway, when I saw all those things in Father Thames's study at Christmas I did begin to wonder,' Rodney went on, 'but by then it was obviously too late to do anything. One could only hope for the best.'

'And do you remember Mr Bason saying that he always must be surrounded by beautiful things?' I added. 'Poor man, I suppose it's a sort of kink — showing the egg to Mr Coleman was surely a sign of that, don't you think?'

'Yes, a gesture of bravado. He couldn't resist showing off, drawing attention to what he'd done. Well, we can't do anything about it *now*,' Rodney yawned. 'We'd better sleep on it.'

Sleeping on a Fabergé egg seemed a simple comic thing and I laughed. Soon, perhaps as a relief from tension, we were all laughing.

'If Father Thames discovered it was missing, would he announce it from the pulpit?' Rodney asked.

'He might. Among the parish notices, I suppose, but after the banns of marriage.'

'It would be like school,' said Rodney. 'No boy shall leave the room until the culprit has owned up.'

CHAPTER SIXTEEN

I T was, to put it mildly, a little embarrassing to come face to face with Mr Bason the very next morning. I had gone out to do some shopping at the large store in our neighbourhood which had a self-service grocery department. I sometimes strayed into it, idly and extravagantly filling my basket with any expensive delicacy that happened to catch my eye. Sybil used to call these little expeditions 'Wilmet's wanderings', for I never chose really sensible everyday things, which we always had sent, anyway.

I had stopped by a shelf of Eastern specialities — bamboo shoots, tinned mushrooms, lime pickle and exotic sauces, when I suddenly saw the head of Mr Bason popping up from the other side. His *egg*-shaped head, I thought, immediately conscious of the unfortunate relevance of the comparison. For a moment I toyed with the idea of moving quickly on, but before I could make up my mind I realized that it was too late, for he had seen me and was coming over to the side of the shelf where I was.

'Isn't it fascinating here,' he said in his rather gushing way. 'I never can resist all these lovely things.'

Did he mean that he could never resist *taking* them? I wondered, unhappy in my new knowledge of his character, for I was sure that the amount of clergy housekeeping money would hardly run to *buying* them.

'Yes, they're very tempting,' I agreed, 'but I suppose Father Thames and Father Bode wouldn't like them really.'

'Father Thames would,' said Mr Bason eagerly. 'He has the most exquisite taste.'

'One can tell that from his collection of objets d'art,' I said boldly. 'There are some lovely things in his study.'

'Exquisite!' agreed Mr Bason enthusiastically. 'And do you know which is my favourite?'

'No?' I waited fearfully.

'Why, the Fabergé egg, of course. Surely there couldn't be two opinions about that?'

During our conversation we had moved away from the Eastern delicacies, and were now for no apparent reason standing by the breakfast cereals. I found myself nervously reading the life story of an Indian chief called Pontiac on one of the packets. Would Mr Bason go on talking about the Fabergé egg? I wondered. And was it my duty to say something to him? Surely not *here*, among the All-Bran, the Grapenuts, the Puffed Wheat, the Rice Krispies and the Frosted Flakes?

'Father Bode *will* have his cornflakes,' said Mr Bason, seizing a giant packet of Kellogg's. 'Of course Father Thames has a continental breakfast, coffee and croissants.'

'My husband likes Grapenuts,' I found myself saying feebly. Then, gathering strength, I asked, 'And what do *you* have? An egg?'

He shuddered. 'Oh no — just black coffee and orange juice. I hate eggs.'

'Not Fabergé eggs, surely?' I said boldly, wondering if his face would change colour in some dramatic way.

'Oh Mrs Forsyth, how did you know about my little peccadillo?' he asked in an agitated tone. 'Did Father Thames speak to your husband? I hoped he hadn't missed it. I was going to put it back — I swear it — I only *borrowed* it because I wanted to look at it. It's so beautiful that I'm carrying it about with me all the time, because I know I must put it back eventually. *Look!*' He opened the canvas bag he was carrying and I peered into its cavernous depths. There, nestling incongruously among an assortment of groceries, I saw the Fabergé egg, its stones winking and glistening in the dim light.

'*Oh — !*' I drew back in a kind of fascinated horror.

'*Such* a lovely thing, isn't it?' he purred, more in his old manner.

I hoped he would not take the egg out and toss it in the air as he had done in the vestry before Mr Coleman.

'Yes, but it's not *yours*,' I said firmly.

He closed up the bag quickly and said rather petulantly, 'I know — and I should appreciate it just as much as *he* does.'

'When are you going to put it back?' I asked, amazed at my boldness.

He turned away and hung his head like a sulky child.

'Shall we go and put it back *now*?' I suggested.

'All right,' he said, suddenly meek. 'But Father Thames may be in his study.'

'Don't worry, I will divert him in some way,' I said, wondering what I could possibly do to achieve such a thing.

We paid for our purchases and then walked slowly back to the clergy house. It was by this time nearly twelve o'clock.

'I suppose you'll be thinking of preparing lunch for Father Thames and Father Bode?' I said chattily. 'What are you giving them today?'

'Well — really — I've been so upset lately, what with one thing and another, that my heart hasn't been in it.'

I must have smiled, perhaps at the culinary associations of the word 'heart', for he said quickly, 'And very delicious a stuffed sheep's heart can be! You mustn't think, Mrs Forsyth, that I'm one to despise offal, as it is called. On the contrary!'

'Will they have heart today?' I asked.

'No, it will be the remains of last night's joint made up. Almost a shepherd's pie,' he added contemptuously, 'though I might put a little garlic into it. And just cheese and biscuits to follow. Twice cooked meat is something I *don't* think much of.'

'Still, one has to have it sometimes,' I said. 'Perhaps the clergy do, more than other people.'

We were now walking up the steps of the clergy house, and I was beginning to feel a little nervous at what lay before us. In the hall we met Father Bode and Mrs Greenhill, the latter holding an untidy brown paper parcel from which a bit of striped material of a pyjama-like nature protruded. They appeared to be deep in conversation.

'I'll do the best I can with these, Father,' I heard Mrs Greenhill say in a low mumbling voice.

'Thank you very much, Mrs G.,' he answered in a louder, more open tone. 'I think there's a good deal of wear in them yet.'

I hung my head, as if I were unworthy of the privilege of seeing Father Bode's pyjamas.

'Why good morning, Mrs Forsyth. Did you want to see me?' he asked, smiling his toothy friendly smile, his eyes gleaming behind his thick spectacles.

'Well, I really wanted to see Father Thames,' I said. 'I believe he's going to Italy soon, and I wanted to ask him something. Is he very busy?'

'Well —' Father Bode hesitated, honesty perhaps struggling with loyalty to his vicar; then, hitting on a happy phrase, he said, 'We clergy are always ready to see our parishioners. I think he's in his study.'

'Shall I go and see?' asked Mr Bason.

I heard him go upstairs, and knock at Father Thames's study door. I followed him up nervously.

When I reached the door Father Thames called out, 'Do come in, Mrs Forsyth. Bason tells me you want to see me.'

'It's really quite a frivolous matter,' I said, entering the room where Father Thames was sitting at his enormous desk, writing something — I could not see what — on a piece of foolscap. 'I was wondering if you were going anywhere near Rome on your holiday, and could perhaps deliver a message to some friends of mine.'

'Alas no — friends in Siena. They have a villa, but — this will surprise you — no motor car! Otherwise I should have been delighted to execute any commission for you. Perhaps we may contrive something, though.'

'No, it's quite all right, thank you very much,' I said lamely. 'I mustn't disturb you, or Mr Bason at his dusting,' I added, seeing that he was over by the window with his back to us.

'Ah — Bason is very houseproud,' said Father Thames. 'He takes such care of my treasures.'

I waited till Mr Bason had left the room before making any comment. I saw that the Fabergé egg was back in its accustomed place.

'They must be rather valuable,' I said at last. 'Will you leave them locked up when you go away?'

'No, they will be quite safe here. Bason would be so hurt if I removed them. It might seem like a reflection on his honesty.'

There was an embarrassed silence, at least on my part. But before I could decide what I ought to say, Father Thames had picked up the Fabergé egg and was saying in an indulgent tone, 'So my egg is back again. I wondered how long it would be away this time.'

'You mean …?' I faltered.

'Oh yes, Bason borrows it every now and then. He doesn't realize that I know, of course. He thinks I don't notice.' Father Thames smiled. 'He is very fond of beautiful things, you know.'

'Yes, I did know,' was all I could think of to say.

'It seems selfish to keep one's possessions too much to oneself, doesn't it, when they can give so much pleasure to others.'

I could hardly fail to agree with him, and after that there seemed to be nothing more to say. Any chatty remarks about Father Ransome's friend, Edwin Sainsbury, having gone over to Rome, would I felt have been out of place. I left the study in some confusion and was waylaid by Father Bode in the hall.

'I hear that Miss Beamish is coming to stay with you,' he said in a confidential tone. 'I'm so glad that she has friends she can be with at this rather difficult time.'

'Yes, I suppose she may feel a little awkward,' I said, 'but I can't help thinking it's all for the best, her coming away from *that place*.' I felt I had given the last words a sinister emphasis which I had not really intended, so I added quickly, 'I thought the convent seemed very nice — it certainly has a lovely garden. I believe they grow all their own vegetables,' I added, for all the world as if it were a hotel advertising 'own garden produce'.

'Yes, but it wasn't the place for *her*. She can do so much good out in the world, you know, and I hope she will realize that now. I have a little plan for her — there's a retreat house in the diocese in need of a housekeeper and I thought she might like the work. I think it would be rather jolly if we could organize a parish retreat, don't you? We might hire a coach.' Father Bode's toothy smile and gleaming eyes now seemed rather alarming.

I must have looked a little dismayed, for he went on quickly, 'Retreats can be rather fun, you know. Had you heard that Father Thames is retiring in the autumn?'

'I had heard rumours.'

'It will be announced in the June magazine,' said Father Bode, 'and of course we shall have a presentation when he gets back from Italy.'

'I wonder who we shall get as vicar. It would be splendid if you were to be offered the living,' I said impulsively.

'It would be a great joy to *me*,' said Father Bode simply, 'but of course the Bishop could so easily find a better man.'

He said this so sincerely that it sounded as if he really meant it.

As I left I could hear Mr Bason singing 'All things bright and beautiful' in the kitchen, and I wondered whether Father Bode, if he became vicar, would keep on Mr Bason as housekeeper at the clergy house. Then my thoughts returned to the strange business of the Fabergé egg. I supposed that Father Thames's attitude towards the 'borrowing' had been the really Christian one, and I could not resist asking Rodney that evening whether the high up female civil servant had adopted a similar attitude when her jade Buddha had been taken.

'I think *not*,' said Rodney emphatically.

'But surely there *is* Christian behaviour among civil servants? Among the higher ranks of women civil servants?' asked Sybil. 'I hope you don't mean to imply that there never could be?'

Rodney sighed. 'Oh, Mother, these searching questions of yours! They're really a bit much at the end of a heavy day. How can I possibly know the answer to that one?'

'Now, Noddy, you know how I like to tease you,' Sybil

laughed. 'Anyway, it's reassuring to find Father Thames behaving as he should. People are too apt to make jokes about the unChristian behaviour of Christians — I'm afraid I do myself sometimes.'

'I also had a talk with Father Bode this morning,' I said, 'and he's very glad that Mary is coming to us when she leaves the convent.'

Rodney looked rather startled, and Sybil smiled indulgently at him.

'We shall be able to see to her material comforts,' she said. 'That's the least we can do.'

'I should have thought it was also the most,' said Rodney. 'Which room is she to have?'

'We thought the front spare room was the obvious one,' I said. 'It has the washbasin and a nice view over the square, and the bed is really more comfortable than the bed in the back room.'

'Will she expect a comfortable bed?' Rodney asked. 'Oughtn't we to break her into the world gradually?'

'I don't see what difference it makes,' I said.

'Wilmet, have you thought what books to put by her bed?' asked Sybil. 'You must make a careful choice.'

'I suppose some anthologies of poetry and good novels by female authors,' I said. 'Not devotional books, obviously.'

'We have just completed an interesting report on the Linoleum Industry,' said Rodney. 'I could let her have a cyclostyled copy — the pages are bound together.'

'Foolscap is awkward to read in bed,' said Sybil. 'Arnold has just published a paper in one of the archaeological journals — that's a handy size for night reading, and there are some excellent drawings of pottery fragments done by an invalid lady who lives in Dawlish.' She paused and then, with an uncharacteristic air of self-consciousness, said, 'By the way, Arnold thinks he would like to come to Portugal with us in September. What do *you* think?'

'Why, that would be delightful,' I said. 'It would make a better-balanced party. But what about his family ties?'

'Well yes, there is his sister of course. They have always stayed at a small private hotel in Minehead and gone for long walks over Exmoor. They've been going there for the past ten years or so, and Arnold feels he would like a change. Apparently a friend of Dorothy's — that's his sister's name — always joins them and they take a packed lunch out every day, wet or fine. Arnold says he is rather tired of it.'

'I should think ten years of packed lunches would become rather a bore after a while,' said Rodney.

'They are very *good* packed lunches,' said Sybil, 'but Dorothy is rather a dreary little woman. I think that's the trouble.'

'And the friend?' I asked. 'Professor Root evidently hasn't felt drawn to her romantically.'

'Evidently not,' said Sybil. 'Perhaps Exmoor is not conducive to romance.'

'No,' said Rodney. 'Sitting on mackintoshes, eating packed lunches over the years, and then tramping home again through the rain — one can see how he would yearn after Portugal.'

Some time later I went up to look over Mary's room and to give it a few little touches — a plant on the table in the window, lavender soap in the washbasin, some new magazines, as well as a careful selection of books by the bed. While I did these things I was thinking that there was now only very little time left in which I could make my expedition to find out where Piers lived, for it was hardly the kind of jaunt on which I could expect, or indeed wish, Mary to accompany me. I should have to pretend to Sybil that I was going shopping or to the cinema. Not that she ever asked outright, but I knew I should feel self-conscious and obliged to make some sort of excuse. It seemed a pity that I should have to lie, almost as if I were doing something wrong.

When I came downstairs I saw that there was a letter on the hall table. It looked almost beautiful — a blue rectangle against the polished mahogany, like some long expected letter for which one had hardly dared to hope. It was addressed to me — Wilmet Forsyth, without any Mrs — in a small neat hand, the kind of writing a clergyman might have.

When I opened it, I saw at once that it was from Piers. And now I realized that I had seen the handwriting before, only much bigger and in white chalk on the blackboard at the Portuguese classes. He began 'Dear Wilmet' and asked me to meet him in the park to go for a walk and have tea with him. I turned over the page eagerly to see how he would end. To my surprise I saw that he had got round what might have been a difficulty or embarrassment by using the — for him — improbable and ridiculous ending 'Yours in haste'. I almost laughed out loud, so incongruous did it seem.

I could not truthfully say that I was in haste myself, though I wrote back quickly enough. After a little thought I used the harmless conventional ending 'with love', for it gave me a perverse kind of pleasure to think that love could be no more than a harmless and conventional thing.

CHAPTER SEVENTEEN

'PERHAPS you will see Piers's lodgings,' said Sybil, when I told her of the invitation, so much more respectable than my secret expedition would have been.

'Lodgings' sounded old-fashioned and sordid, and for a moment I felt as if it were wrong to be looking forward to the afternoon so much.

'He's asked me to have tea with him, but I suppose we may go to some public place,' I said.

'It's a pity the Derry Roof Gardens aren't open on Saturday afternoons,' said Sybil drily, 'but I expect you'd enjoy a tea he had prepared himself better than anything else. Women like to see men doing domestic things, especially if they are not done very well — if the tea is too weak or too strong, or the toast burnt.'

'I don't suppose Piers is very domesticated,' I said happily, imagining the sort of tea we might have. Perhaps not toast, as it was a hot day, but roughly cut bread and butter and sickly bought cakes. 'It won't be like having tea with Mr Bason.'

'I should think not indeed,' Sybil laughed. 'Well, you look very nice and I hope you will enjoy yourself. Give Piers my kindest regards and tell him that I have composed six sentences showing — I hope correctly — the use of the personal infinitive.'

If it had seemed odd, and it had a little, for Sybil to send me off to Piers with her blessing, I was now reminded that to her he was after all our Portuguese teacher and the brother of my best friend. She could not know the delicious walking-on-air feeling that pervaded me as I hurried across the park, hardly able to bear being even the prudent few minutes late.

May has always seemed to me, as indeed it has to poets, the most romantic of all the months. There are so many days when the air really is like wine — a delicate white wine, perhaps

Vouvray drunk on the banks of the Loire. This afternoon had about it something of the quality of that day when Piers and I had walked through the Temple and seen the cat crouching among the tulips and the new leaves covering up the old sad fruits on the fig tree.

I was wearing a dress of deep coral-coloured poplin, very simple, with a pair of coral and silver earrings, and a bracelet to match. I always like myself in deep clear colours, and I felt at my best now and wondered if people were looking at me as I passed them. They seemed to be mostly lovers absorbed in each other, and I did not mind this, but when a drab-looking woman in a tweed skirt and crumpled pink blouse looked up from her sandwich and *New Statesman*, I felt suddenly embarrassed and was reminded of poor Miss Limpsett in Piers's office. What could her life have held? What future was there for her and the woman in the crumpled pink blouse?

I was glad when I reached our meeting place and saw Piers standing with his back to me, apparently absorbed in a border of lupins. I wanted to rush up to him with some silly extravagant gesture, like covering his eyes with my hands; and my hands were outstretched, waiting to be taken in his, when I called his name and he turned round to face me.

'I hope I'm not late,' I said, discarding as one does the other more exciting openings I had prepared.

'Not very,' he said, evading my outstretched hands without seeming to do so in any obvious way. 'You look very charming. That colour suits you.'

I had hoped he would say this, but I was pleased when the words actually came. We stood for a few moments looking at the lupins.

'How I should love to get right in among them and smell their warm peppery smell!' I said exuberantly. 'I do so adore it!'

'My dear, it isn't quite you, this enthusiasm,' said Piers. 'You must be cool and dignified, and behave perfectly in character — not plunging in among lupins.'

'Oh.' I was a little cast down. 'Is that how I am — cool and dignified? I don't mind being thought elegant, of course — but cool and dignified. It doesn't sound very lovable.'

'Lovable? Is that how you want to be?' He sounded surprised.

'I should have thought everyone did on this sort of an afternoon,' I said, rather at a loss. It was evident that his mood did not quite match mine, and that I should have to — as women nearly always must — damp down my own exuberant happiness until we were more nearly in sympathy.

'Wilmet, what's the matter with you? You're talking like one of the cheaper women's magazines.' Piers's tone was rather petulant.

Love is the cheapest of all emotions, I thought; or such a universal one that it makes one talk like a cheap magazine. What, indeed, was the matter with me?

'I shouldn't have thought *you'd* know much about those,' I said.

'We don't read them at the press, certainly, but one sees them somehow. Have we been long enough at these lupins? Shall we walk on?'

'Yes,' I said, for I could think of nothing else to say.

'Poor girl,' he said teasingly, after we had been walking in silence for some time. 'Don't mind my ill-humour. You said yourself that I was a moody person.'

'All people are strange,' I said crossly. Then I began telling him about Mr Bason and the Fabergé egg. The story seemed to amuse him, and by the time we had walked across the park to the end of the Bayswater Road he was in a much better temper and I was feeling almost happy again.

'Imagine that scene in the choir vestry!' he exclaimed. 'Taking the egg out of the pocket of his cassock and tossing it into the air. How I should love to have seen that! Now, Wilmet, what would you like to do next? Go to the pictures, have a nice sit down in a deckchair, or what?'

'I should like to see where you live,' I said firmly.

'All right. Tea at home then. But don't expect too much. We must get a bus to Shepherd's Bush, first of all.'

'Goodness — is it a very long way then?'

'*You* would think it a long way — certainly too far to go by taxi.'

'I always like a long bus ride,' I said. 'Do you remember Father Lester who was at Rowena's cocktail party? He'd been at a church in Shepherd's Bush. He and his wife spoke so nostalgically of it.'

'It's rather that kind of place, though it's a *nostalgie de la boue*, really.'

'I suppose theirs wouldn't be that,' I said. 'I do hope they have settled down better now.'

'It will be hard going for them there,' said Piers. 'I think that in some ways religion in the country *is* harder going than in town. Has it ever occurred to you that it's really the country words that rhyme with God in our language?'

'Yes, I suppose they do — clod, sod and trod — what heavy words they are!'

'How hymn writers have struggled with them, poor things — it's a wonder all hymns aren't harvest hymns or for the burial of the dead. Those are really the only kind that the rhymes would fit.'

'This must be Shepherd's Bush Green,' I said. 'Do we get out here?'

'No, we must go on a little way and then walk.'

'Will your colleague be at home this afternoon?' I asked, as we stood on an island amid a swirl of trolley buses.

'My colleague?'

'The person you share the flat with.'

'Oh, of course. Yes, it's quite likely he'll be doing the weekend shopping at this very minute.'

We walked along a street full of cheap garish looking dress shops, their windows crammed with blouses and skirts in crude colours, and butchers' and greengrocers' smelling sickly in the heat. When we came to a grocer's, Piers went into the doorway and looked inside.

'Yes, there he is,' he said.

We went into the shop. I had imagined that I would immediately recognize the colleague when I saw him, but although there were several people at the counter none of them seemed quite right. There were two men and three women, two elderly and the other young and flashily dressed with dyed golden hair and long earrings. Surely, I wondered in horror, it couldn't be *her*? But no, Piers had said 'he', so it must be one of the nondescript looking men.

'Oh there you are — I thought we'd probably find you here.' Piers had gone over into a corner where a small dark young man wearing black jeans and a blue tartan shirt, whom I had not noticed before, was peering into some biscuit tins.

'Wilmet, this is Keith — I don't think you've met before,' said Piers in a rather jolly tone which did not seem quite natural to him.

Keith gave a stiff little bow and looked at me warily. He was about twenty-five years old, with a neat-featured rather appealing face and sombre brown eyes. His hair was cropped very short in the fashionable style of the moment. I noticed that it glistened like the wet fur of an animal.

'No, we haven't actually met, but I've heard a lot about you, Mrs Forsyth,' he said politely.

'I think we've spoken on the telephone, haven't we?' I said, recognizing the flat, rather common little voice as the one which had answered me the evening I had tried to ring up Piers. I could not reciprocate by saying that I had heard a lot about him, when I had heard nothing whatsoever. Indeed, I was so taken aback and confused by the encounter that I did not know what to say or even what to think. I stood rather awkwardly, my hand mechanically stroking a large black and white cat which was asleep on a sack of lentils. So *this* was the colleague.

Keith turned to Piers with some question about bacon.

'What do you think, Wilmet?' asked Piers. 'Which is the best kind of bacon?'

'I don't know,' I said, unable to give my attention to bacon. 'It depends what you like.'

'These two gentlemen will never make up their minds,' said the motherly looking woman behind the counter. 'I have to help them choose every time. Now, what's the matter with that, dear?' she said to Keith. 'Is it too fat for your liking?'

'We like it more striped, as it were,' said Piers.

'*Striped!* Isn't that sweet — did you ever!' She turned to me. 'You mean *streaky*, dear — that's what we call it. Let me cut you some off here — this is nice.' She thrust a side of bacon towards us and then placed it in the machine.

It began to go backwards and forwards with a swishing noise, while the three of us stood in silence watching it. There was an air of unreality about the whole scene — Keith, with his absurd clothes, and bristly hair like a hedgehog or porcupine, was almost a comic figure. And yet I felt sad, too, as if something had come to an end. The sadness, however, was underneath, and my most conscious feeling as I waited for somebody to break the silence was one of indignation.

'Have we finished yet?' Piers asked rather impatiently.

'I think we need custard powder,' said Keith.

'*Custard powder?*' exclaimed Piers in horror. 'Good God, whatever do we want custard powder for?'

'To make custard,' said Keith flatly.

'You mean *you* want to make custard with it. Well, all right then, as long as you don't expect *me* to eat it.'

'He'll eat anything, really,' said Keith to me in a confidential tone, gathering his purchases together into a canvas bag not unlike Mr Bason's. 'I always think custard is nice with stewed fruit, don't you, Mrs Forsyth?'

His respectful manner and constant use of my name were a little disconcerting, I found.

'Yes,' I said inadequately, 'I do.'

We walked along the pavement, Keith and I together with Piers a little in front. Nobody seemed to be saying anything and perhaps conversation is not always necessary; but I felt that there was a kind of awkwardness about our silence, so I said to Keith, 'You're not really at all as I'd imagined you.'

'Had you imagined me, Mrs Forsyth?' There was a note of eagerness in the flat little voice. 'How did Piers describe me?'

Perhaps if I had said 'he didn't' he would have been hurt, and it was lucky that Piers broke in rather impatiently before I had time to think of a tactful answer.

'We cross the road here,' he said, 'and take this turning opposite.'

We were soon in a street of peeling stuccoed houses, which were not even noble in their shabbiness. I saw that some of them had been painted, while others which had presumably been bombed had had their façades rebuilt in a way which did not harmonize with the rest. There were rather a lot of children running about, and old women in bedroom slippers sunning themselves on ramshackle balconies crowded with plants in pots. Various kinds of music were blaring from the open windows.

'It's rather continental here, isn't it,' I said. 'It reminds me of Naples, you know.'

'Thank you,' said Piers. 'That's really the best one can say about this district, and it's nice of you to say it.'

'Where do you live, Mrs Forsyth?' asked Keith.

I told him.

He paused a moment in what seemed a respectful silence, then said seriously, 'I should think rents are very high there.'

'Wilmet doesn't have to bother about dreary things like that,' said Piers.

'No — I mean, the house belongs to my husband's mother, so I've never had to.'

'I wish we could get a nice place, somewhere in a cleaner district,' said Keith. 'I have to wash the paint every week here.

I just use plain soda and water — detergents make it go yellow. Do you find that, Mrs Forsyth?'

'Well, I don't know,' I said, ashamed of my ignorance.

'Keith, you must realize that Wilmet wouldn't know about dreary things like that,' said Piers. 'I don't suppose she's ever washed paint in her life.'

'No, I haven't,' I said crossly, 'except perhaps when I was first in the Wrens. But am I any the worse for that? I could do it if I had to.'

'But do remember about not using detergents,' said Keith.

'Well, here we are,' said Piers, with a note of relief in his tone.

We had stopped outside one of the newly painted houses. It had a flight of steps up to the front door and three bells, two of which had cards by them. One had HALIBURTON written in block capitals, the other a Polish name of daunting complexity on a printed visiting card.

'I suppose yours is the top bell, as it has no card on it,' I said.

'Yes, we've got the top flat,' said Keith chattily. 'Two rooms with kitchenette, and we share the bathroom with Mr Sienkiewicz.'

'No relation to the author of *Quo Vadis*, as far as we know, but the name is comforting in a way,' said Piers.

We entered the hall and began to walk upstairs. I remembered how I had imagined the narrow hall with prams and bicycles and the smell of stale cooking or even other things, but there was a kind of deadness about this house on this fine Saturday afternoon. People were either out or behind closed doors, and I had the feeling that I ought to walk on tiptoe up the stairs, carpeted in maroon with a white squiggle pattern. And yet the silence was somehow unlike that of the clergy house, though I could not have said exactly why.

At last we reached the top floor.

'Where are we to have tea?' Piers asked. 'My room is the obvious one, but I think I may have forgotten to make my bed, and I don't think Wilmet could stand the sight of that.'

'I shouldn't mind,' I said, for I had been preparing myself for the unmade bed — perhaps littered with galley proofs — for the bottle of gin, the unwashed glasses and cups, and the unemptied ashtrays.

'I tidied and cleaned your room while you were out,' said Keith primly. 'And I've laid tea in there.'

'Good heavens!' Piers flung open a door. 'It's hardly recognizable. Flowers, too.' He glanced over to the bookcase where some blue irises were arranged in a cut glass vase. 'Did you do all this?'

Keith smiled but said nothing.

I had wanted so much to see where Piers lived, and was disappointed that Keith should have tidied away the more obvious personal touches. The room was, of course, full of books; but I have rather ceased to regard books as being very personal things — everybody one knows has them and they are really rather obvious. It was no doubt significant that Mary Beamish should have the novels of Miss Goudge while Piers had those of Miss Compton-Burnett, but I should have been able to guess that for myself without actually seeing. I suppose I really *had* hoped for the pyjamas on the unmade bed and the shaving things on the mantelpiece, though perhaps, as Piers had said, I could not really have stood the sight of them.

Keith came back from the kitchen with the teapot and kettle, but he had evidently made most of his preparations in advance. There was a check tablecloth on a low table, and plates of sandwiches and biscuits and a pink and white gateau arranged on plastic doilies. Each plate had a paper table napkin laid across it. It was not at all like Mr Bason's tea, but I had the feeling that it had been even more anxiously prepared and that I must therefore eat more than I wanted — which was really nothing — and praise it judiciously or even extravagantly. It was quite obvious that I was going to find it impossible to dislike Keith.

After we had finished tea I was taken on a tour of the flat.

'Of course the flat is furnished,' Keith explained, 'so we can't

196

really have exactly what we want, but I got this contemporary print for my divan cover — do you like it, Mrs Forsyth?'

I said that I did, though it was not particularly distinguished. His room was painfully neat and unlived in, as if everything had been arranged for effect. There were only two books on the table by the divan, a French grammar and a paperbacked novel with a lurid cover. A trailing plant of a kind which had lately become fashionable stood on another table, its pot in a white painted metal cover. A print of Van Gogh's irises in a light oak frame hung on one wall.

'You're much tidier than Piers,' I said. 'And I think your room has a nice view, hasn't it?' I went over to the window hopefully.

'Yes, it is rather nice, isn't it, Mrs Forsyth?' said Keith in a pleased tone. 'You can even see trees in the distance.'

'It's amazing how one can in London, isn't it?' I said.

'Yes,' said Piers, 'even in the worst parts of London there is always a distant glimpse of some trees or Battersea power station or the top of Westminster Cathedral.'

'I expect Mrs Forsyth sees *many* trees where she lives,' said Keith wistfully.

'Why don't you call her Wilmet?' Piers suggested. 'I'm sure she wouldn't mind?'

'No, of course I shouldn't,' I said, rather embarrassed.

'I expect your home is very nice, Wilmet,' said Keith.

'You must come and have tea one day,' I found myself saying, as I suspected I was meant to.

'Thank you, Wilmet,' said Keith with quiet satisfaction. 'I should like that.'

He stood on the doorstep and waved as Piers and I went out of the house. I was surprised that he should be so friendly towards me, but then it occurred to me that he had no reason to be otherwise. It was a situation I had not met before, and I did not know what to say to Piers as we walked along the hot noisy street.

We were silent for a while, then I said rather stiffly, 'So that is the person with whom you live.'

'Yes. He's obviously taken a great fancy to you,' Piers smiled, 'do you like him?'

'He seems a nice boy,' I said, 'but rather unexpected.'

'In what way unexpected?'

'You said you lived with a colleague from the press. I suppose I'd imagined a different sort of person.'

'*You* always said that I lived with a colleague. But aren't we all colleagues, in a sense, in this grim business of getting through life as best we can?'

I said nothing, so he went on, 'My dear girl, what's the matter? Do you think I've been deceiving you, or something absurd like that?'

'No, of course I don't,' I said indignantly. But of course, in a way, he had deceived me. 'It would have been more friendly if you'd told me, though,' I added.

'Well, now you and Keith have met I'm sure you'll like each other. You really will have to ask him to tea, you know. He's dying to see your home, as he calls it.'

I noticed that there was no malice in this last remark.

'Of course I shall,' I said. 'Where did you meet him, if I may be so inquisitive?'

'Why — at my French class.'

'I see — that accounts for the French grammar by the bed, then.'

'Yes — imagine it, Wilmet. The pathos of anyone not knowing French — I mean, not at all!'

'It does seem strange,' I admitted. 'So he was one of your pupils! Of course I had no idea ...'

'No, why should you have?'

'But Piers, why did you choose him of all people? I shouldn't have thought you had anything in common.'

'This having things in common,' said Piers impatiently, 'how overrated it is! Long dreary intellectual conversations, capping

198

each other's obscure quotations — it's so exhausting. It's much more agreeable to come home to some different remarks from the ones one's been hearing all day.'

'I'm sure you get *those*,' I said spitefully. 'What does Keith do for a living, anyway?'

'Various things. At the moment he's working in a coffee bar in the evenings, and he sometimes gets modelling jobs.'

'Good heavens!' I suppose I must have been unable to keep the note of horror out of my voice, for Piers said sharply, 'Well, hasn't it ever occurred to you that somebody must pose for those photographs of handsome young men you see in knitting patterns and women's magazines?'

'Yes, but not people one actually *knows*.'

'Not people *you* know, you mean, but there *are* others in the world — in fact quite a few million people outside the narrow select little circle that makes up Wilmet's world.'

I had a dreadful feeling that I might be going to cry, but even that seemed impossible in the hot garish street with the Saturday evening shopping crowds and trolley buses swirling around us.

Piers looked at me curiously. 'I'm sorry,' he said more gently. 'Perhaps I've gone too far. After all I didn't really mean to imply that you're to blame for what you are. Some people are less capable of loving their fellow human beings than others,' he went on in an almost academic way, 'it isn't necessarily their fault.'

'You're being horrid,' I protested.

'But I often am — you should know that by now.' He was smiling most charmingly as he spoke, which increased the confusion of my feelings still further. Perhaps I had never really known him, or — what was worse — myself. That anyone could doubt my capacity to love! But strangely enough my immediate thought was that I could not bear to go home by bus. I must get a taxi.

'This will take you most of the way,' said Piers, as a bus approached the stop.

'I think I'd rather find a taxi.'

'Dear Wilmet, so deliciously in character! Don't ever try to make yourself any different.'

He waved to a passing taxi. They were no doubt easier to get here than in the better districts, I reflected.

'I've just remembered that Mary Beamish is coming back from the convent today,' I said, trying to pull myself together. 'She's coming to stay with us for a while and I must be home before she arrives.'

'Whatever will you say to her?' Piers asked. 'Do you often have this kind of experience?'

'No,' I said, 'it will make two new experiences in one day.'

'I hope they will both have been equally interesting and rewarding,' said Piers. 'Well, all experience is said to be that, isn't it?'

I got into the taxi and we waved goodbye. I could now imagine Piers going back to the house, climbing the stairs, perhaps sitting down heavily in an armchair, letting out an exaggerated sigh, while Keith's flat little voice began discussing me, criticizing my clothes and manner. I felt battered and somehow rather foolish, very different from the carefree girl who had set out across the park to meet Piers. But I was not a girl. I was a married woman, and if I felt wretched it was no more than I deserved for having let my thoughts stray to another man. And the ironical thing was that it was Keith, that rather absurd little figure, who had brought about the change I thought I had noticed in Piers and which I had attributed to my own charms and loving care!

I lay back in the taxi and lit a cigarette. Into my temporarily blank mind there came a sudden picture of Father Bode, toothy and eager, talking about hiring a coach for the parish retreat. It was obscurely comforting to let my mind dwell on such things, and I suppose I must have been unconsciously preparing myself to meet Mary, covering up the humiliation and disappointment to be looked at later when I had more time.

I had hoped to be back before she arrived, but as soon as I opened the front door I knew that she had forestalled me. A suitcase and a brown canvas bag stood in the hall. I wondered irrelevantly that she should have so much luggage.

'Is that Wilmet?' I heard her eager voice say, and soon we were embracing and apologizing — she for being early, I for being late. I was glad to have something to do, to show her her room and sit with her while she unpacked the drab clothes she had worn in the convent — including the dyed black dress with the dye showing up the worn patches, which I should so much have disliked wearing myself.

'I really shall have to do some shopping,' she said. 'I've no summer things. Will you help me, Wilmet, please?'

I saw us shopping together, having lunch or tea in a restaurant, perhaps going to the pictures. It gave me the same comfortable feeling as thinking of Father Bode hiring a coach for the parish retreat. I knew that time would pass and that I should feel better.

After dinner we sat — Sybil, Mary and I — in the drawing-room by the open window, looking out at the trees in the square. I heard again Keith's wistful voice saying, 'I expect Mrs Forsyth sees *many* trees where she lives'. Rodney had decided to be out; he was rather nervous of meeting Mary, perhaps fearing that his conversational powers would not be up to the situation. It might be, after all, that I with my sheltered life was in some ways more fitted to deal with certain things, for which Rodney's, with public school and university, the war in Italy, and the Civil Service, was inadequate. For there could, I felt, be situations for which even these varied experiences might have failed to equip him.

As it happened Mary went to bed quite early, and Sybil and I were left alone, feeling that we could hardly discuss her the moment she had left the room. In any case she had seemed to be so very much her old self that there was little we could have said, especially when another more important and interesting subject was on our minds.

'So you saw Piers's lodgings,' said Sybil, in the tone she used to invite discussion of a topic when no information had yet been offered.

'Yes, he has quite a nice flat, not properly self-contained but on the top floor, which does make it *seem* more self-contained,' I found myself saying quickly.

'And the mysterious colleague — was he there?'

'Oh yes — we all had tea together.'

'What is he like?'

'Younger than I'd expected — rather nice, really.'

'I suppose he works at the press?'

'I'm not sure what he does,' I said. For if I had ever thought that Sybil and I might enjoy a good laugh over Keith not knowing French, and posing for photographs of knitting patterns, I now realized that he had aroused in me some kind of — protective or maternal? — instinct which would save him from being turned into an object of ridicule.

Sybil yawned and rolled up her knitting.

'Well, it doesn't seem to have been a very exciting afternoon,' she said. 'I suppose I was hoping for some little bit of scandal — very wicked of me, I know, and wickedness is particularly distressing in *old* people don't you think? Do you want that knitting book, dear?'

'I thought I'd look through it and see if there's anything I could make for Rodney. I seem to want to knit when I see other people doing it.'

I took the book up to my room and put it on the table by my bed. As I sat brushing my hair I caught sight of the little box which Harry had given me at Christmas.

> If you will not when you may
> When you will you shall have nay ...

I pondered over the words in the light of the new character Piers had given me. How had Harry meant them to be taken? As a rather naughty little joke, or had there been a grain of truth in the words? I put the box into a drawer, not wanting to have to look at it every time I went to my dressing table.

In bed I turned the pages of the knitting book, looking for Keith. I soon found him, on the opposite page to a rugged looking pipe-smoking man who was wearing a cable stitch sweater which took thirty ounces of double knitting wool. Keith was leaning against a tree, one hand absently playing with a low-hanging branch. He wore a kind of lumber jacket with a shawl collar, knitted crossways in an intricate and rather pleasing stitch. 'For Leisure Hours', the pattern said, 'to fit a 36-38 inch chest. Commence at right cuff by casting on 64 sts. on No. 11 needles ...' It seemed as if he might have stood there patiently while some busy woman knitted the jacket on to him. The expression in the dark eyes was sombre and unfathomable, the lips unsmiling. If one ignored the slightly ridiculous setting, it was easy to see how he could become an object of devotion. This thought led me to consider the religious and secular meanings of the word devotion, and how 'devout' did not mean the same as 'devoted'. I was not sure why this was but it seemed suitable that my life should have this confusion in it.

I went on looking at the patterns, comparing the expressions, and finding that though most were smiling and jolly the sort of men one could imagine pottering about in the garden at the week-end or playing a round of golf, some were a little shamefaced, as if they hoped nobody they knew would come upon them posing for knitting patterns. None seemed to me to have Keith's air of romantic detachment. Was he thinking of French verbs, dreaming of the day when he could read Baudelaire with ease, I wondered? Or was his mind a blank, in the way that the minds of beautiful people are sometimes said to be? I began to want to know more of his origins and history. I thought he might be a colonial, perhaps a New Zealander; I remembered clever moody passionate girls, like Katherine Mansfield, striving to break away from the narrowness of their environment, almost nineteenth-century Russian in their yearnings, hating the traditional English

Christmas in the middle of summer and the sentimental attitude towards the Mother Country. They would come to London and live wretchedly, perhaps starving in an attic, exulting in their freedom, and yet keeping underneath everything their innate primness and respectability. Was Keith like this, or did he just come from Fulham or Brixton or some dreary English provincial town? I supposed that if I kept my promise to ask him to tea I should be able to find out all about him.

I closed the knitting book and took a sleeping pill. I was just conscious of Rodney coming in very much later, but I did not open my eyes or speak to him.

CHAPTER EIGHTEEN

I was glad in the days that followed to have Mary with me. Her companionship was soothing and at the same time a kind of discipline, for there could be no question of discussing Piers or my feelings about him when I was with her. Our conversation was either about her immediate future or, of course, about church matters. She was to take up residence at the retreat house as a kind of housekeeper at the beginning of June. We had quite an interesting time choosing clothes for her — summer dresses that might be regarded as suitable for greeting parties of devout men and women (mostly women, we suspected) arriving to make a retreat.

'Perhaps it's one's demeanour rather than one's dress that matters,' I suggested, as we walked to church for the Corpus Christi evening service. 'I'm sure you would know how to greet the retreatants, whatever you wore, whereas I should be quite hopeless.'

'Of course you wouldn't,' said Mary warmly. 'You're always belittling yourself lately.'

'Meaning that I used not to?'

'Well, you seem different since I came out of the convent.' She hesitated. 'As if — well — you'd been disappointed in some way about something, perhaps lost confidence in yourself a bit. And yet I don't see how that could be.'

No, she would not see, and I could hardly tell her. It was funny to remember that Harry had once said something rather like it when we had been having lunch together, but he had seen my air of sadness as something appealing. To have Mary notice it made me feel dreary and depressed.

'Life isn't always all it's cracked up to be,' I said rather frivolously. 'And then sometimes you discover that you aren't as nice as you thought you were — that you're in fact rather a horrid person, and that's humiliating somehow.'

'What nonsense — that couldn't possibly apply to you!' Mary took my arm in an affectionate gesture. 'And even if it did, I suppose a person would be even nicer if they could make a discovery like that and admit the truth of it.'

I was glad that at this point we reached the church, for I was beginning to fear that I might go too far in talking about myself.

'It's very crowded already,' Mary whispered. 'We shall have to go rather near the front.'

The service had attracted quite a number of strangers, for there was to be a procession with candles, followed by refreshments in the church hall. It had been advertised in the *Church Times*, with a list of buses, not strictly accurate, which were said to pass the door. It would be Father Thames's last public appearance before leaving for his holiday in Italy, but the preacher was a stranger to me — Father Julian Malory, the vicar of a church in Pimlico — and I supposed that he would draw some of the congregation from his own parish. No doubt it was they who were occupying our usual seats, making us go uncomfortably near the front.

The church was looking very beautiful, and Mary and I had helped with the decorating of it in the morning. Her presence had made it easy for me to enter the charmed circle of decorators, and I had even been allowed to help to lay down the carpet of leaves and flowers which covered the nave and looked almost as striking as the altar with its many candles embowered in green leaves, lilies and carnations.

Julian Malory was a dark, rather good looking man in his late forties. There was something about him that reminded me a little of our own Father Ransome, though perhaps it was nothing more subtle than the angle of his biretta. While he was preaching I found myself wondering whether he was married or not, until I remembered Miss Prideaux having said that he lived with his sister.

The procession round the church with lighted candles reminded me of a scene from an Italian opera — *Tosca*, I suppose.

There was something daring and Romish about the whole thing which added to one's enjoyment. It should have been followed, I felt, by a reception in some magnificent palazzo, where we would drink splendid Italian wines with names like Asti Spumante, Làchryma Christi and Soave di Verona. That it seemed to go equally well with the tea and sandwiches and cakes in the church hall was perhaps a tribute to the true catholicity of the Church of England.

'So beautiful, all those candles,' said Miss Prideaux, as we found ourselves standing together in the crush waiting to get into the hall, 'but rather dangerous. I am always so afraid of fire, and Sir Denbigh's candle was burning dangerously low.'

'Now, Augusta, that remark might be taken in more ways than one,' said Sir Denbigh, with his hollow, diplomat's laugh.

'I do want to have a word with Father Malory,' said Miss Prideaux. 'I thought his sermon was splendid, so very much to the point. I suppose I could hardly tell him that in so many words.'

'He would not mind if you implied that other clergy seldom do preach to the point,' said Sir Denbigh. 'He seems to be surrounded at the moment. I wonder if everybody is telling him that.'

'I think clergymen always are surrounded at functions like these,' I said.

'Yes,' Sir Denbigh agreed. 'It makes one wonder whether it would really be proper to admit women to Holy Orders. Is it likely that a woman would be surrounded by men at a parish gathering and would it be seemly if she were?'

'I suppose one visualizes rather plain-looking middle-aged and elderly women taking Orders,' said Miss Prideaux.

'Surrounded by men of the same type or perhaps not surrounded at all?' said Sir Denbigh. 'Yes, I see your point — perhaps it would be like that. What do you think, Miss Beamish?'

'Oh, I don't think women should be admitted to Holy Orders,' said Mary. 'Perhaps I'm old-fashioned, but it wouldn't seem right to me. Now, Sir Denbigh, I'm going to get you and Miss Prideaux some tea. You sit and wait here and Wilmet and I will bring it to you.'

'I might have taken Orders,' said Sir Denbigh regretfully. 'One often hears of an elderly man retiring into the church — particularly an army man — but I don't think I should have been able to manage the singing.'

Mary and I pushed our way as gently as we could through the crowds to the table where the refreshments were. Mrs Greenhill, looking quietly triumphant, was dispensing tea assisted by Mrs Spooner. Mr Bason stood near them, a scornful expression on his face.

'He's imagining how much better he could have done it,' I whispered to Mary. I still felt a slight awkwardness on meeting him, but his jaunty wave to me indicated that he felt none himself which was all to the good. After all, it was he who had stolen the egg, not me.

'A good thing Sir Denbigh likes it stewed,' he whispered to me, as I passed with a cup of tea in my hand, 'though it beats me why somebody who must have passed his life in the *highest* circles should have such taste.'

After we had taken tea and cakes to Sir Denbigh and Miss Prideaux, I found myself standing next to Mr Coleman, whose smile was rather more embarrassed than Mr Bason's had been.

'I just wanted to tell you that it was all right about the egg,' I said, lowering my voice. 'I daresay you heard? Mr Bason put it back where it belonged.'

'I'm glad to hear it, Mrs Forsyth — that *is* a relief. I hope Father Thames will keep it locked up in future.'

'I hope the Husky is well?' I asked, feeling rather foolish.

'Yes, thank you, Mrs Forsyth.' His tone grew warmer. 'You'd hardly know where that scratch had been now. I didn't have to have the whole side resprayed after all. Eddie Fowler — he was thurifer tonight — works in a garage and he fixed it for me.'

'I'm so glad,' I said. 'You must be tired after all your exertions

208

in the Sanctuary this evening. Everything seemed to go very well. And such a lot of strangers here, too.'

'Yes, this kind of service is very popular,' said Mr Coleman, rather in the manner of a salesman recommending some particular line of goods. 'I think some people come to see the procession; it's really something of a spectacle.'

If only I had had the courage to ask Piers, and perhaps even Keith, to come this evening, I thought. They might have enjoyed it. And what a beautiful acolyte Keith would make! And yet his world was probably too far removed from that of the church to make it feasible. It was both exciting and frightening to think how many different worlds I knew—or perhaps 'had knowledge of' would be a more accurate way of putting it. I could not say that I really *knew* the worlds of Piers and Keith, or even of Mr Coleman and his Husky if it came to that. It seemed as if the Church should be the place where all worlds could meet, and looking around me I saw that in a sense this was so. If people remained outside it was our — even *my* — duty to try to bring them in.

'Won't you have a sandwich before they all go?' A voice at my side interrupted my noble thoughts.

It was Father Ransome.

'I'm afraid our guests have taken the best of the food,' he said, 'I suppose we ought to feel gratified.'

'They do seem to be tucking in,' I said, looking over to a corner where a stout woman in a grey uniform, presumably a sort of deaconess, sat crouched with two other ladies over a large plate of sandwiches. 'I suppose they feel less shy among strangers.'

'Sister Blatt wouldn't be shy anywhere,' said Mary. 'She's a splendid person and such a great help to Father Malory, I believe.'

'Is his parish a particularly difficult one?' I asked.

'Not more than most,' said Father Ransome, a little jealously, I thought. 'There is a rowdy element, of course, as there must inevitably be wherever one tries to bring in the young people,' he added in a professional tone. 'Poor Edwin had a good deal of trouble with that sort of thing.'

'That's your friend who became a Roman Catholic, isn't it?' asked Mary.

'Yes. Poor Edwin, that was a great blow to me.'

'What is he doing now?' I asked.

'He's gone to Somerset for a holiday. He will take long walks over Exmoor and try to think out his future,' said Father Ransome seriously.

I wondered, though luckily I did not ask, whether he would be taking out a packed lunch every day; for I had remembered Professor Root and his sister and her friend who had apparently been doing this for ten years.

'That may bring him some peace and consolation,' said Mary. 'The country is so very lovely in that part of the world.'

'It will be a change from London,' said Father Ransome tritely.

'Where was he received?' Mary asked.

'At Westminster Cathedral, which seems a little less sinister than Farm Street, don't you think?' said Father Ransome, recovering his usual manner. 'I met him afterwards and — oh *dear*, it was so difficult to decide what to *do*!' He wrung his hands as if reliving the embarrassment of the occasion. 'One couldn't very well suggest the pictures, and yet the idea of going back to the vicarage to pack up his things was somehow *too* depressing.'

'What *did* you do?' I asked.

'Well, in the end we went and had tea at some rather ghastly help-yourself place. We had egg and chips, I remember.'

'It seems difficult to suggest a suitable meal for such an occasion,' I said.

'Yes, life has to go on, and I suppose a cup of tea does make it seem to be doing that more than anything,' said Father Ransome.

'Couldn't the Romans have welcomed him with a party, or at least some kind of refreshment?' I suggested.

'They've been coming so thick and fast lately — the converts, I mean — I suppose they couldn't welcome each one individually.'

He was interrupted by a banging on the floor, and I saw that Father Thames had mounted the platform. He looked very distinguished in a caped cassock, the waist encircled by a wide band of moiré silk.

'My friends,' he began, 'how very glad I am to see so many of you here this evening. As some of you know, I am shortly leaving for a holiday in Italy. There seems something a little unsuitable, does there not, about a clergyman going for a holiday in Italy in these difficult days? When we hear about such a thing perhaps we remember our *Barchester Towers* — the older ones among us, that is.' He seemed to be looking at Sir Denbigh Grote and Miss Prideaux as he said this, perhaps feeling that they alone were old enough to remember a century ago or literate enough to have read Trollope. 'We think of Canon Vesey Stanhope and his villa on the shores of Lake Como — or was it Maggiore? *Not* Garda, I think — I forget the details. As I was saying, we remember that, and it might be thought that there was a parallel there.' Father Thames paused for laughter, which came a little uncertainly, though one elderly choirman clapped his hands and guffawed perhaps too heartily for such a gathering. Father Thames held up his hand and went on, '*But*, and this will surprise you, who can say that there might not be something in it after all?' His hearers were now mystified and awaited his next words with considerable interest. 'I am an old man,' he went on. 'Oh yes, you may protest and say that you have seen older priests carrying out their duties perfectly capably — indeed Father Fosdick, who has sometimes assisted us here at holiday times, is nearly ninety, and a great joy it has always been to have him with us — but I have passed my threescore years and ten, and it may be that the time has come for me to make way for a younger man. *It may be.*' He paused impressively, then went on in a more confidential tone, 'I was talking to the Bishop at luncheon the other day — he knows full well the rigours of this parish. Now *you* know, most of you, that I have friends — kind friends they are — near Siena whom I visit every year for rest and refreshment, to enable me to *carry on*, as it were. *Well'* — there was another impressive pause — 'what do you think? A villa has fallen vacant there! *Da affittare!* A small villa with just four bedrooms and a delightful garden — the Villa Cenerentola. What a delightful name that is, and perhaps not altogether inappropriate'.

Mary sighed and turned to me. 'What *is* he talking about?'

'He plans to retire in the autumn,' whispered Father Ransome.

'Cenerentola — Cinderella, isn't it,' said Miss Prideaux. 'I don't see how that is at all appropriate.'

The speech went on for some time longer, and at its conclusion it was felt that tea was needed again. I saw Mrs Greenhill come hurrying in with more cakes, while Father Bode staggered under the weight of the urn.

'What a good man he is, helping Mrs Greenhill like that,' said Mary. 'I do hope he will get the living here. It would be a very popular choice.'

'Do you think so?' said Mr Bason spitefully. 'I'm afraid the clergy house would become a *very* dreary place if Father Bode was vicar. He has no taste at all.'

I remembered his room and saw what Mr Bason meant. His exquisite continental cooking would be wasted on Father Bode and there would be no Fabergé eggs lying around. And yet would it not perhaps be more suitable if the clergy house did become more dreary than it was at present? Didn't one really prefer to think of the clergy eating plain food and cod on Fridays?

'I expect there will be some changes when Father Thames goes,' said Mary, as we walked home.

'Yes, I shouldn't be at all surprised if Mr Bason found himself out of a job,' I said, 'and then the worry of finding him something suitable will begin all over again. How would you like to have him as cook at the retreat house?'

Mary looked doubtful.

'No, it wouldn't do,' I said. 'You couldn't very well get a reputation for excellent cooking, though I suppose there might be no harm in it. But now, in a way, I feel responsible for Mr Bason.'

'Yes, I can understand that,' said Mary, 'and in a strange way I feel responsible for Marius.'

'You don't think he is still toying with the idea of Rome?'

'No. I think he has been put off it by being with his friend at the time when he went over,' said Mary thoughtfully.

The embarrassment and the dreadful tea, I thought, and the prospect of those long walks over Exmoor.

'I feel,' Mary went on, 'that Marius talks rather lightly about these things, perhaps too flippantly in a way, but how does one know what he is *feeling*?'

'One never knows what men are *feeling*,' I said rather brutally. 'Have you fallen in love with him?'

'Oh, *no*! That would never do,' Mary sounded genuinely shocked.

'Perhaps not. But it might happen,' I said.

CHAPTER NINETEEN

I HAD not liked to probe any more deeply into Mary's feelings for Marius Ransome and we had not discussed the subject again when she left our house. It seemed such a hopeless and hackneyed situation — dowdy parish worker in love with handsome celibate priest — and I hoped she would not brood too much over it. Her new position in the retreat house seemed to me to be very little better than that in the convent, for neither place would be likely to provide the kind of company that might take her out of herself. The trouble was that there were so few eligible men of the right age to whom one could introduce her. Sir Denbigh Grote was obviously much too old, and rather Miss Prideaux's property, one felt, and Mr Coleman was too taken up with his Husky and not quite suitable socially. Piers was not to be considered at all, even had he been the kind of man who might marry.

I was able to smile now when I remembered my extravagant dreams about him only a few weeks ago; but when I went to spend a weekend with Rowena and Harry I found that I was self-conscious about mentioning him, though I knew that we should discuss him in the way that we invariably did.

As it happened, Rowena raised the subject quite naturally.

'We had Piers here last weekend,' she said, 'with his friend Keith. I gather you went to tea with them and that the whole thing was a great success.'

I should not have described it quite like that myself, but that was obviously how it was to be.

'Yes, I saw the flat at last,' I said.

'What did you think of Keith?'

'Oh, rather a nice little thing,' I said warily.

'He's certainly an improvement on some of Piers's friends,' said Rowena.

'I think I'd expected somebody older and — well — different,' I said. 'I'd somehow imagined that he lived with a colleague from the press.'

Rowena burst into laughter, which made me feel that I had been rather naive in my imaginings. 'Poor Piers,' she said, 'it would be a bit much to expect him to live with the kind of people we saw in that dreary place. I liked Keith very much, and he was so helpful in the house.'

'Did Harry like him?'

'He didn't quite know what to make of him. Of course we *didn't* tell him about Keith being a model and posing for knitting patterns — I thought it better not, though goodness knows lots of most respectable-looking men seem to do that. All those solid pipe-smoking types — '

'In double knitting wool,' I giggled. 'Yes, I'd noticed that too, but I didn't tell Rodney, either.'

'No, *much* better not, I think. Men are so narrow-minded and catty,' said Rowena. 'But it was all right about Keith working in the coffee bar — you see, the daughter of a man Harry *knows* does that. It's rather a chic kind of job, though perhaps not very manly, and I think Harry is beginning to realize that men needn't necessarily always do manly jobs.' She smiled. 'He travels up in the train every day with this man whose daughter works in a coffee bar. He comes from Oxted, so it seems *very* much all right, really.'

Later that evening, as we sat in the garden having drinks, I caught Harry looking at me with a kind of doggy devotion in his eyes. I leaned back in my chair, well satisfied, both with my drink in such pleasant surroundings and with his devotion. It seemed like a balm to heal the little wound inflicted by Piers's unkindness. I might be incapable of loving my fellow human beings in a dreary general way, but I could inspire love in others. This picture of myself was not at all unpleasing to me. I began imagining future luncheons in town, the great joints of meat being wheeled up to the table in an unending procession, the chefs standing deferentially with carving implements poised ... a smile twitched the corners of my mouth.

'Wilmet, you're getting tiddly,' said Rowena enviously. 'Did Harry give you one of his specials?'

'Just the same as I gave you, darling,' said Harry virtuously. 'But you're being slow — drink up!'

Rowena drank with steady concentration and soon we were all very merry. Rodney joined us later in the evening; and we had two days of perfect weather, and could almost have imagined ourselves back in Italy in our carefree youth at the end of the war.

When we returned to London I rang up Keith and asked him to come and have tea with me.

I had arranged a bowl of sweet peas on the table in the window, and the dress I wore, a romantically blurred wild silk print, seemed to harmonize with their colours.

As he came into the room I experienced again the curious painful sensation I had felt on seeing him in the grocer's. His clean white shirt and black velvet jacket showed that he, too, had been anxious to look his best.

'I love those dark purply ones,' he said, going over to the bowl of sweet peas. 'Purple's rather a sad colour, isn't it?'

'Yes,' I said feebly.

'Well, Wilmet, this *is* nice of you,' he said, in a rather carefully social tone. 'Piers told me you had a lovely home, and now I can see for myself.'

He sat down on the edge of a chair, and I began to wonder what on earth we were going to talk about once we had exhausted the beauties of my home. Rhoda brought the tea in, and it occurred to me that she must be wondering too.

When I had poured out, and Keith had admired the silver teapot and the cups and saucers, he said in a cosy confidential voice, 'I believe we're going to be great friends, Wilmet. I think you're very nice — and very attractive, too, if you'll excuse my mentioning it.'

'Thank you,' I murmured, but either my tone was wrong or

irony was wasted on him. I wondered what I should do or say now that this new relationship had been established between us. But as it turned out I did not have to exert myself at all, for Keith now began to open his heart to me, to tell me his life history from the early days in Leicester up to the present moment. The little flat voice went relentlessly on, hardly allowing me even a formal murmur of sympathy or astonishment.

I began to feel a little drowsy — I may even actually have closed my eyes — but really it was better to keep them open, for only by resting them on the beauty of Keith's face could I forget that he was really rather a bore. Yet the recognition of this fact was a kind of solace, for it made him much less alarming and glamorous, and seemed to bring Piers's world nearer to my own, where people seldom looked like Keith but were often as boring.

'And then you decided to learn French?' I heard myself saying.

'Yes, and *that* was how I met Piers. Then I had a row with my landlady. At least it wasn't me, really. There were two other boys sharing the flat with me — they were in the ballet, but resting at the time — Tony and Ray their names were. Well, one night we had a party and Tony threw an ornament out of the window. Actually it was a big blue and gold vase with a picture of a Grecian lady on it — you know how excitable stage people are,' he added primly. 'Anyway, the landlady thought it was me that did it, though I was always *very* quiet, but I didn't trouble to vindicate myself because I knew that Piers was on his own and had a spare room — he'd had some domestic upset too — so I went there. And Wilmet — the *mess* in that place!' He lowered his voice confidentially. 'That woman in the basement was *supposed* to keep it clean, but she never went *near*. You remember that big table in Piers's room?'

'Vaguely,' I said.

'Well, I wrote my name in the dust on that.'

'Fancy that,' I said cosily.

'There was plenty for me to do *there*. I really don't know how

Piers ever managed without me. Do you know, the kitchen was so full of empty bottles you could hardly open the door properly?'

'Really?'

'Yes! And he never used to make his bed. Some days he didn't even cover it up. And he wasn't getting proper food, either. Do you know, Wilmet —' the dark eyes looked so seriously into mine that I wondered what horror was going to be revealed next — 'he hadn't even got a *teapot*?'

'Goodness! How did he make tea, then?'

'He didn't — he *never made tea*! Just fancy!'

'Well, one doesn't really associate Piers with drinking tea,' I said.

'He drinks it now,' said Keith, in such a governessy tone that I began to feel almost sorry for Piers.

'I expect you've been very good for him,' I said. 'I always think there's something pathetic about undomesticated men living on their own, and Piers is rather difficult to help.'

'Oh, he's a difficult person altogether,' said Keith, with understandable complacency. 'But you mustn't take too much notice of what he says, Wilmet. He can be very unkind sometimes, but he doesn't really mean it.'

I was extremely embarrassed, and a little annoyed, too, for this could only mean that Piers had told Keith what he had said to me in our last conversation.

'I never mind what he says,' I said quickly, anxious to keep my end up.

'I'm glad to hear it, Wilmet, because really it *was* a nasty thing to say.'

'Did you know what he said?' I asked.

'Did I know?' Keith seemed surprised. 'But of course. Piers doesn't really think you're unlovable, you know, and *I* certainly don't.'

I was too astonished to point out that Piers hadn't exactly said that, or even to make any other kind of comment, but perhaps astonishment was not a bad note on which to end our tea party,

218

for Keith had now risen to his feet and was saying that he really must be going because he liked to be in when Piers got home from the press.

'Wilmet, I *have* enjoyed myself,' he said, fingering the curtains and turning them back to see if they were lined. I saw him give a little nod of approval when he discovered that they were. 'I do hope you will come to my coffee bar one evening, if you ever go to such places.'

'Yes, I should be interested to see it. What's its name?'

'It's quite near you, really — nearly at Marble Arch. It's called the Cenerentola.'

'La Cenerentola!' I exclaimed. 'What a strange coincidence.'

'Why — do you know it?'

'No, but it's the same name as the villa which our vicar is retiring to in Italy.'

'Oh well, *we* have Italian décor,' said Keith.

I remembered thinking what a beautiful acolyte he would make, so I asked him if he ever went to church.

'No, Wilmet, I'm afraid I never do,' he said. 'Church services are so old-fashioned, aren't they? As a matter of fact, I once knew a boy who went to church. He used to wear a vestment — he looked ever so nice.'

I felt it was hardly worth the trouble to point out that it was only priests who wore vestments. Unless, of course, the friend had been a priest, which seemed unlikely.

'Of course he was a Catholic,' Keith went on, 'very devout.'

I have often noticed that it is only *Roman* Catholics who are spoken of as very devout, just as it seems to be only Romans who are lapsed, but again it seemed useless to argue the point.

'You see, Wilmet, I don't believe in God,' said Keith simply. 'Goodbye and thank you for a lovely tea. I hope we'll meet again soon.'

'Give my love to Piers,' I said; for now I could send it in the casual meaningless way one did to all and sundry, when it no longer mattered.

Keith tripped away across the square while Sybil and Professor Root approached the house with more measured steps.

'Who was that beautiful young man who didn't believe in God?' asked Sybil.

'Did you hear him say that?'

'Yes. We wondered if you had been having a little evangelizing tea party, and were sorry that you had apparently been unsuccessful,' said Professor Root.

'Actually he is a friend of Piers's,' I said.

'*Ah*,' said Sybil, in a meaningful tone.

I changed the subject, but when we were having dinner she brought it up again.

'Wilmet has been entertaining a friend of Piers's to tea,' she said.

'Really?' said Rodney, in a not very interested tone.

'Yes. I see now the clue to Piers's lack of success in this world. I believe that he has loved not wisely but too well.'

'Mother, that's such a hackneyed quotation, and it really tells one nothing. I suppose we've all of us done that in our time, if you come to think of it.'

I looked at Rodney in surprise. He so seldom indulged in these generalizations about love. I saw that he had gone a little pink.

'Noddy, I think you misunderstand me,' said Sybil.

'Anyway,' I said, 'I should have thought that Piers's inability to make a success of his life springs from all sorts of causes — he's so lazy, for one thing. I believe that Keith has been very good for him, even making him drink tea. And *has* he been so unsuccessful? Not really, you know.'

'At least he has taught us a little Portuguese,' said Sybil. 'I wonder how we shall get on with our speaking.'

'Are we *all* going to Portugal?' asked Rodney.

'That's really what I wanted to talk about,' said Sybil, laying down her knife and fork, and glancing over towards Professor Root. He bent lower over his lobster mayonnaise and, like

Rodney earlier, seemed to grow a little pink in the face. Or was it my imagination that both men seemed slightly embarrassed this evening?

'Arnold, will you speak?' she asked. 'Or shall I?'

'We have a piece of news,' said Professor Root, raising his head. 'A joyful one, as far as we are concerned, and we hope you will find it agreeable too. I am happy to tell you that Sybil has consented to be my wife.'

I can hardly describe how I felt on hearing this news. My first feeling was that I must have heard wrongly, my second that it was some outrageous joke. Sybil to be Professor Root's wife! But she was Rodney's mother and my mother-in-law — how could she ever be anything else?

'Wilmet is overcome,' said Sybil kindly. 'Perhaps she is also astonished and a little shocked to hear that two old people have decided to marry.'

'It's such a surprise,' I stammered.

'Yes, my dear, I thought it would be,' said Professor Root. 'But for many years I have had the deepest regard for your mother-in-law. Of late it has become so deep that we both felt —' he paused and made an expansive gesture with his lobster pick.

'But of course it's lovely news,' I said, pulling myself together. 'Nothing could have pleased me better.'

'After all, I might have brought disgrace on us all by marrying a man half my age,' said Sybil. 'The kind of thing that gets headlines in the lower daily papers.'

'Really, Mother, I can't imagine that you have ever had the opportunity of doing *that*,' said Rodney, smiling indulgently.

Sybil smiled mysteriously, for which I did not blame her. 'Arnold *is* eighteen months younger than I am, as it happens,' she said. 'I am sixty-nine and he is only sixty-seven. But we have the seventies before us, and perhaps even the eighties.'

'And you can go to Portugal for your honeymoon. Obviously you won't want Rodney and me to accompany you,' I said lightly, for I did not want to dwell too much on the honeymoon aspect, feeling that it might embarrass them. I imagined them going about quietly together looking at buildings, and in the evenings drinking wine in the open air and talking about the kind of abstract subjects they usually discussed when Professor Root came to the house.

'No, we shall let you have Portugal to yourselves this year,' said Rodney in a relieved tone. 'Wilmet and I will go to Cornwall. James and Hilary Cash go to a very good hotel near Penzance — I must get the address from James.'

My heart rather sank but I said nothing. 'When is the wedding to be?' I asked brightly.

'We thought some time in August. In a registrar's office, of course, with a quiet family luncheon afterwards,' said Sybil. 'It will be a rather sober affair, as is fitting.'

'I hope we need not take that too literally,' said Professor Root. 'The sobriety, I mean.'

'Oh no, we'll make it a jolly party,' said Rodney rather stiffly.

Sybil caught my eye and we began to laugh. I suddenly realized how much I should miss her if she left the house and went to live with Professor Root. But she would never do that — obviously we should all live here together. The only difference would be that Professor Root would be here always, instead of just rather often. But even as I was thinking these thoughts Rodney was saying something about changes and asking where they were going to live.

'I shall go on living here, of course,' said Sybil, 'in my own house. Arnold has been living at his club lately, as you know, and could not take a wife there. He will come here to me.'

'Not quite the usual thing, perhaps, but by no means unknown. Matrilocal or uxorilocal residence, they call it,' said Professor Root drily, 'where the husband goes to the wife's village — in certain tribes which follow the system of matriliny, that is.'

'In that case —' Rodney began.

222

'Yes, Noddy, I shall be turning you out. You and Wilmet will buy a house of your own. I think Wilmet will enjoy that.'

Rodney looked so dismayed that I couldn't help teasing him and saying lightly, 'Darling, is it so very dreadful, the prospect of living alone in a house with me?' But really I was a little dismayed myself. It had never occurred to me that Sybil and Professor Root would want the house to themselves.

Later that evening, when we were alone, Rodney began to talk in a rather gloomy way about Wembley, Ealing, Walton-on-Thames, Beckenham and other outlying parts of London. He dwelt in turn upon the horrors of the Central Line, the impossibility of getting to Waterloo or Charing Cross in the rush hour, the inaccessibility of London Bridge or Cannon Street from the Ministry.

'That Mother should do *this*,' he said. 'It's a most unnatural thing.'

'But you can't blame her,' I said. 'And after all it seems rather appropriate that Sybil should act in this way. I've always seen her as being rather like a character in Greek tragedy, doing some unnatural thing.'

For my part I had no intention of moving to any of the places Rodney had been talking about. I saw us settled in a nice little house or flat still within easy reach of St Luke's and the clergy house.

CHAPTER TWENTY

MARY had been anxious that I should go and see her at the retreat house as soon as she was settled there, and I was really glad to get away from the preparations for Sybil's wedding and Rodney's agonized speculations as to where we were going to live. The only thing settled was that we should go for a holiday in August, staying at the hotel in Cornwall which James and Hilary Cash had recommended. It seemed that Rodney had been extremely fortunate in getting accommodation there — only the mention of James's name had made it possible — and I foresaw that we should be carrying with us a burden of gratitude, having to exclaim continually about how lucky we had been.

I did not expect to see many clergy or obvious looking re-treatants on the bus, as I was going in the middle of the week and the retreats were usually held at weekends.

'There *is* a party of clergy coming on Saturday,' Mary said, when she met me at the bus stop in the village. 'Last weekend we had women — my first experience from the domestic side.'

'Were they troublesome?' I asked.

'Yes, one or two of them were a little. One had brought a Primus stove with her to make tea in her room, and it flared up and burnt the curtains; another left old bits of bread and cake in a drawer — so messy.'

'Poor Mary! It seems odd that their misdemeanours should be concerned with eating and drinking, though I suppose these things assume greater importance when you're supposed to be mortifying the flesh — the woman with the Primus stove had to have her tea, and the other couldn't exist without her extra bits of food.'

'There are gas rings in some of the rooms, and I could have given her a kettle, and if anyone wants extra food they've only to ask for it.'

'Perhaps they'd be ashamed to admit their weakness,' I suggested. 'But fancy having to take a Primus about with one — so awkward! Let's hope the clergy will be better.'

'There's no reason why they should be,' said Mary, 'they're only human after all. Marius told me that he once fused all the lights at a retreat by using his electric razor.'

'The clergy ought not to have such luxuries,' I said sternly. 'But I always imagined that you were one of those people who regard the clergy as being better than other beings.'

'Me?' Mary seemed surprised and smiled. 'Perhaps I was like that once, but I don't think I am any more. Such surprising things seem to happen.'

I wanted to pursue the subject further, but we had now reached the house and I felt bound to utter some exclamation of wonder or disbelief. As it happened it was disbelief, for it seemed hardly possible to imagine how this elaborate Victorian gothic building could have got itself put up in an unpretentious little village.

'It used to be the vicarage,' Mary explained, 'but of course it was too big, so the vicar before last built himself a kind of bungalow. Then the diocese took over the house, first as a home for unmarried mothers and then as a retreat house. Oh, and it was also a boys' prep school at some time, I can't remember exactly when.'

'It looks right for all the horrors of a school,' I said. 'Do you have enough domestic help?'

'Oh yes, we have a woman living in besides myself — she does most of the cooking — and women come in from the village to clean, and the sexton stokes the boiler and does the garden.'

'Do you like it here?' I asked.

'Yes. It's busy but very peaceful, though I still feel rather useless, as if the life were too pleasant to be a really good one.'

Mary's remark irritated me because it made me feel guilty myself; but I could understand that after her life of committees and parish work, and the tyranny of her mother, and then her stay in the convent, she might feel like this. Indeed, when I had been at the retreat house a day, I began to feel it myself. I tried to make myself useful but there was very little for me to do. The weather was glorious, but it seemed wanton to be lying in a deckchair in the mornings while Mary was arranging things for the coming retreat, so I took an upright canvas chair, or sat on a hard wooden seat of the kind that looks as if it might have been given in memory of someone. I half expected to see an inscription carved on the back. The only task Mary could find for me was to pick and shell some peas for lunch, and to put the pods on the compost heap under the apple trees at the bottom of the garden. Here, in a kind of greenish twilight, stood a pile of grass cuttings and garden rubbish, and as I added my pods to it I imagined all this richness decaying in the earth and new life springing out of it. Marvell's lines went jingling through my head.

> My vegetable love should grow
> Vaster than Empires and more slow ...

There seemed to be a pagan air about this part of the garden, as if Pan — I imagined him with Keith's face — might at any moment come peering through the leaves. The birds were tame and cheeky, and seemed larger than usual; they came bumping and swooping down, peering at me with their bright insolent eyes, their chirpings louder and more piercing than I had ever heard them. I wondered if people who came here for retreats ever penetrated to this part of the garden. I could imagine the unmarried mothers and the schoolboys here, but not those who were striving to have the right kind of thoughts. Then I noticed that beyond the apple trees there was a group of beehives, and I remembered the old saying about telling things to bees. It seemed that they might be regarded as a kind of primitive confessional.

I went slowly back to the lawn, but to a deckchair now; the hard wooden seat seemed out of keeping with my mood.

It was not until the evening of my second day there that Mary and I had a real heart to heart talk. We were in her bed-sitting-room after supper, and I had been telling her about Sybil's forthcoming marriage and what an upheaval it was going to make in our lives.

'Yes,' Mary said, 'marriage does do that, doesn't it? — and death, too, of course.'

'But not birth.'

'No — people seem to come more quietly into the world. It isn't until they've really become personalities that they make changes and upheavals.'

'I suppose I was surprised, and perhaps even a little shocked, that Sybil should think of marrying again,' I admitted.

'I think I should have felt that too. Yet it's nice for older people to marry, to be able to comfort each other in their old age. I think people do need help and comfort from others, you know.'

I remembered with a pang Piers saying that we were all, in a sense, colleagues in the grim business of getting through life. It seemed as if Mary was leading up to something — Marius Ransome, I supposed.

'Drinking coffee is supposed to keep one awake,' she said. 'Do you mind, Wilmet?'

'No, I'm not tired,' I said. 'I've done nothing all day.'

'I always used to wish I could have gone to college where people sat up half the night talking about life,' she said eagerly, 'but I suppose it's too late now.'

'What — to go to college?'

'I didn't mean that — I meant that people don't talk when they're older in the way they do when they're young.'

'I suppose not,' I said, feeling rather uncomfortable.

'Wilmet, I want to ask you something. Will you give me an honest answer?'

'Yes, of course, if I can,' I said, wondering as one does when challenged in this way whether it would be at all possible.

She clasped her hands round her coffee cup and looked down

at the tiles in the fireplace. I noticed that they had a curious pattern of bulrushes alternating with brownish-coloured irises.

'Do you think it wrong for a priest to marry?' she asked in a low voice.

'Do you mean as a general principle?' I asked, in order to gain time.

'Yes, I suppose I do.'

'Well, I don't see how it can be *wrong*,' I said. 'After all, there are a great many married priests.'

'Yes, there are, aren't there!' she said quickly. 'Though most of the ones I've known haven't been married. I mean, it would be unthinkable to have a married priest at St Luke's.'

'Father Thames probably wouldn't approve of it,' I laughed, 'but he's retiring in the autumn and I daresay Father Bode thinks on other lines.'

'But you couldn't have a married priest living at the clergy house,' Mary persisted. 'Surely the idea of a clergy house is that the priests should be celibate?'

'Yes, but don't you remember Father Thames saying that it was originally built as a vicarage, and that the first incumbent had lots of children?'

Mary smiled. 'You see, Wilmet, Marius has asked me to marry him — that's what I've really been wanting to tell you. Do you think it so very dreadful of him?'

I could hardly confess my first reaction to her news, which was the perhaps typically feminine one of astonishment that such a good looking man as Marius Ransome should want to marry anyone so dim and mousy as Mary Beamish. But as soon as I had pushed aside this unworthy thought I realized what a good wife she would make for a clergyman, especially one as unstable as Marius appeared to be. Mary was obviously just the person he needed to steady him, and the novelty and responsibility of marriage would surely take his mind off Rome.

'I think it would be a very good thing,' I said. 'Have you given him your answer, as they say?'

'Not in so many words,' Mary smiled, 'but I think he knows what it will be.'

'When did he propose to you?' I asked. 'There seems to have been so little opportunity — first of all you were with us, and then you came here —'

'Just before you arrived,' said Mary. 'He came down for the afternoon on his scooter.'

'On his scooter?' I echoed in amazement. 'But I didn't know he had one.'

'He suddenly bought it about a week ago. As a matter of fact, Mother left him a little legacy and I think he used some of that to buy it. It will be awfully useful for visiting and that kind of thing,' Mary added eagerly.

It seemed to me highly frivolous and unsuitable, but I could not help being amused after all his talk about being able to do good with money. Then I remembered that we had decided that five hundred pounds was perhaps only enough to do good to oneself. What with the scooter and Mary, I felt that he now had enough to keep his mind firmly on the good Anglican path.

'Did you fall in love with him that evening at the parish hall?' I asked. 'It would be wonderful to think that love could blossom in such surroundings.' I thought of the chipped Della Robbia plaques, the hissing of gas fires and tea urns and the curious smell of damp mackintoshes that seemed to pervade it, and perhaps all parish halls everywhere. Why, indeed, shouldn't love blossom here rather more than in conventional romantic surroundings?

'Not really,' said Mary. 'I never thought of myself as marrying. You see, I've never had any boy friends' — she brought out the words self-consciously. And what *does* one say, what word can one use, to describe what she meant? Lovers, admirers, suitors, followers — none seems to be quite right.

'I thought I might have a vocation for the religious life,' she went on, 'but I suppose I should have discovered that I hadn't even if I'd never met Marius.'

'I think it will be an excellent thing, and I hope you'll be very happy,' I said. 'I suppose Marius will get a living somewhere?'

'Yes, that would be best. Better than staying on at St Luke's, really. Of course he'll have to break the news to Father Thames when he gets back from Italy.'

That interview should be an interesting one, I thought. Perhaps Mr Bason would listen at the door and let out what he should not have heard. It was wrong of me, I know, but I hoped that he might do this.

'Goodness, Wilmet, do you know what time it is? Nearly two o'clock! And a clergy retreat coming tomorrow. I shall never be up in time to get things ready.'

We then went to bed, but I lay awake for rather a long time, either because of the coffee or my confused thoughts. It seemed as if life had been going on around me without my knowing it, in the disconcerting way that it sometimes does, like the traffic swirling past when one is standing on an island in the middle of the road. Sybil and Professor Root, Piers and Keith, Marius and Mary — the names *did* sound odd together — all doing things without, as it were, consulting me. And now Rodney and I would have to set up house on our own, a curious and rather disconcerting thought. I tried to remember our time in Italy, but all that came into my mind were curious irrelevant little pictures — a dish of tangerines with the leaves still on them; the immovable shape of Rodney's driver as we held hands in the back of some strange army vehicle on our way home from a dance; the dark secret face of a Neapolitan boy who used to come to stoke the fire in winter; then Keith's face peering through leaves, one hand resting lightly on the low bough of an orange tree; and a comfortable looking woman, using number 11 needles and commencing by casting on 64 stitches ...

I was woken by bright sunshine and Mary standing by my bed with a cup of tea.

'There's quite a lot to do,' she said, 'though they won't actually be arriving till the late afternoon.'

'Arriving?' Why, the priests for the retreat, of course. I was fully awake now and anxious to help, though it wasn't at all like preparing for ordinary guests. The small cell-like rooms needed no last minute feminine touches, the single rose in a glass on the dressing table or the glossy magazine by the bed. They didn't even, I imagined, need to be particularly clean. The coarse sheets and rough greyish blankets like the skins of donkeys *were* doubtless clean, but presumably the priests would not have noticed or complained had they not been.

When we had done all we could there seemed to be a little time to sit on the lawn in deckchairs, but Mary did not feel that she ought to be discovered thus and was ready to spring up as soon as the first sign of a clergyman should appear in the drive.

'Most of them will be here for tea, I imagine, won't they?' I asked. My own train back to London left just after five o'clock and I was to have my tea alone and secretly before going.

'Yes, I think that will be a good start for them, a cup of tea,' said Mary.

I began idly to plan a sort of retreat tea, with everything in dark colours; but the darkest, greyest food I could think of was caviare, which seemed unsuitable, so I got no further.

'One train should be in now,' said Mary, looking at her watch. 'I daresay most of them will come on this one.' She stood up and folded up her deckchair. 'I think I'll just go into the drive and see if they're coming.'

She left me, but I could no longer lie back and enjoy my laziness, so I put away my chair and began to stroll round the garden. I was walking among the vegetables when I suddenly saw an agitated figure gesticulating and running towards me. It was one of the village women who came in to help with the cleaning.

'Miss — Madam — come quickly!' she cried. 'The bees are swarming!'

'But what can *I* do?' I called out, looking around me helplessly. 'I don't know anything about bees. Isn't the gardener here?'

231

'Oh Madam, he's digging a grave!' came the agitated answer.

'Perhaps Miss Beamish will know what to do,' I suggested hopefully. 'She's gone down the drive to meet the priests.'

A sound like a snort — though perhaps it can hardly have been that — came from the woman, and we ran together down the drive. We had not gone very far before we saw Mary rounding a bend by some rhododendron bushes, accompanied by the priests. There seemed to be a great many of them carrying small suitcases and canvas holdalls.

'Mary,' I called, 'the bees are swarming! What does one do?'

'Goodness, I don't know! Isn't the gardener anywhere about?'

'Somebody will have to take the swarm, madam,' said the woman who had first told me about the bees. She glanced around her in a challenging manner.

At her words an elderly bent shabby priest, carrying a very old Gladstone bag, stepped forward out of the little throng surrounding Mary.

'I can do it,' he said quietly. 'Have you a veil and smoke gun? I am afraid I did not bring mine with me' — he indicated the Gladstone bag apologetically. 'I did not really expect — of course one *does* not, does one?' He smiled a sweet absent sort of smile, as if he really *ought* to have expected bees to swarm at a retreat. 'Perhaps you will show me where they are?'

So we all trooped down into the bottom of the garden to the part where the beehives stood. They had swarmed in the gnarled trunk of an old apple tree.

The elderly priest put on the hat and veil, and a pair of thick gloves, and started to manipulate the smoke gun.

'He is the conductor of the retreat,' Mary whispered to me, 'a very saintly old man.'

'Fancy his knowing about bees,' I said. 'I can imagine it might be a test of saintliness — certainly of patience.'

Standing there watching the old man, I amused myself by wondering how the St Luke's priests would have dealt with the situation. I could not see Father Thames or Father Ransome as being very efficient, but I felt that Father Bode might manage it.

'They must find the queen, that is the thing,' said one of the priests, 'then they will follow her to the hive.'

I saw him take out a little note book and jot something down. It pleased me to think that here in this pagan part of the garden he might have found an idea for a sermon.

CHAPTER TWENTY-ONE

IT was, one might say, a far cry from the garden of the retreat house and the saintly old priest taking the swarm of bees to the Cenerentola coffee bar, where Piers's friend Keith worked in the evenings. And yet, in a way, it was not such a very far cry. For the Cenerentola, with its dim lighting and luxuriant greenery, reminded me of that part of the garden where the compost heap stood in the mysterious green twilight under the apple trees, and where the bees had swarmed. I was not prepared to go further with the analogy, or even quite as far as this comparison might suggest. The people sitting or standing around us were all in the fresh bloom of youth; they were the young people one saw and read about but seldom met. They made a person who was only ten or so years older feel very old indeed.

'Good heavens,' said Rodney in a low voice, 'this *is* life, isn't it! I always felt we should perhaps get out and about more, but I hadn't realized *quite* how out of touch we were.'

Sybil and Professor Root had been married that morning at Caxton Hall, a simple pagan ceremony not without its own dignity and beauty. After the quiet family luncheon, which had consisted of ourselves and Professor Root's sister Dorothy, the newly married couple had taken a plane to Lisbon — Sybil armed with her Portuguese grammar and Arnold with a sheaf of introductions to professors in Lisbon and Coimbra. Piers had given them letters to some of his friends, who would be able to take them to places that the learned professors might not care to visit, as he put it.

After they had gone, and the effects of the champagne had worn off, Rodney and I had hung about aimlessly until it was time to go to the theatre to see a fashionable gloomy play; after which I, feeling in need of amusement and cheering up, had suggested a visit to Keith's coffee bar.

'I suppose all this keeps young people from doing worse things,' said Rodney, brushing aside a trail of greenery as we squeezed ourselves into two vacant places.

I looked eagerly for Keith and soon caught sight of him, his dark eyes peering, as in my imagination, through a screen of leaves. He was wearing a tangerine-coloured shirt and looked very animated. On seeing us he let out a little squeak of pleasure.

'Ooh, Wilmet, how lovely!'

I introduced Rodney, and Keith hurried away to get us some coffee.

Rodney began to laugh. 'So *that* is Piers's "colleague"! Now I can see what Mother meant. Is Piers himself here this evening? Perhaps he's helping behind the scenes with the washing up.'

'Is Piers here?' I asked, when Keith brought the coffee.

'He's just come in now,' said Keith. 'Look — in the doorway by that lady in the lemon jumper. Shall I make room for him at your table? I expect he'd like to sit with you,' he said cosily. 'I'll fetch another chair.'

I looked over to where Piers was standing, a little older and more careworn than most of the young people around him but so much more distinguished and interesting. The sight of him gave me a pang, the very slightest twinge of pain around the heart.

'Hullo, Piers,' I said. 'Do come and sit with us.'

'Gloomy, isn't it,' he said, 'sitting drinking non-alcoholic beverages with people of a younger generation. There's really nothing for people of our age but the pubs, and they're closed now.'

'Yes,' said Rodney, looking at his watch in an academic sort of way, 'I suppose they must be.'

'Keith seems to be very busy,' I remarked. 'It must be rather tiring work.'

'He loves fussing round after people. His energy is too exhausting — for other people, I mean. When I got home this evening, I found that he'd scrubbed the kitchen floor and washed all the drying-up cloths, and everything else he could lay hands on.'

'Yes, I boiled them in Tide,' said Keith in a satisfied tone. 'Now, Wilmet, would you like something to eat? We have some very nice sandwiches, or would you prefer a pastry? Danish pastries, we call them.'

I was just hesitating before making up my mind when Rodney clutched me by the arm.

'Oh my God, do you see who's standing in the doorway now?' he muttered.

I looked and saw Mr Bason, his egg-face beaming, casting around for a vacant seat or a person on whom he could fasten himself for a chat. It was inevitable that he should see us, and I waited for the raising of the eyebrows and the surprised look of recognition as he made his way over to where we were sitting.

Rodney groaned.

'Ooh,' said Keith, bringing up another chair, '*everybody* seems to be here tonight. Hullo, Wilf! I wondered what had happened to you — you're later than usual.'

Mr Bason hit Keith playfully on the side of the head with his rolled-up evening paper.

'So you two know each other,' I said, rather taken aback at hearing Mr Bason addressed as 'Wilf'.

'Oh yes, Wilf's a regular,' said Keith. 'He keeps house for a lot of clergymen.'

'Yes, I know,' I said, thinking how odd it was that all the time I had been wondering about Piers's domestic life such an unlikely person as Mr Bason could probably have told me all about it.

'One gets a really good cup of coffee here,' said Mr Bason confidentially, 'almost as good as I make myself.'

'I should think so indeed,' said Keith cheekily. 'Isn't it nice, you all knowing each other. Now you'll be able to have a nice chat.'

'Yes, I think we shall,' I said, for I could see that Mr Bason had a kind of secret bursting look about him, as if he had something to tell and could hardly wait to get it out. Here in the Cenerentola, its hissing coffee machine tended by two handsome young men who seemed as devout as any acolytes, it would not be inappropriate to speak of church and clergy house matters.

'I suppose Father Thames will be back any day now,' I began.

'Oh, he came this afternoon — quite bronzed, he was, and things going *very* well at the villa. He's having an extra bathroom put in, with a bath of Carrara marble — quite an elaborate thing, I gather. He was full of it! It seemed a shame that Ransome had to spring *his* bit of news on him the first evening he was back.' Mr Bason paused and took a sip of coffee.

If he had expected any response from Rodney or Piers he must have been disappointed, and he could not have been very pleased when I said, 'You mean the news of his engagement to Miss Beamish?'

'So you knew then?' The egg-face fell.

'Yes, I've been staying with Miss Beamish and she told me about it.'

'Well, you can imagine what a shock it was to *us* at the clergy house.'

'I suppose it was.'

'*We* had hardly envisaged such a thing,' said Mr Bason grandly. 'Celibacy of the clergy has always been *our* motto.'

I heard Piers utter a stifled sound, and his eyes met mine for a moment in agonized amusement.

'But why shouldn't Father Ransome marry Mary Beamish?' asked Rodney in a casual layman's tone. 'I should think it will be a very good thing for both of them.'

'Ah, my dear Forsyth,' said Mr Bason. 'You don't quite get the point, if I may say so.' And then, having dismissed Rodney, he went on, 'The way Ransome broke it to him — casually, before dinner, and with the door wide open!'

This sounded promising.

'I suppose Father Ransome took the first opportunity he could find,' said Piers. 'No doubt he wanted to get it over — one knows the feeling so well.'

'Yes,' I agreed, imagining him rehearsing the interview, going over his opening sentence like an actor practising an entrance. 'What did he say?'

'That is perhaps hardly for me to let out here and now, in such a place as this,' said Mr Bason, glancing around him at the absorbed groups of young people glimpsed dimly through the greenery.

'I don't see why not,' said Rodney smoothly.

'You could give us the general gist of the conversation,' said Piers, 'though such accounts are usually improved by an imaginative retelling.'

'Oh, there will be no necessity for *that*, I can assure you!' said Mr Bason, his voice becoming shrill with indignation. 'I heard every word, as I could hardly have failed to. Father Thames likes his glass of Tio Pepe before dinner — as who does not? And I was about to take the decanter in to him, having cleaned it — not *washed* it, I hasten to add — during his holiday, when I became aware of voices coming through the open door of the study.'

'Whereupon you became rooted to the spot, as one naturally would,' Rodney suggested.

'Well, I could hardly move, could I, or my presence would have become known and general embarrassment would have ensued. I *had* to stand there outside the door with the decanter in my hand. Ransome must have slipped into the room without my realizing it, for the first thing I heard was his voice saying, "Father, I feel I ought to tell you that I have decided to get married." Father Thames is a little deaf in the right ear, you know, and Ransome's tone was of such a loudness that I judged him to be standing on Father Thames's right. "Married, did you say?" Father Thames repeated. "Yes," said Ransome. Then there was silence for a minute, during which Father Thames must have made some gesture of surprise or disgust, for he then said, "Well, Ransome, this *is* a shock, I must say. No sooner is my back turned than this happens. It is really *too* bad. First it was the South India business and doubts about the validity of Anglican Orders, and now *this*. Oh, it is *too* bad, *too* bad." ' Mr Bason paused and waited as if for applause.

I felt he had been rather overacting the part of Father Thames, though I could believe that the conversation had in general been faithfully reported.

'I could tell that Father Thames was upset,' Mr Bason went on, 'and when Ransome told him that it was Miss Beamish he was going to marry, he said, "I blame myself for this. Had I been able to have you to live here at the clergy house, this would never have happened." '

'There's some truth in that,' I said. 'Poor Father Ransome was rather pushed about, wasn't he? First living at the Beamishes, then with his friend Father Sainsbury, and now in the guest room at the clergy house.'

'But surely,' said Rodney, 'if people are going to marry, they will. He would have met Mary Beamish, anyway, in the course of his work.'

'I suppose so,' said Mr Bason. 'But one does feel it is letting the side down, to use a slang expression.'

'How did the interview end?' I asked.

'Unfortunately just at that moment I heard Bode coming downstairs so I had to move, though it was extremely awkward. I shouldn't have liked Father Thames to feel that I'd been listening at the door. So I didn't hear the end. But the atmosphere at dinner was a little strained. Bode was gassing away about parish matters — oh, the most trivial things, hiring a coach for the social club outing to Runnymede, and getting the piano in the church hall tuned, or something — I don't believe any of them noticed what they were eating.'

'What had you given them, Wilf?' asked a flat little voice, and I realized that Keith had come back to our table.

'Eggs in aspic and a dish of lasagne verde — in compliment to

Father Thames's Italian holiday, you know — but I might just as well not have bothered.'

'What a shame,' I said.

'I'm not staying there when Father Thames goes, I can tell you,' said Mr Bason indignantly. 'Bode can have Mrs G. back and welcome to her — tea after every meal with two spoons of sugar in it, except in Lent. It's a real penance for *him* to give up sugar, I can tell you.'

'Then it seems a praiseworthy thing to do,' said Rodney evenly. 'I suppose you'll be looking for another job, then?'

'Yes, and I think I've found it,' said Mr Bason. 'Antique shop in Devon that does teas as well in the season. I'm going down there at the end of the month.'

'You'll find it ever so tiring being on your feet all day, won't you, Wilf?' asked Keith. 'I'm just about worn out now, I don't mind telling you, and I haven't got your corns.'

'I'm not sure that I shall be doing *that* kind of work,' said Mr Bason grandly, ignoring the reference to corns. 'I see myself more on the antique side.'

'You will be surrounded by beautiful things,' said Rodney, with a sideways glance at me, 'which is just what you like, isn't it?'

'Let's hope they really *will* be beautiful,' said Piers. 'So many antique shops seem to have nothing but junk in them these days, especially in seaside towns.'

'Oh, this is a most reputable and old-established business,' said Mr Bason. 'They tell me that Queen Mary often used to pop in — in the old days, of course.'

'That does sound reassuring,' I said. 'Any connection with royalty is that, don't you think?'

'With *our* royal family certainly,' Mr Bason agreed, 'though some one could mention wouldn't inspire quite the same confidence.'

'Will your mother be joining you?' I asked.

'No, Mother prefers to stay in Harrogate, and of course it's useful for me to have a pied à terre up there.'

'Well, Bason, you do seem to have fallen on your feet as far as jobs go,' said Rodney. 'How did you hear of this one.'

'An advert in the *Church Times*. One does feel that if one sees something *there* it will be all right, and so it has proved to be. Very convenient all round — A.-C. Church two minutes,' he added chirpily. 'Reservation.'

'Ooh, I *am* tired,' said Keith petulantly.

'If you've finished we can go home,' said Piers, looking up at him.

'Do we leave him a tip?' Rodney whispered to me.

'I don't see why not,' I said. 'I suppose we should be going home now.' I turned to Piers. 'You must come and see us some time,' I said lamely.

'He's generally here in the evenings nowadays,' said Keith rather bossily. 'So you must pop in and have a chat.'

I could not quite see myself doing that, but perhaps at this time of night and after the exhausting day we had had I could not imagine myself doing anything.

'And I'm going to help you choose curtain materials,' said Keith, 'don't forget?'

'No, of course I won't,' I said.

It seemed impossible to avoid giving Mr Bason a lift in our taxi, and he made us promise to call and see him should we be anywhere near his antique teashop on our holiday.

'We can easily be not all that near,' said Rodney, after he had left us. 'I should think it will be impossible to turn off from the stream of holiday traffic — you know how it is.'

I looked at the closed door of the clergy house and imagined Mr Bason creeping quietly up the stairs, perhaps pausing outside doors to listen for a moment. I wondered if any of the clergy would still be up at this late hour, praying or meditating, or just lying awake reading a thriller. It was not the kind of thing one could expect to know.

The next morning I met Father Ransome in the square. It was the first time I had seen him alone since Mary had told me the

news of their engagement, so I hastened to offer him my con-
gratulations and best wishes.

He thanked me and sighed heavily.

'But *what* a business it's been,' he said wearily. 'Father Thames
took it badly, as I feared he might.'

I said that I was sorry to hear it.

'It was a difficult interview, and to make matters worse I knew
that Bason was listening outside the door. I hadn't anticipated
an audience so I didn't really do myself justice. Still, it's all
settled now.'

I began to wonder, as one so often does, whether in spite of
his being a clergyman he was really good enough for Mary, but
I could hardly ask that question in so many words.

'You're very lucky,' I said. 'Mary is such a splendid person.'

'Yes, isn't she,' he agreed. 'She'll be able to do so much for
me. And of course we have both been bruised by life, as it
were.'

'Have you?' I asked doubtfully, for I couldn't quite see that
this applied to him, unless he had suffered more from his doubts
and uncertainties than I had given him credit for.

'We all have been, come to that, haven't we?' he said rather
lamely.

'That's what life does, of course — bruises one,' I said, thinking
of Piers. 'One shouldn't assume that one has a monopoly of
suffering.

        Rolled round in earth's diurnal course
        With rocks and stones and trees ...'

'I shouldn't have thought that of *you*,' he began almost accusingly.

'All right then,' I said, beginning to laugh.

'Of course it's a bit embarrassing, Mary being rather well off,'
he said.

'But just think of all the good you'll be able to do with the
money,' I said quickly.

'Yes, we shall, shan't we?' he said thankfully. 'Money need not always be an embarrassment.'

'When you have a parish of your own you'll need a car,' I said. 'A scooter is all very well for a curate to go visiting on, but a vicar should be more dignified.'

'People have been so kind,' he said. 'Do you know, Coleman even offered to lend me his Husky for the honeymoon?'

'Could you accept such an offer?' I asked.

'I suppose not, in the end. It will be like Abraham and Isaac. I could not ask that sacrifice of our good friend Bill. I think we shall buy a car quite soon. Of course the wedding will be *very* quiet.'

I reflected that the marriage of two people who had almost taken vows of celibacy, as it were, ought not to be a riotous affair, but I managed not to say so.

CHAPTER TWENTY-TWO

'I SUPPOSE this must be it?' I said, leaning out of the car window. 'It's definitely an antique shop, and I can see people sitting at tables inside.'

'I can't park *here*,' said Rodney, in the irritable, slightly agitated tone common to motorists in England in the holiday season. 'You'd better get out quickly and I'll join you when I've found somewhere to put the car.'

I went in through the low door, and sat down at a small round table in a corner filled with lustre jugs and horse brasses. I noticed that the walls were hung with old prints and engravings, framed in a contemporary style with white frames and coloured mounts; warming-pans, fire-dogs, toby jugs, ships in bottles and other objects of antique and tourist interest were displayed on shelves. I wondered what it was that Queen Mary had often popped in for, or if she had perhaps bought all the better pieces — for such furniture as I saw was not noticeably good.

The other tables were nearly all filled, but the occupants appeared to be talking in whispers as if ashamed of their conversation; and they may have had cause to be, for some were giggling in a rather unseemly way.

'Should we leave him a tip, do you think?' I heard one woman ask another.

'I suppose so,' tittered her companion, 'though they might have a box for staff gratuities somewhere — quite a lot of places do now.'

I thought that they were probably talking about Mr Bason, though it was quite likely that all the staff had that rather superior manner which makes one hesitate to leave a little heap of pennies or a sixpence under the plate. I waited with some curiosity for him to appear, which he did very soon from behind a Jacobean chintz curtain, carrying a tray of tea. He did not see me immediately, so I was able to get over the first shock of his appearance and compose my features before greeting him. He had grown a beard — egg-shaped, I suppose one might have called it, to match his face — and was wearing a loose blue smock, corduroy trousers and sandals.

When he saw me and Rodney, who had now joined me, he gave a cry of recognition and pleasure.

'Wilmet and Rodney — but this is *delightful*!'

Now we really have got down to Christian names, I thought, and wondered when I should dare to utter the first 'Wilfred' or even 'Wilf'.

'Now what can I get you?' he asked.

'Oh, just tea, thank you,' I said.

'Ah, but *which* tea? Shrimp, Lobster, Crab, Devonshire, Carlton or Plain, though I hope you won't want *that*.'

'Carlton sounds interesting,' I said. 'What is it?'

'Pot of tea, China or Indian, scones, jam and cream, lobster salad and fruit — but the fruit is tinned,' he added in a low voice.

'I think that sounds rather too substantial for us,' said Rodney doubtfully. 'Could we have a plain lobster tea?'

'You would be difficult! We don't really have a *plain* lobster tea, but seeing that it's *you* ...' he slithered off in his flapping sandals, but was soon back again with our tea.

'They made me dress up like this,' he said, indicating his costume. 'It adds a novelty touch, doesn't it, and people do seem to be attracted by something unusual.'

'Was the beard your own idea?' I asked.

'Yes, it was, really. I thought my face just needed something, and a beard did seem to provide the finishing touch, as it were.'

'Splendid!' said Rodney heartily, his hand going up to his own beardless chin. 'And you like the work here?'

'Oh, *immensely*!'

'You've got some nice things,' I said, picking up a pink and gold lustre jug from the shelf behind our table.

'Would you like that?' asked Mr Bason enthusiastically.

'Well, it's probably rather expensive, isn't it?'

'But I should like you to have it as a present from me,' said Mr Bason, pressing the jug into my hands. 'It is so very much *you*, I feel.'

I threw a doubtful and perhaps appealing glance towards Rodney, who tactfully drew out his notecase and said calmly, 'That's very kind of you, Bason, but you'll never make a living if you're going to be so generous. I should like to buy it for Wilmet — I insist.'

'Well, perhaps that *is* a husband's privilege,' Mr Bason agreed. 'Now *do* tell me about those poor things at the clergy house. I suppose Mrs Greenhill's back there now?'

'Yes, she agreed to go back — mainly because she's so devoted to Father Bode. And of course when Father Thames retires in October she'll have him all to herself, until another priest comes, I suppose.'

'The poor things,' Mr Bason sighed. 'Cod on Fridays, and those *endless* cups of tea.'

'I met Mrs Greenhill the Friday before we came away and couldn't resist asking her what she was giving them, and of course it *was* cod! I couldn't help feeling a little sad, remembering scampi and all the lovely things they had when you were there.'

'*Remembering Scampi*,' said Rodney thoughtfully. 'Surely that ought to be the title of a novel?'

'Yes,' I agreed, 'though it might be a little too esoteric for a book about a clergy house. People would never guess, would they? *Cod on Fridays* would be too obvious, on the other hand.'

'And you are to live even nearer to the clergy house now, I hear,' Mr Bason went on.

'How did you know?' I asked.

'Oh, I heard,' said Mr Bason airily, and went away to give the bill to a tableful of ladies who had been trying to attract his attention for some time.

'I suppose he would always know things that one thought were known only to oneself,' said Rodney, 'but in this case it doesn't really matter.'

Our search for somewhere to live seemed to have brought us closer together than we had been for years, though it had taken us a long time to decide whether it was to be a house or flat, and in town or suburban country. After visiting Mary at the retreat house I had had a hankering for the country, the dim compost heap under the apple trees and the drama of bees swarming at unexpected times. But Rodney could see only the winter mornings, struggling to the Ministry in gumboots over two ploughed fields, wearing a duffle coat with his bowler hat — an abomination, he thought. Then there had been the tempting advertisements — self-contained wings of Georgian rectories in Wiltshire or Hampshire, suburban residences in favoured positions, with tiled cloakrooms and double garages. I think I must have invented the one which advertised 'disused clergy house — would convert' — so unlikely does it seem now.

In the end we had done something safe and dull, and bought the lease of a flat a stone's throw from Sybil's house and a good hundred yards nearer the clergy house than we had been before. I had enjoyed choosing carpets and curtains, and had found Keith a tireless, and sometimes rather tiring, companion. 'Wilmet, *I* like the lime green. It goes well with antique furniture — sets it off, doesn't it? These chairs are old-fashioned in a way, but they're nice — would you say they were antique?...' I smiled as I remembered him chattering away, at once comic, boring and cosy. I had really grown quite fond of him.

'Why, if you had a telescope you could see into the clergy house windows,' said Mr Bason, as we parted at the door of the antique teashop.

'One feels there will be less to see now,' I said a little sadly.

'Don't you believe it,' said Mr Bason confidently. 'Dash it, there's another customer — bye-bye!'

'*He* seems all right,' said Rodney with a sigh, as we walked through the narrow streets to the rather distant place where he had parked the car.

We drove soberly to the Trust House where we had arrranged to stay the night, for we were on our way home now. Dinner was a rather silent meal in the great dining-room with its tall windows looking out on to the rainswept main street.

'Portugal might have been better than this,' said Rodney. 'Next year, perhaps.... Or even Italy — how would you like that?'

'I think I should like it very much,' I said. 'It would be better to go to the parts we don't already know. After ten years they might be too sad.'

'Like these little pictures,' said Rodney, for we had discovered a little lounge upstairs which nobody else seemed to know about, whose walls were hung with delicate nineteenth-century water-colours of Neapolitan scenes — Posillipo, Vesuvius, Pompeii and Pozzuoli.

'How did these come to be here?' he asked.

'Somebody's aunt did them, or perhaps they were bought in a lot at some country house sale and regarded as being suitable decorations for a hotel lounge,' I suggested.

'In the damp gloom of the west country the traveller is reminded that there is sunshine somewhere,' said Rodney. 'And how very different this is from Posillipo!'

'Yes. Do you remember the funny guide book we found — ' "the Via de Posillipo, recently ampliated"?'

'Of course, and the name meaning "pause of every sorrow".'

'And the caves in the Via Chiatamone where some citizens went for pastimes that ended in scandal,' I laughed.

Rodney sighed. 'Those were good days, weren't they?' he said. 'Perhaps better than we shall ever know again.'

'Well, we were young then. But life is supposed to get better as one grows older — even married life,' I added, not consciously cynical.

'Wilmet, I'm afraid it may not have been like that for you this

248

last year or two. I've often wondered ...' Rodney hesitated and looked down intently at the patience which I had laid out on the table. 'This summer particularly,' he went on.

I could feel embarrassment creeping over me, and I wondered what he was going to say next. Could it be that he had noticed something of my ridiculous so quickly nipped in the bud infatuation for Piers and was going to have it out with me? Nervously I took a card from one of my long lines, only to find that the intricate move I had planned was now blocked by another card I had failed to notice.

'This summer?' I asked, to gain time.

'Yes. Do you remember hearing me talk about a woman principal in our department?'

'Yes — with cotton stockings,' I laughed quickly, with a mixture of relief and curiosity as to what could be coming next.

'I believe I did mention Eleanor's cotton stockings,' Rodney smiled, 'rather unkind of me, really. But do you also remember that she had a friend?'

'Even a woman civil servant can have a friend,' I mocked. 'What's so remarkable about that?'

'Don't you remember my telling you that I had met her?'

'Oh yes, Miss Bates — I remember now. And her christian name was Patience.'

'No — Prudence, actually,' said Rodney. 'I took her out to dinner once or twice,' he added casually. 'That evening when you heard about Bason stealing the Fabergé egg, and another time later on when Mary Beamish came to stay.'

My hands stopped moving the cards about. So he had taken Miss Bates out to dinner. At the time when I had been occupied with foolish thoughts of Piers, my husband had been taking the attractive friend of a woman civil servant out to dinner.

'I see,' I said stiffly.

'Darling, it was no more than that,' said Rodney, his manner becoming almost agitated. 'I can't think why I didn't tell you at the time — it was stupid of me.'

'It doesn't matter,' I said. 'Why should you have told me? After all, I've had lunch with Harry and Piers several times, but I doubt if I've always remembered to tell you.'

'Lunch, yes. But dinner *is* rather different somehow.'

'Well, if you insist, perhaps it is. Was she nice, Miss Bates?'

'In a way. The funny thing is she reminded me of you. Sitting there on that little Regency sofa thing, rather cool and distant —'

'Where was the Regency sofa? In her flat?'

'Yes. She has a nice little place near Regent's Park,' said Rodney seriously.

'How uncomfortable,' I said coolly.

'Regency furniture isn't exactly cosy.' Rodney's mouth began to twitch, and suddenly we had both dissolved into helpless laughter, so that an elderly woman coming into the lounge to retrieve the knitting she had left there before dinner, retreated quickly and with a look of alarm on her face.

'What a funny place to choose to tell me such a thing,' I said weakly. 'And I have told you about Harry and Piers, so now all is revealed.'

But after I had stopped laughing I began to think that perhaps it wasn't so funny after all. I had always regarded Rodney as the kind of man who would never look at another woman. The fact that he could — and had indeed done so — ought to teach me something about myself, even if I was not yet quite sure what it was.

CHAPTER TWENTY-THREE

'ARE you robing, Father?' I heard one clergyman ask another, as we filed into the suburban church where Marius Lovejoy Ransome was to be instituted and inducted as vicar that afternoon.

'Rather!' came the enthusiastic answer from his colleague. And saw that they were both carrying small suitcases, from which I imagined crushed cottas being taken out.

There were rather a lot of us, for two coachloads of friends and wellwishers had come from St Luke's, as well as Mr Coleman's Husky-full; and we began to fill up the front of the church, conscious that we were usurping the places of many of he regular members of the congregation but not worrying overmuch about it. Indeed, shortly after I had taken my place beside Miss Prideaux, and was kneeling to say a prayer, I became aware of a little whispering group at the end of the row, and when I at up two ladies squeezed their way past us and then sat looking around them suspiciously, like animals in unfamiliar surroundings.

'I do love an induction,' whispered Miss Prideaux, as sentimentally as if she were talking of a wedding. 'And Father Ransome's *first* parish, too — such a *great* occasion.'

'Yes, let's hope he stays here a long time,' I said. Then wondered if I should have said that, for it was not after all quite like a wedding, in which one hopes that the parties will stay together for many years, even for ever.

The church was not beautiful, but I was glad to detect a faint smell of incense in it. I began studying the rows of clergy already seated and trying to pick out any that I knew. I wondered if Marius's poor friend Edwin Sainsbury, now a shabby Roman Catholic layman no doubt, was hidden away somewhere at the back of the church — or would he not be allowed to attend such a service? It would be bitter for him to watch his friend, all doubts now resolved, being inducted into this flourishing suburban parish with its comfortable looking modern vicarage and endless 'opportunities', as the religious papers called them. I could not see him anywhere, and then I remembered that he might still be tramping on Exmoor, thinking things out in the autumnal mists.

I noticed Mary sitting quite near us, looking already like a vicar's wife in her grey coat and rather too sensible hat. I had decided that the occasion called for something a little gay, and was wearing an emerald green feather cap with my black suit.

'Look!' Miss Prideaux plucked at my elbow. 'They're bringing him in.'

'The churchwardens shall conduct the Vicar-Designate to a seat in the Nave, near to the entrance to the Chancel,' I read in my service paper; and Marius, looking very handsome and serious, came in, towering over the two rather dumpy churchwardens who led him to his seat. Then we began to sing a psalm, and the Bishop and more clergy came in. When we reached the stage where the new vicar was led to various parts of the church and promised to do all kinds of things, the Lord being his helper, I found myself wondering whether Marius would not find it all rather too exhausting. But perhaps with a good wife and a comfortable home, not forgetting the embarrassment of old Mrs Beamish's money, he would struggle through somehow.

The Bishop's address was short and to the point. He told his congregation that last week he had inducted a priest as vicar of a very beautiful old church in the diocese. The church we were in this afternoon was not beautiful, but we must not think that beauty was everything. It was not *nothing* — he certainly would not go so far as to say that — but it was not so very much, not nearly so important as people imagined.

At this point my thoughts wandered, and I found myself thinking that Marius's looks made up for the shortcomings of the church; though the Bishop could hardly make this point, it might well be that it was not lost on the congregation.

Soon we were singing very heartily the hymn 'The Church of

God a kingdom is', and then the service was over and we were moving with politely controlled impatience to the hall where tea was to be served.

Mary came running up to me through the crowds, full of her usual eagerness and enthusiasm.

'Wilmet, how lovely to see you! I'm so glad you were able to come. And so many of our friends from St Luke's, too. Two coachloads. We never imagined ...'

'How pleased Father Thames looks,' I said, 'in spite of everything. He must see that it was all for the best.'

'Yes, I think he has come round to the idea of Marius being married. He sent us a very pretty piece of china as a wedding present — Dresden or something, you know, like those bits he has in his study.'

'Did your furniture come out of the depository all right?' I asked.

'Yes, of course — everything was in excellent condition.'

'I suppose it would be,' I said thoughtfully, for I was remembering my walk past the depository with Piers, and our wild imaginings — the dramatic decay, the baroque horror of it all. It would not be like that in reality, and perhaps it was just as well.

'And you're really happy?' I asked Mary, unnecessarily, for her face was radiant.

'Oh Wilmet, life is perfect now! I've everything that I could possibly want. I keep thinking that it's like a glass of blessings — life, I mean,' she smiled.

'That comes from a poem by George Herbert, doesn't it?' I said.

> 'When God at first made man,
>   Having a glass of blessings standing by ...'

'But don't forget that other line,' said Marius's charming languid voice, 'how, when all the other blessings had been bestowed, rest lay in the bottom of the glass. That's so very appropriate for a harassed suburban vicar. *What* an afternoon! I'm simply exhausted.'

'I like to think of you as a harassed suburban vicar,' I mocked. 'And you'll have to read the Thirty-Nine Articles on Sunday, won't you?' I added unkindly.

'Goodness, yes. I suppose there's no escaping it. I wonder if my voice will hold out?'

'I think you can divide them between morning and evening, can't you?' said Mary practically. 'Ah, tea is coming. How lovely!'

A beaming woman, wearing pince-nez and a rather unusual hat trimmed with fur animals' tails, came up to us with a tray of tea. I saw Mrs Greenhill, who had also been given a cup, tasting it suspiciously, either fearing it might be poisoned or merely comparing it with her own brew.

'*Not* Lapsang, I'm afraid, or even Earl Grey,' said Marius in a low voice. 'But luckily, unlike Father Thames, I am able to *take* Indian tea. Did he ever tell you that? Over forty years a priest and not able to take Indian tea!'

'Yes, indeed he did,' I began. But seeing that the new vicar and his wife were being approached by a rather important looking lady in a purple hat and musquash cape, I tactfully moved away and found myself beside Mr Coleman who, in spite of our shared experience of the Fabergé egg, I still found difficult to talk to.

'What did you think of the church?' I asked hopefully.

'Quite nice, Mrs Forsyth,' he said. 'I was agreeably surprised, really. Rather cramped for a High Mass, but I daresay they manage all right with a bit of manoeuvring. I was just talking to the M.C. here.'

'I suppose you were able to compare notes.'

'Yes, and he told me a piece of news.'

'A piece of news?'

'Apparently they've discovered fungus on the wall in the choir vestry,' Mr Coleman's blue eyes gleamed.

'Fungus?' I said uncertainly. 'You mean toadstools and that sort of thing?'

'Yes, that's it. Of course it's very interesting. It's nearly always a sign of dry rot.'

'Oh dear,' I said conventionally. And then it occurred to m͏
that here was something for Marius to tackle, and a use for some
of Mrs Beamish's money. It would make a man of him, as they
said.

'Fascinating thing, dry rot,' continued Mr Coleman.

I wondered if he made a hobby of its study, so enthusiastic
did he seem. How full his life must be!

'It *is* Mrs Forsyth, isn't it?' said a rather booming man's voice,
and I turned to see a tall man in an expensive looking overcoat
at my side. I recognized him as one of Mary's brothers, the one
who had run after me on that January afternoon of Mrs Beamish's
funeral and tried to make me persuade Mary not to enter the
convent.

'This is a *very* different occasion from the last one on which
we met,' he went on.

'It's a much pleasanter one,' I agreed. 'It looks a very friendly
parish, and I'm sure Mary and Marius are going to be very happy
here.'

'So I was right after all,' chuckled Gerald Beamish, 'and they
talk about *woman's* intuition! It didn't take *me* long to see which
way the wind was blowing. Mary was keen on this fellow, but
he had ideas about celibacy and all that kind of thing, as these
young parsons sometimes do have; so off she goes into a convent
and he very soon realizes he's missed the boat. Quite a clever
move of Mary's that—I'd never have thought her capable of
such cunning. It only shows we should never underestimate
women, doesn't it?'

'Men should never do that,' I agreed. 'But of course that
wasn't the reason why Mary went into the convent. She was
really convinced that it was the best life for her.'

'But a good looking husband's even better, eh?' he chuckled,
stuffing a last bit of cake into his mouth. 'Well, I've had enough
of this bun fight now—only came to see Mary, really—family
support and all that, you know. I suppose one can slip away
quite easily?'

Oh, yes, I think so,' I said. 'I shall have to stay a little longer ᵉcause we all came from St Luke's in a coach.'

Soon after this the party — for I suppose that was what it was — began to break up. I said goodbye to Mary and she asked me to go over to tea one day the following week. She and Marius came out into the road as we took our places in the coach, and waved to us as we started off on what seemed the long journey back through tree-lined suburban roads, past ugly new-looking shops and little houses, the sight of which filled me with despair. Ahead of us Mr Coleman's grey Husky shot like an arrow from a bow and had soon left us far behind.

'Quite a nice tea,' I heard Mrs Greenhill say to her friend Mrs Spooner.

'Yes; they've not got much in the way of conveniences in that church hall, though,' said Mrs Spooner. 'No proper sink, really, or I didn't see one.'

'How do they manage the washing up then?' asked Mrs Green-hill. 'That must be awkward, with no proper sink.'

Here was another use for Mrs Beamish's money, I thought. Soon, what with the car and the dry rot and the sink, there would be none left, and Mary and Marius would be suitably poor.

But Mary would be happy whether they had money or not. I turned over in my mind her description of life as being a glass of blessings, and that naturally led me to think about myself. I had as much as Mary had — there was no reason why my own life should not be a glass of blessings too. Perhaps it always had been without my realizing it.

The coach drew up outside St Luke's church hall.

'Well well,' said Father Bode, smiling his toothy smile. 'All very satisfactory, I think. Ransome should do well there.'

I turned into the street where our new flat was, and where I knew Rodney would be waiting for me. We were to have dinner with Sybil and Arnold that evening. It seemed a happy and suitable ending to a good day.

256

ABOUT THE AUTHOR

A writer from the age of sixteen, Barbara Pym made a substantial reputation for herself from 1950 to 1961 as an author of graceful comedies about the British middle classes. She was rediscovered in England in 1977, when she was named the most underrated writer of the century and *Quartet in Autumn,* her first novel in sixteen years, was published to unanimous critical acclaim. Barbara Pym completed two more novels before her death in January 1980.